WEREWOLF ACADEMY BOOK 1

Strays

By Cheree L. Alsop

STRAYS

Copyright © 2014 by Cheree L. Alsop
All rights reserved. This book or any portion thereof may not be reproduced or used in any manner whatsoever without the express written permission of the author except for the use of brief quotations in a book review.
This is a work of fiction. Names, characters, places, and incidents are a product of the author's imagination. Any resemblance to actual persons, events, or locales is entirely coincidental.
ISBN 1500840106
Cover Design by Robert Emerson and Andy Hair
Cover Image Natureaction4 by Martin Knight
www.ChereeAlsop.com

ALSO BY CHEREE ALSOP

The Werewolf Academy Series-
Book One: Strays
Book Two: Hunted
Book Three: Instinct
Book Four: Taken
Book Five: Lost
Book Six: Vengeance
Book Seven: Chosen

The Silver Series-
Silver
Black
Crimson
Violet
Azure
Hunter
Silver Moon

Heart of the Wolf Part One
Heart of the Wolf Part Two

The Galdoni Series-
Galdoni
Galdoni 2: Into the Storm
Galdoni 3: Out of Darkness

The Small Town Superheroes Series-
Small Town Superhero
Small Town Superhero II
Small Town Superhero III

STRAYS

Keeper of the Wolves
Stolen
The Million Dollar Gift
Thief Prince

Shadows
Mist- Book Two in the World of Shadows

PRAISE FOR CHEREE ALSOP

The Silver Series

"Cheree Alsop has written *Silver* for the YA reader who enjoys both werewolves and coming-of-age tales. Although I don't fall into this demographic, I still found it an entertaining read on a long plane trip! The author has put a great deal of thought into balancing a tale that could apply to any teen (death of a parent, new school, trying to find one's place in the world) with the added spice of a youngster dealing with being exceptionally different from those around him, and knowing that puts him in danger."
—Robin Hobb, author of the Farseer Trilogy

"I honestly am amazed this isn't absolutely EVERYWHERE! Amazing book. Could NOT put it down! After reading this book, I purchased the entire series!"
—Josephine, Amazon Reviewer

"Great book, Cheree Alsop! The best of this kind I have read in a long time. I just hope there is more like this one."
—Tony Olsen

"I couldn't put the book down. I fell in love with the characters and how wonderfully they were written. Can't wait to read the 2nd!"
—Mary A. F. Hamilton

"A page-turner that kept me wide awake and wanting more. Great characters, well written, tenderly developed, and thrilling. I loved this book, and you will too."

—Valerie McGilvrey

"Super glad that I found this series! I am crushed that it is at its end. I am sure we will see some of the characters in the next series, but it just won't be the same. I am 41 years old, and am only a little embarrassed to say I was crying at 3 a.m. this morning while finishing the last book. Although this is a YA series, all ages will enjoy the Silver Series. Great job by Cheree Alsop. I am excited to see what she comes up with next."

—Jennc, Amazon Reviewer

The Galdoni Series

"This is absolutely one of the best books I have ever read in my life! I loved the characters and their personalities, the storyline and the way it was written. The bravery, courage and sacrifice that Kale showed was amazing and had me scolding myself to get a grip and stop crying! This book had adventure, romance and comedy all rolled into one terrific book I LOVED the lesson in this book, the struggles that the characters had to go through (especially the forbidden love)...I couldn't help wondering what it would be like to live among such strangely beautiful creatures that acted, at times, more caring and compassionate than the humans. Overall, I loved this book...I recommend it to ANYONE who fancies great books."

—iBook Reviewer

"I was pleasantly surprised by this book! The characters were so well written as if the words themselves became life. The sweet romance between hero and heroine made me root

for the underdog more than I usually do! I definitely recommend this book!"
—Sara Phillipp

"Can't wait for the next book!! Original idea and great characters. Could not put the book down; read it in one sitting."
—StanlyDoo- Amazon Reviewer

"5 stars! Amazing read. The story was great- the plot flowed and kept throwing the unexpected at you. Wonderfully established setting in place; great character development, shown very well thru well placed dialogue- which in turn kept the story moving right along! No bog downs or boring parts in this book! Loved the originality that stemmed from ancient mysticism- bringing age old fiction into modern day reality. Recommend for teenage and older- action violence a little intense for preteen years, but overall this is a great action thriller slash mini romance novel."
—That Lisa Girl, Amazon Reviewer

"I was not expecting a free novel to beat anything that I have ever laid eyes upon. This book was touching and made me want more after each sentence."
— Sears1994, iBook Reviewer

"This book was simply heart wrenching. It was an amazing book with a great plot. I almost cried several times. All of the scenes were so real it felt like I was there witnessing everything."
—Jeanine Drake, iBook Reveiwer

"This book was absolutely amazing...It had me tearing at parts, cursing at others, and filled with adrenaline rushing along with the characters at the fights. It is a book for everyone, with themes of love, courage, hardship, good versus evil, humane and inhumane...All around, it is an amazing book!"
—Mkb312, iBook Reviewer

"Galdoni is an amazing book; it is the first to actually make me cry! It is a book that really touches your heart, a romance novel that might change the way you look at someone. It did that to me."
—Coralee2, Reviewer

"Wow. I simply have no words for this. I highly recommend it to anyone who stumbled across this masterpiece. In other words, READ IT!"
—Troublecat101, iBook Reviewer

Keeper of the Wolves

"This is without a doubt the VERY BEST paranormal romance/adventure I have ever read and I've been reading these types of books for over 45 years. Excellent plot, wonderful protagonists—even the evil villains were great. I read this in one sitting on a Saturday morning when there were so many other things I should have been doing. I COULD NOT put it down! I also appreciated the author's research and insights into the behavior of wolf packs. I will CERTAINLY read more by this author and put her on my 'favorites' list."

—N. Darisse

"This is a novel that will emotionally cripple you. Be sure to keep a box of tissues by your side. You will laugh, you will cry, and you will fall in love with Keeper. If you loved *Black Beauty* as a child, then you will truly love *Keeper of the Wolves* as an adult. Put this on your 'must read' list."
—Fortune Ringquist

"Cheree Alsop mastered the mind of a wolf and wrote the most amazing story I've read this year. Once I started, I couldn't stop reading. Personal needs no longer existed. I turned the last page with tears streaming down my face."
—Rachel Andersen, Amazon Reviewer

"I truly enjoyed this book very much. I've spent most of my life reading supernatural books, but this was the first time I've read one written in first person and done so well. I must admit that the last half of this book had me in tears from sorrow and pain for the main character and his dilemma as a man and an animal. . . Suffice it to say that this is one book you REALLY need in your library. I won't ever regret purchasing this book, EVER! It was just that GOOD! I would also recommend you have a big box of tissues handy because you WILL NEED THEM! Get going, get the book..."
—Kathy I, Amazon Reviewer

"I just finished this book. Oh my goodness, did I get emotional in some spots. It was so good. The courage and love portrayed is amazing. I do recommend this book. Thought provoking."
—Candy, Amazon Reviewer

Thief Prince

"I absolutely loved this book! I could not put it down. . . The Thief Prince will whisk you away into a new world that you will not want to leave! I hope that Ms. Alsop has more about this story to write, because I would love more Kit and Andric! This is one of my favorite books so far this year! Five Stars!"
—Crystal, Book Blogger at Books are Sanity

". . . Once I started I couldn't put it down. The story is amazing. The plot is new and the action never stops. The characters are believable and the emotions presented are beautiful and real. If anyone wants a good, clean, fun, romantic read, look no further. I hope there will be more books set in Debria, or better yet, Antor."
—SH Writer, Amazon Reviewer

"This book was a roller coaster of emotions: tears, laughter, anger, and happiness. I absolutely fell in love with all of the characters placed throughout this story. This author knows how to paint a picture with words."
—Kathleen Vales

"Awesome book! It was so action packed, I could not put it down, and it left me wanting more! It was very well written, leaving me feeling like I had a connection with the characters."
—M. A., Amazon Reviewer

"I am a Cheree Alsop junkie and I have to admit, hands down, this is my FAVORITE of anything she has published.

In a world separated by race, fear and power are forced to collide in order to save them all. Who better to free them of the prejudice than the loyal heart of a Duskie? Adventure, incredible amounts of imagination, and description go into this world! It is a 'buy now and don't leave the couch until the last chapter has reached an end' kind of read!"

—Malcay, Amazon Reviewer

"I absolutely loved this book! I could not put it down! Anything with a prince and a princess is usually a winner for me, but this book is even better! It has multiple princes and princesses on scene over the course of the book! I was completely drawn into Kit's world as she was faced with danger and new circumstances...Kit was a strong character, not a weak and simpering girl who couldn't do anything for herself. The Thief Prince (Andric) was a great character as well! I kept seeing glimpses of who he really was and I loved that the author gave us clues as to what he was like under the surface. The Thief Prince will whisk you away into a new world that you will not want to leave!"

—Bookworm, Book Reviewer

Small Town Superhero Series

"A very human superhero- Cheree Alsop has written a great book for youth and adults alike. Kelson, the superhero, is battling his own demons plus bullies in this action packed narrative. Small Town Superhero had me from the first sentence through the end. I felt every sorrow, every pain and the delight of rushing through the dark on a motorcycle. Descriptions in Small Town Superhero are so well written the reader is immersed in the town and lives of its inhabitants."

—Rachel Andersen, Book Reviewer

"Anyone who grew up in a small town or around motorcycles will love this! It has great characters and flows well with martial arts fighting and conflicts involved."
—Karen, Amazon Reviewer

"Fantastic story...and I love motorcycles and heroes who don't like the limelight. Excellent character development. You'll like this series!"
—Michael, Amazon Reviewer

"Another great read; couldn't put it down. Would definitely recommend this book to friends and family. She has put out another great read. Looking forward to reading more!"
—Benton Garrison, Amazon Reviewer

"I enjoyed this book a lot. Good teen reading. Most books I read are adult contemporary; I needed a change and this was a good change. I do recommend reading this book! I will be looking out for more books from this author. Thank you!"
—Cass, Amazon Reviewer

Stolen

"This book will take your heart, make it a little bit bigger, and then fill it with love. I would recommend this book to anyone from 10-100. To put this book in words is like trying to describe love. I had just gotten it and I finished it the next day because I couldn't put it down. If you like action, thrilling

fights, and/or romance, then this is the perfect book for you."
—Steven L. Jagerhorn

"Couldn't put this one down! Love Cheree's ability to create totally relatable characters and a story told so fluidly you actually believe it's real."
—Sue McMillin, Amazon Reviewer

"I enjoyed this book it was exciting and kept you interested. The characters were believable. And the teen romance was cute."
—Book Haven- Amazon Reviewer

"This book written by Cheree Alsop was written very well. It is set in the future and what it would be like for government control. The drama was great and the story was very well put together. If you want something different, then this is the book to get and it is a page turner for sure. You will love the main characters as well, and the events that unfold during the story. It will leave you hanging and wanting more."
—Kathy Hallettsville, TX- Amazon Reviewer

"I really liked this book . . . I was pleasantly surprised to discover this well-written book. . .I'm looking forward to reading more from this author."
—Julie M. Peterson- Amazon Reviewer

"Great book! I enjoyed this book very much it keeps you wanting to know more! I couldn't put it down! Great read!"
—Meghan- Amazon Reviewer

"A great read with believable characters that hook you instantly. . . I was left wanting to read more when the book was finished."
—Katie- Goodreads Reviewer

Heart of the Wolf

"Absolutely breathtaking! This book is a roller coaster of emotions that will leave you exhausted!!! A beautiful fantasy filled with action and love. I recommend this book to all fantasy lovers and those who enjoy a heartbreaking love story that rivals that of Romeo and Juliet. I couldn't put this book down!"
—Amy May

"What an awesome book! A continual adventure, with surprises on every page. What a gifted author she is. You just can't put the book down. I read it in two days. Cheree has a way of developing relationships and pulling at your heart. You find yourself identifying with the characters in her book...True life situations make this book come alive for you and gives you increased understanding of your own situation in life. Magnificent story and characters. I've read all of Cheree's books and recommend them all to you...especially if you love adventures."
—Michael, Amazon Reviewer

"You'll like this one and want to start part two as soon as you can! If you are in the mood for an adventure book in a faraway kingdom where there are rival kingdoms plotting and scheming to gain more power, you'll enjoy this novel. The characters are well developed, and of course with Cheree there is always a unique supernatural twist thrown into the story as well as romantic interests to make the pages fly by."

Karen, Amazon Reviewer

When Death Loved an Angel

"This style of book is quite a change for this author so I wasn't expecting this, but I found an interesting story of two very different souls who stepped outside of their "accepted roles" to find love and forgiveness, and what is truly of value in life and death."

—Karen, Amazon Reviewer

"When Death Loved an Angel by Cheree Alsop is a touching paranormal romance that cranks the readers' thinking mode into high gear."

—Rachel Andersen, Book Reviewer

"Loved this book. I would recommend this book to everyone. And be sure to check out the rest of her books, too!"

—Malcay, Book Reviewer

The Shadows Series

". . . This author has talent. I enjoyed her world, her very well developed characters, and an interesting, entertaining concept and story. Her introduction to her world was well done and concise. . . .Her characters were interesting enough that I became attached to several. I would certainly read a follow-up if only to check on the progress and evolution of the society she created. I recommend this for any age other

than those overly sensitive to some graphic violence. The romance was heartfelt but pg. A good read."
—Mari, Amazon Reviewer

". . . I've fallen for the characters and their world. I've even gone on to share (this book) with my sister. . .So many moments made me smile as well as several which brought tears from the attachment; not sad tears, I might add. When I started Shadows, I didn't expect much because I assumed it was like most of the books I've read lately. But this book was one of the few books to make me happy I was wrong and find myself so far into the books that I lost track of time, ending up reading to the point that my body said I was too tired to continue reading! I can't wait to see what happens in the next book. . . Some of my new favorite quotes will be coming from this lovely novel. Thank you to Cheree Alsop for allowing the budding thoughts to come to life. I am a very hooked reader."
—Stephanie Roberts, Amazon Reviewer

"This was a heart-warming tale of rags to riches. It was also wonderfully described and the characters were vivid and vibrant; a story that teaches of love defying boundaries and of people finding acceptance."
—Sara Phillip, Book Reviewer

"This is the best book I have ever had the pleasure of reading. . . It literally has everything, drama, action, fighting, romance, adventure, & suspense. . . Nexa is one of the most incredible female protagonists ever written. . .It literally had me on pins & needles the ENTIRE time. . . I cannot recommend this book highly enough. Please give yourself a wonderful treat & read this book... you will NOT be disappointed!!!"

—Jess- Goodreads Reviewer

"Took my breath away; excitement, adventure and suspense. . . This author has extracted a tender subject and created a supernatural fantasy about seeing beyond the surface of an individual. . . Also the romantic scenes would make a girl swoon. . . The fights between allies and foes and blood lust would attract the male readers. . .The conclusion was so powerful and scary this reader was sitting on the edge of her seat."

—Susan Mahoney, Book Blogger

"Adventure, incredible amounts of imagination and description go into this world! It is a buy now, don't leave the couch until the last chapter has reached an end kind of read!"

—Malcay- Amazon Reviewer

"The high action tale with the underlying love story that unfolds makes you want to keep reading and not put it down. I can't wait until the next book in the Shadows Series comes out."

—Karen- Amazon Reviewer

"Really enjoyed this book. A modern fairy tale complete with Kings and Queens, Princesses and Princes, castles and the damsel is not quite in distress. LOVE IT."

—Braine, Talk Supe- Book Blogger

". . . It's refreshing to see a female character portrayed without the girly cliches most writers fall into. She is someone I would like to meet in real life, and it is nice to read the first person POV of a character who is so well-round that she is brave, but still has the softer feminine side that defines her character. A definite must read."

—S. Teppen- Goodreads Reviewer

"I really enjoyed this book and had a hard time putting it down. . . This premise is interesting and the world building was intriguing. The author infused the tale with the feeling of suspicion and fear . . . The author does a great job with characterization and you grow to really feel for the characters throughout especially as they change and begin to see Nexa's point of view. . . I did enjoy the book and the originality. I would recommend this for young adult fantasy lovers. It's more of a mild dark fantasy, but it would definitely fall more in the traditional fantasy genre . "

—Jill- Goodreads Reviewer

To build and rebuild,
To create castles in the sky,
To reach those castles by
Dreaming and believing;
This is love.

Thank you to my husband and my family
For making every day one of castles.

STRAYS

Chapter One

"Don't do it, Alex!"

Alex glanced over his shoulder at his twin sister Cassie. Her dark blue eyes were pleading. He looked back at the older boys as they jumped one at a time off the cliff.

"They're Alphas," Cassie pointed out. The wind tangled in her curly brown hair; she shoved a strand behind her ear. "It's not worth it. Think about what you're going to do! You'll suffer consequences they can get away with."

She always had a way of sounding older than their fourteen years. Alex clenched his hands into fists for a moment, torn. He couldn't take her imploring gaze, but the last of the boys was about to jump.

"You coming, Alex?" Raynen asked, glancing over the edge. A hint of uncertainty touched his gaze.

"Sorry, Cass," Alex called over his shoulder. He leaped off the cliff before either his sister or Raynen could move. The wind rushed past him, bringing scents of evergreens, rocks far older than any who dwelled in the forest, and the crisp reminder that winter was soon to come.

The cold, sharp grasp of the water enveloped him. It stole the breath from his lungs and peppered his exposed flesh with merciless pinpricks of pain. He kicked as soon as his feet touched the bottom. He rocketed up; his lungs burned, aching to draw in a breath. He wondered if he would make it in time.

Alex broke the surface of the lake with a gasp.

"Hey, it's the little guy!" someone exclaimed from the bank.

"I didn't think he had the guts," another said.

"I didn't think he had the coat," someone else replied. Everyone laughed.

Alex swam to the shore. The irony of dogpaddling wasn't lost on him, but it was the only way he knew how to swim. His sneakers grazed rocks and he stumbled forward until he fell to his knees on the shore.

"Good job, Alan," Torin said, slapping him on the back hard enough to make him cough. The older boy flicked wet brown hair out of his eyes.

"It's Alex," Alex corrected. They had been at the Academy together for almost six years and Torin still didn't know his name. He couldn't understand why everyone followed the Alpha; it must have been more for brawn than brains.

"Is Raynen gonna jump?" Sid, Torin's Second, asked.

"I don't know," Alex told them. He shaded his eyes with one hand and gazed back up the cliff. Now that he was beneath it, the distance looked even more intimidating. A normal human wouldn't survive a drop like that. The voice in the back of his mind whispered that a Gray shouldn't, either.

Cassie glared down at him. He could only imagine the scolding he would receive when they returned to the Academy. He hadn't had a choice; not really. It was Choosing Day and he really didn't want to be chosen last yet again. His heart stuttered. He put a hand to his chest as he stood.

A bell rang. It echoed through the forest, bouncing off trees and reaching the werewolves loud enough to make them cover their sensitive ears.

"Think they can ring it a bit quieter?" Sid asked.

"I think Professor Nikki likes to torture us," Torin replied, rolling his eyes. "It's another one of her tests."

Alex fought back to urge to bare his teeth at the tone Torin used to talk about the dean's wife. She had always been nice to him.

"Come on," Torin said. "Last one there's got latrine

duty." The Alpha took off through the trees with the rest of the older werewolves close behind.

Alex glanced back up at the cliff, but Cassie was gone. He sighed and ran after the others.

It would have been faster and more fun to phase to wolf form, but the dean would definitely frown upon werewolves arriving naked at the Choosing. Alex could hear the others ahead of him. He slipped through the trees to the right, darted around a huge boulder, and found the steep decline. It was a shortcut that cut the time weaving down the switchback trail in half. The only downfall was that was also littered with poison ivy.

Alex jumped, using his werewolf strength to propel himself to a rock, then to a fallen tree. One more jump and he would be back on the path. It was far, further than a Gray should be able to leap. He ran along the tree trunk, bent his knees, and jumped at the last possible second. He was almost there. He was falling short.

Alex landed a few feet from the path. His foot clipped a root and sent him rolling. He put up his arms to protect his face from the poison ivy, and came to a painful stop against a massive tree.

The sound of footsteps running in a tight cadence approached.

"Nice jump, Alex," Torin said as they jogged past.

"Dweeb," Sid said behind him. The others laughed.

Alex pushed to his feet. He brushed off his pants and pulled leaves from his hair. A prickling pain ran up his arms and the back of his neck. He shook his head and continued down the path at a slower pace.

He stepped through the tree line and the Academy spread out below him. If he hadn't lived there for the last five years, he would have been impressed by the reaching spires that were caught in the last of the mist as it was burned away by the morning sun. Dark green walls, huge white-framed windows, and wooden doors carved and stained the color of red cedar dwarfed the gathering of students and teachers below. To Alex, it wasn't a home, nor a school. It was somewhere in-between. His heart gave another stutter. He ignored it and jogged down the grassy decline.

"Hey Alex, wait up!"

Alex slowed so Raynen could reach him. The Alpha sounded out of breath. As much as Alex hated the Choosing Ceremony, he wanted to ensure that things went his way this time.

"Hi Raynen," he said in his happiest voice. "Glad you made it down. Don't worry about the jump. It wasn't that bad."

"Yeah," Raynen replied, trying to hide his embarrassment. "I'm not too fond of heights, but I figured it wasn't worth the way they pump it up."

"You're right," Alex agreed, though his heart still raced from the jump and he had to fight back a smile. "So today's going to be different, huh," he said. "I think everything is going to change."

"I think so, too," Raynen replied.

Alex's heart leaped. "Imagine how strong your pack would be if you evened out the Choosing, picking members who have strengths in every area."

Raynen nodded thoughtfully as they made their way around the Academy. "I was thinking that, too. I'm going to change things up this year. It's going to be good."

Alex couldn't help the grin that spread across his face. "I'm looking forward to it."

"Me, too," the Alpha replied with a matching grin.

They reached the courtyard. Raynen broke away to join

the other Alphas near the front.

"I just wanted to address you before the buses arrive," Dean Jaze Carso was saying. His eyes followed Alex as the boy took a place near the back of the students. Alex met his gaze and the dean smiled. "It's always fun to start a new year, and we want it to begin right," he continued.

Alex fought back a sigh and shoved his hands in his pockets. It was the same lecture every year. Be nice to the Termers. Help them fit in. He glanced at Torin. The Alpha pushed a small Fourth Year into the group of older students in front of him. The students turned with angry glares and the Fourth Year shrank back.

"That was really stupid," Cassie said in a loud whisper.

Alex was faintly surprised she had braved the crowd to seek him out.

"It wasn't that bad," he replied.

Cassie glanced around, anxiously shuffling her feet.

"You can go," Alex whispered. "I'll fill you in on what happens."

She gave him a grateful smile. Her gaze shifted to his arms and her eyes widened. "Alex!"

"I know," he replied, crossing his arms in front of his chest. He winced and dropped them to his sides again. "It'll go away."

She studied him for a minute before shaking her head. She turned away and disappeared through the crowd.

Dean Jaze was about to speak again when howls cut through the air. A shiver ran down Alex's back and he smiled. The piercing cries echoed across the clearing, bouncing from the high walls of the Academy back down to the students.

An answering smile broke out across the dean's face. "They're here," he announced.

The students rushed around the school. Alex caught a

glimpse of Cassie flanking them through the trees. She hated crowds and preferred to stay in the forest on Choosing Day, even though she would be forced to come out when it was her turn. He couldn't blame her as he turned the last corner to find students pouring out of school buses.

Alex took his usual place at the base of the great wolf statue that stood in the middle of the courtyard. A rush of warmth filled him at the familiarity of the black sculpture. He reached up and set a hand on the silver seven that had been emblazed on the wolf's shoulder. Reassurance filled him. He crossed his arms and leaned against the base.

People spoke near the head of the statue. He recognized the voices of Dean Jaze and his wife without looking over.

"We'll have one hundred and fifty students," the dean was telling Professor Nikki. "That's fifty more than last year."

Alex could hear the concern in Nikki's voice when she replied, "Parents are seeing the advantage of having their children here safe through the school year, especially with the Extremists getting so aggressive."

Dean Jaze's brow creased as he watched the students mass on the lawn. "General Jared's tracing bloodlines. They aren't safe at home any longer. I wonder how many more will have to die before the rest of the parents realize what we are offering."

Professor Mouse, a skinny werewolf with thick glasses and a smile whenever his wife, Professor Lyra was at his side, leaned over and said, "We're getting more of the seven year olds who haven't phased yet. I guess they figure here is a much safer place to see if their children will turn into wolves."

The dean nodded. "I agree, and if they don't phase, at least they'll know their heritage."

"And at least our new lesson format supports larger

classroom sizes," Professor Nikki replied.

"Five to one," a voice said, tearing Alex's attention away from the conversation the leaders of the school were having.

His gaze shifted to Trent, a small Gray who barely reached Alex's shoulder despite being a year older. "What?" Alex asked.

Trent ran a hand across his buzzed head. He had begun prematurely balding last year and decided to handle it himself. Alex thought it made him look like a pencil eraser. Unfortunately, Torin did too, and made sure Trent knew it. "Five to one," Trent repeated. "At my count, there are one hundred and twenty-two students that just came from those buses. That's a five to one ratio for Termers versus Strays."

Alex bristled. "Don't call us that."

"Uh, sorry," Trent apologized. "Lifers. For every Lifer, there are five Termers. We're getting more outnumbered every year."

Alex let out a breath. "Tell me about it," he grumbled. He hated sharing the Academy with the Termers. They came for the school year, and then went home to their families during holidays and the summer. The intrusion wasn't something he could prevent, but like most of the orphans for whom the Academy was their permanent home, he already couldn't wait until they left again.

The dean and professors crossed to the stairs in front of the school where they could be seen by the arriving students. Alex remembered seeing Dean Jaze for the first time years ago. Jaze had been so young and confident despite everything he was going through. Now, the early signs of gray brushed the temples of the dean's black hair, and though his eyes still had smile lines around them, there was weight behind his gaze as he looked out over the students he was in charge of protecting and educating.

Excited talking filled the air. Dean Jaze raised a hand and the noise in the courtyard quieted. "Welcome to Vicki Carso's Preparatory Academy!" he said. His words and the applause that followed them echoed off the sheltering walls behind him. "We are happy to see all of the new faces, as well as those students who are returning for another term at our school. As some of you know, this academy was named after my mother, who," his voice cracked slightly, "Gave her life to sheltering and caring for any who needed a place to call home." He smiled past the emotions that filled his gaze. "I'm pleased to announce that this is the sixth year for the Academy, and I welcome back all of the Sixth Years who have been here since we started!" Another cheer rang out.

Jaze smiled at the students around him. "As you know, we have a very different way of teaching our students due to the *special nature* of our student body." Several chuckles sounded. The dean continued, "Instead of being divided by age, you will be taught with a group of students who will act as your support group and peers. This way, everyone can help each other with classes, and each has the opportunity to experience all of the learning opportunities offered here, those academically related and others that are more, as we say, intrinsic to your heritage."

Alex chuckled inwardly at the way the dean avoided using the term werewolf. It was said profusely throughout the year, but with the school bus drivers and a few parents who had come along for the ride and were still milling about the courtyard, his efforts to tiptoe around the delicate subject was humorous.

Jaze continued, "I'd also like to inform you that here at Vicki Carso's Preparatory Academy, we are little less formal than many other schools. You can call me Dean Jaze, and I will attempt to remember all of your names." He glanced back at Professor Nikki and smiled. "Though it'll probably take me all year to do so, and then next year there will be more of you. Our professors use their first names instead of their last, generally because they don't like to feel like old geezers," the professors behind him laughed, "And because we have a few who have either forgotten their surnames entirely, or choose not to claim them." He smiled at the students. "You can start over here at the Academy. Be who you are, or who you have always wanted to be." He winked. "The best is if both of those end up being the same thing."

It was the same joke he told every year, and worked to bring a few smiles to the faces of the werewolves watching from below.

Jaze waved a hand to indicate the building. "Welcome to your new home."

Applause from both the students and faculty rose in the courtyard. Alex gave a few halfhearted claps to support Jaze. The dean glanced in his direction and smiled. Alex wondered if the smile was meant for him or for the statue he leaned against.

Jaze's wife stepped forward. Professor Nikki's long black hair was caught back with a headband that sparkled in the sunlight. Her blue eyes creased with her smile as she watched the students below. "We'll now invite the bus drivers and parents to depart so we can commence with the Choosing Day Ceremony," Nikki told the crowd.

Alex watched as the parents who had traveled with the buses gave hearty goodbyes. Many students looked sad to see their parents go. A few appeared glad. One in particular, a girl with white-blonde hair, glowered at both her parents and the school. Her mother looked anxious to get away from the forest, casting glances in all directions as if the trees were going to crawl over the walls attack her at any time. Her father sat in the car and merely nodded when the tall boy standing near the girl waved.

Alex's heart sank. The tall, blond-haired boy was Boris, a Sixth Year and the Alpha leader of the Termers. Alex had hoped the boy wouldn't return. It looked like instead of fulfilling his wish, Boris had brought his sister. Alex felt at least a bit of consolation at the fact that the sister didn't appear pleased with the arrangement, either. She stomped to the car and tried to open the back door, but the driver locked it. Her father watched impassively from the back seat, giving the merest wave of his fingers to thwart off his angry daughter.

"Kalia," her mother called. The girl crossed her arms and glared at the ground. Her mother threw her arms around her daughter despite her stony expression. "Maybe they can fix this and you can return home," Alex heard the mom say.

"I'm not like *them*," Kalia replied, her disgust clear as she gestured flippantly toward the group waiting in the courtyard. "I can't believe you're leaving me here."

"We talked about this," her mom said.

Her father unrolled the window. "Get in the car, dear," he called before rolling it back up again.

"It's not fair," Kalia protested. Her blonde hair swished just above her shoulders when she shook her head. "You can't do this."

"Kalia, I—"

Her mother was cut off by the opening of the back window. "Marnie, now," Kalia's father said in a stern tone.

Kalia's mother kissed the top of her head before hurrying to the car. Both Kalia and Boris watched it follow the path the buses had already taken. When the car reached the wall, two staff members shut the wrought iron gates intricately worked in the shape of two wolves howling at the half-moon on either side that connected to make it full when the gates closed. The sound sent an ominous chill through the new students, while Alex breathed a sigh of relief. Though his home was overrun by students, at least they were through with the bombardment.

"Take this time to mingle with your fellow students," Professor Nikki encouraged the group. "This will become very important in the Ceremony. Get to know those you want to have in your pack. The contacts you make now may very well become your pack later. Learn the Alphas, learn the Grays. Everyone is important in a pack. I'll encourage you to not waste this time."

The Alphas began to mingle through the crowd as was expected of them. Alex watched Grays and younger years talk with enthusiasm, hoping to catch the eye of someone who would watch their back at the Academy. Alex had long ago given up mingling. He only hoped Raynen would hold true to what he had said. Trepidation filled Alex's chest at the thought that things might stay as they always had been.

"What's your name?"

Surprised, Alex glanced up from his brooding to see a tall, brown-haired boy watching him. Alex hadn't seen the werewolf before. He must have been a First Year, but the way he held himself said that he was an Alpha.

"Alex," he answered.

"I'm Jericho," the Alpha replied. He tipped his head toward the statue. "That's awesome."

Alex nodded without speaking.

"You been here long?" Jericho asked.

"Six years," Alex replied.

Jericho nodded. Another werewolf caught his eye and he wandered away. Alex clenched his hands into fists, then caught himself and shoved his hands in his pockets.

A few minutes later, Professor Nikki climbed to the top step of the Academy again. "Let's adjourn to the meeting hall for the Choosing Ceremony," she said. She and Dean Jaze held hands as they led the way through the huge front doors. Alex trailed behind the crowd. His patience was rewarded when Cassie eventually gave up her vigil at the edge of the forest and joined him.

"There are so many of them," Cassie whispered.

"It's just for the term," Alex reassured her. "They'll go home soon enough."

"I sure hope so," she replied.

Chapter Two

Alex fought down the rush of anxiety he always felt at the Choosing Ceremony. His efforts to find an in with Torin's group had failed miserably when he tripped on the forest path. He had put his trust in Raynen. If the Alpha didn't pull through, Alex would have to resign himself thought of being chosen last and staying with the same group of Lifers he had been with every term since he was eight.

Dean Jaze waited until everyone found a seat on the cushioned red chairs. Rows of the comfortable seats had been set out in a semi-circle around the dais that took up one end of the Great Hall. It took some time for the new students to find seats and for the group to quiet down. The Lifers kept to one side of the hall while the Termers sat as far away from them as the seating allowed.

"Don't get too comfortable," the dean warned with a smile that made it a joke. "You're going to get shuffled around soon enough." He nodded at the dark-haired, red-eyed werewolf near the middle of the stand. "I'll turn the time over to Professor Kaynan for the Ceremony," Jaze said.

Kaynan smiled at the group. Many of the new students looked uncomfortable under his red gaze, but Alex smiled back. Professor Kaynan taught English and art with his wife Grace. He and his sister Colleen, a wilderness education teacher, were also the only two genetically created werewolves as far as Alex knew.

He wasn't sure of the specifics except that when he was younger, he had asked Kaynan how it happened. The look of sadness that filled the werewolf's face was enough to prevent further questions, but Kaynan's kindness had helped Alex through a few rough times and he was grateful for the werewolf.

"Wolves run in packs," Kaynan began. "Werewolves run in bigger packs." Laughter rang through the room. Kaynan held up a hand. "Here at the Academy, your pack is your safety net, your security blanket, your go to, and your family. Your pack is your support and your biggest cheerleader. Starting with a strong connection to your pack means you will have a good year. Choosing Day is the most important day of your term here at the Academy."

Kaynan glanced over his shoulder. "Sorry, professors, but it's true. Your classes only make a strong second." They chuckled with the camaraderie of true friends. He turned back to the students. "Packs in the wild are not forced; they are made of family units who have each other's backs and work together for the defense of their territory and security of their members. Here at the Academy, the Alpha students will choose you."

Kaynan's voice lowered, "You have the right to refuse your pack, but you do so at the risk of not being taken in by another pack. If that is the case, you will become part of a pack that has the fewest members. We will have ten packs led by ten Alphas, thanks to the addition of Jericho, our new First Year Alpha. Choosing will go in order of years at the Academy."

Kaynan motioned for Torin to step forward. As a Lifer, he was given precedence over Boris for the first choosing. He crossed to the center of the stage.

"Sid Hathaway," he called without hesitation, choosing the werewolf who was always his Second. The linebacker-built werewolf crossed calmly to stand below his Alpha.

Boris took the stage. "Parker Luis," he called."

Though the choosing of the Alpha's Second was expected, Alex caught a hurt expression on Boris' sister's face. Kalia crossed her arms and stuck her feet on the back of the chair in front of her. The student who sat there turned around and gave her a disgruntled look, but she ignored him.

Kaynan motioned to Maliki, a Fifth Year Alpha, the second from the Lifers.

"Jordan Smith," the Alpha called.

Shannon, the Fourth Year Alpha, walked up to the dais next. She looked out over the group and a smile crossed her face. "Shaylee," she called.

The duo was twins, the only other set of twin students Alex knew of beside him and Cassie. The sisters were actually Alphas, but chose to stick together instead of making eleven packs at the Academy. Shaylee practically ran to the stage to join her sister.

Raynen was called next. After Alex's mishap with Torin's group, his only hope of being a Second was with Raynen, the last Alpha of the Lifers. Alex hoped the Alpha wouldn't let him down. He had never been a Second before, but both he and Raynen had spent a lot of time tagging along at the back of Torin's group trying to fit in. They were the same age. Perhaps the Alpha would pick him.

Raynen's eyes flitted over the crowd in his usual anxious way. He met Alex's gaze for a moment, then moved on. Alex's chest was tight. As a Gray, the highest position he could ever hope for was a Second. He hadn't cared about it before; it surprised him how much he wanted it this time.

"Cherish Mayland," Raynen called out.

Alex's heart fell. He slouched in his seat and glared at the worn knees of his pants. He had never needed new clothes. His needs had always been provided for by the Academy; but it was hard not to compare his clothes to the brand new shirts and pants worn by the Termers.

"I hate this," Cassie said in a whisper.

Alex nodded without looking at her. No doubt they

would be chosen as the last two of Raynen's or Miguel's packs. It wouldn't matter either way. The Alphas chose their pack mates based on familiarity. Alex wished he was an Alpha like his brother had been so he could show them what a true pack should look like. Strengths needed to counterbalance each other. Torin and Boris made their packs out of the physically strongest Grays, ignoring the fact that some of the weakest had strengths in areas other than physique.

Drake chose, then Jessilyn and Kelli. Miguel was silent for several minutes, but Alex didn't look up. The Second Year Alpha had formed a close pack the previous term. There was no doubt he would make the same choices again.

"Daniel Adamson ," he called. The round Second Year hurried up to the stage.

None of it made sense to Alex. Miguel and Daniel had pretty much exactly the same skillsets. Why choose someone like that as a Second? Different points of view meant better decisions for the pack. It was easy to choose someone who would be a yes man and never second-guess decisions, but isn't that what a Second was for? Obviously they needed to take Rafe's course on pack survival again.

"Alex Davies."

Alex's head jerked up. Jericho, the new First Year, was on the dais. Surely there was another Alex in the group of new students. But when Alex looked at the stage, Jericho was staring directly at him.

"He called you," Cassie said, her whisper loud in her amazement.

"He did?" Alex questioned. He didn't want to be the one who stood up only to be laughed at when the Alpha was referring to someone else.

Jaze caught Alex's eyes and motioned for him to step forward. Alex obeyed numbly, making his way between the chairs and then down the aisle without realizing he was doing so. He stopped in front of the stage and looked up at Jericho. The Alpha gave him a tight smile. By Alex's estimations, there was at least a two year gap between them, but the older boy gave Alex a nod as though grateful he had accepted.

Alex had never been a Second. It was unusual for a Termer to pick a Lifer to be his Second. Generally, the two groups didn't mix. Actually, the two groups never mixed. They were rivals, and fierce ones at that. Alex had always viewed them as separate entities. He realized he could learn something from Jericho as he surveyed the assembly. It was strange watching the crowd from the front of the Great Hall instead of the back. Everyone looked anxious and tried to cover it up by whispering to their friends or ignoring whoever was up next, but when Torin took the stage again, all eyes locked on him.

"Brace Jacobs."

Everyone followed the Lifer's path to the stage.

"Boris," Professor Kaynan said.

The Alpha Lifer sounded almost annoyed when he called out, "Kalia Dickson."

She made her way to the front without glancing to either side; it was as though nobody existed but her and her brother. She made a face when she reached him. "You pick me *after* Parker? Really?"

Boris motioned for her to be quiet. A slight hint of embarrassment showed on his face. Alex wondered if the Alpha regretted choosing his sister at all. At least Jericho's pack wouldn't have to worry about ending up with her. She turned with a sharp shake of her head that sent her hair swishing across her shoulders before she glared out above the crowd, oblivious to those who watched her as if pretending they didn't exist would make it happen.

"Boris," Professor Kaynan said.

The Alphas went through the choosing cycle again. When they reached Jericho, the Alpha surprised Alex by leaning down and asking, "Who should I choose?" Whispers rushed through the crowd at the unprecedented event. No Alpha had ever asked his Second who to pick in a Choosing.

"Cassie Davies," Alex said.

"I choose Cassie Davies," Jericho repeated.

Cassie's face flushed with relief as she made her way to the front. She stood there next to Alex with her head bowed so she didn't have to look at the faces watching her. He could see her trembling. It was the same every Choosing. As much as she hated crowds, she had to stand there. He knew she fought the urge to phase and run away.

"It's okay," Alex whispered softly as Boris chose his next pack mate.

"It'll be better when it's over," Cassie whispered back.

Alex studied the faces of the werewolves still waiting to be chosen. If Jericho asked him who to choose next, he needed to be ready. His gaze fell on Trent. The Sixth Year was great with numbers, but poor socially. He could help out in the classroom, but they would need someone to counterbalance him when they were outside of the Academy.

"Who next?" Jericho asked on cue.

"Trent Rushton," Alex replied without hesitation.

The werewolf's face lit up when his name was called. He hurried to the front, excited because he had never been chosen so early. Alex saw something in the boy's face that surprised him. There was a measure of self-esteem there as if being called so early gave him a bit more respect for himself. The grin he gave to Alex when he reached the group was relieved, but also carried a hint of pride. Alex made a note of that. If he could instill pride in his pack mates by helping them know their place, perhaps the pack would be stronger.

The rounds were gone through again. For the first time, pack mates who had been chosen began to submit requests to their Seconds and Alphas for others from the crowd. Brothers and sisters from lesser years joined their older siblings. The younger kids began to find places among the packs. Alex glanced back at the professors and staff members watching the Choosing. Jaze caught his gaze and gave him a thumb's-up. A smile spread across Alex's face as he turned around again.

"Terith Rushton," he said when Jericho asked him.

Trent's younger sister skipped through the waiting students. Everyone smiled at her. It was hard not to with her curly blonde hair and sweet smile. She was the counterpart to Trent's antisocial bookworm disposition. Perhaps having her in the pack would help Cassie as well, Alex hoped.

Alex went next with Von and Amos. Von was great in Biology despite his tendency to pick his nose. Amos was a huge, hulking werewolf who had much more in the way of brawn than brains, but would be a big asset when it came to defending the scrawnier members of the pack.

Torin glowered at Alex. The Alpha usually chose Amos as his ninth or tenth pick. Alex ducked away from the glare as he was supposed to being a Gray, but he didn't feel a bit sorry about messing up the Alpha's plans. Perhaps choosing Amos sixth would boost the behemoth's self-esteem as well.

Raynen was up next. "Pip Jacobs," he called.

Alex found the small Second Year werewolf at the back of the Great Hall. The boy stood, but instead of walking forward, he hesitated. Alex's senses sharpened. The boy looked like he was going to be sick.

Instead, Pip shook his head. "I deny the Choosing." His small voice rang clearly across the Great Hall. The twelve-year-old looked as though he wanted to disappear into the floor when one hundred and fifty-one heads plus the faculty and staff turned to stare at him.

"That's never happened before," Alex heard Professor Thorson, the human history teacher, whisper loudly.

"It is his right," Kaynan replied so the entire assembly heard. Alex glanced back to see the professor nod. "Your decision stands," Kaynan concluded.

Pip quickly sat back down and disappeared within the mass of taller bodies.

"Fine," Raynen replied with a hint of anger. "Tessa Mathews, then."

When it came to their turn, Alex told Jericho to choose Pip. The werewolf was a Termer, and it was odd to mix Termers with Lifers, but Jericho had done away with that precedence when he chose Alex. The Alpha hesitated, worried at being denied, but at Alex's encouraging nod, he declared, "We choose Pip Jacobs."

The entire crowd watched the tiny werewolf pick his way through the students to stand in front of Alex. No one had ever denied an Alpha's Choosing. Alex felt a deeper respect for the brave student.

"Welcome to the pack," he whispered.

"Thanks," Pip replied, relief clear in his voice.

Three more times, werewolves chosen for other packs declined only to accept Jericho's Choosing. By the end, Alphas were glaring at the members they chose in case the person dared to decline. Alex felt a stir of satisfaction in his chest at the thought that everyone in Jericho's pack wanted to be there. It was the strangest Choosing Ceremony he had ever been to, and that was saying a lot because he had been to them all.

"The Choosing Ceremony is over," Kaynan declared

when all students had taken their places with their packs. Boris and Torin had one more werewolf in each of their packs, and everyone else stood at fifteen. The packs were a lot larger than Alex was used to. "Pack quarters have been assigned within the dormitory wing. Take this time to find your quarters, get settled, and get to know one another before the dinner bell rings."

"I take it that was an unusual Choosing Ceremony," Jericho said as soon as they left the Great Hall.

"You can say that again," Terith replied, her blonde hair bouncing on her shoulders. "I've never seen Torin so upset! You'll have to watch your back after taking Amos, Alex."

"I watch Alex's back," Amos replied, his deep voice a low rumble that vibrated through Alex like a bass drum.

Alex was surprised by the hulking werewolf's offer. "Uh, thanks, Amos," he replied.

"No one pick on my pack," Amos said.

Terith slipped her hand into the older werewolf's. His fingers engulfed hers as if she was a child. He smiled down at her fondly like she was a puppy.

"Careful," Trent, Terith's brother, warned.

"It's okay," Terith replied, skipping beside Amos. "He's in our family now, right Amos?"

The big werewolf gave a huge smile, the first Alex had ever seen on his face. "Right."

"We ruffled a few feathers, huh?" Jericho asked quietly so only Alex could hear.

Alex nodded. "A few. First of all, even though it's allowed, no werewolf has ever denied a Choosing, and second, we've mixed Lifers and Termers. That never happens."

Jericho was silent for a few minutes as they made their way up the wide staircase and took the left wing to the dormitories. The long dormitory hall had names inscribed on the doors. Torin and Boris had the first two residences across the hall from each other. That always led to a few scuffles. Alex and Jericho continued down the hall with their pack behind them. They passed the other rooms set in the same order as the Choosing, and stopped by the last door. Everyone else had fallen away to their own quarters, leaving Jericho's pack to themselves.

"Guess this is it," Jericho said. He turned the knob and pushed the door open.

Wide windows spilled afternoon sunlight onto the thickly carpeted floors. There was a main meeting and living area complete with couches and a huge table. Two hallways branched off so that each member of the pack had his or her own room. The girls took the left hall while the boys chose the right. Jericho went into the first room while Alex took the second because it was his rightful place.

The furnishings were sparse but sturdy, a four poster bed, a dresser, a desk, and a closet. Alex had been in enough rooms to know that they all matched. Usually during the summer when the Termers went home, everyone could choose whatever room they wanted and generally gave each other space to do as they wished. Though Alex was loath to give that up, there was a sense of accomplishment to sharing quarters with a pack he had chosen.

"This isn't bad," he heard Jericho say from his room.

Alex walked back to the hall. The Alpha had left his door open. Alex leaned against Jericho's door frame. "They'll bring your belongings and the personal items you brought from home up while we eat."

"Room service," Jericho replied with a pleased smile.

Alex found himself warming to the tall Alpha. "First class."

Jericho glanced at Alex over his shoulder. "Do you think mixing Lifers and Termers is a bad idea?"

Again, Alex was struck by the fact that the Alpha was asking his opinion as if it mattered. He thought about his answer, knowing it was important that he give the full truth. "You broke precedence by picking a Lifer as your Second. It definitely caused a bit of an uproar. I figured continuing to shake things up would show my support of your decision."

Jericho snorted and turned to face Alex. "So you're setting everything on my shoulders."

Alex shrugged. "Everyone heard you ask my opinion for the Choosing. It's already on my shoulders. Pretending it's on yours won't make it so."

A smile ran across Jericho's face. "You like to ruff feathers, then."

Though the Alpha was smiling, the statement bothered Alex. He didn't want Jericho to think he was just trying to cause trouble. "I stand behind every decision I made," Alex replied firmly. "Our pack's strengths and weaknesses counterbalance each other in all areas including socially and intellectually. Thanks to Amos and Don, we won't have to worry about being picked on, and picking both Lifers and Termers will keep us out of the never-ending battle between Torin and Boris' packs."

"Or it may give them a shared enemy," Jericho suggested.

"I'm not afraid of them," Alex replied with more vehemence than he meant to use.

Jericho nodded. "I believe you," he said, his tone thoughtful as if he guessed more than Alex let on.

Alex was unable to keep the question in any longer. "Why did you choose me as your Second?"

Jericho clasped his hands behind his back. "I'm new to the school. I knew I needed someone as a Second who was familiar with the traditions but who wasn't caught up enough within a clique that he would deny my Choosing. You stood alone by the statue, and didn't seem completely daunted at being addressed by an Alpha. I needed someone who wasn't afraid to give me his opinion. I figured after talking to you that you were the one."

Alex opened and closed his hands, suddenly uncomfortable. As if on cue, the dinner gong rang. The sound bounced off the walls through the main room with enough strength to rattle the pictures of scenery on the walls.

Jericho winced at the sound. "Is it going to be like that every night?"

Alex nodded. "You get used to it; sort of."

The rest of the pack spilled out into the main room.

"Thanks for picking us," Trent said. Gratitude showed on the faces around them as the others nodded.

"I know this is a strange pack," Jericho replied. "And I'm new to the whole Alpha thing. My dad is an Alpha and leads our pack back home, so I haven't had to take on the leadership role before now."

Alex felt a growing respect for the Alpha. He had never heard an Alpha address those under him with such familiarity instead of looking down on them from an upper level. Jericho held the air of authority of an Alpha, but the smile he gave Cassie seemed to calm her nervousness about the changes. Cassie stood close to Terith. Alex hoped they would become friends.

"Give me a bit of leeway while I learn the ropes of being your leader, and I'll give you leniency if you slip up once in a while," Jericho said. "I am grateful I had Alex's guidance when choosing this pack, and I feel like we're going to have an excellent term."

Everyone nodded and smiles began to appear on faces.

"Let's go eat," Jericho suggested. He led the way to the door. When he tried to open it, the door refused to budge. He pulled harder.

"He's going to rip off the doorknob," Cassie whispered next to Alex.

"Let me try," Amos offered. "I break door down."

Jericho held up a hand. "I don't think we want to ruin our door. Someone needs to figure out what's wrong with it."

"I'll go around," Alex said. He went to the window despite everyone's protests. Two floors up wasn't that high. He had often skirted the walls while exploring the Academy. He pushed the windowpane up.

"Be careful," Cassie said.

Alex nodded and stepped onto the ledge. Fourteen heads stuck out of the windows and watched him as he hugged the wall and made his way carefully to the next window. He tapped on the pane.

A form crossed to the window. "What are you doing?" Raynen demanded.

"Permission to come inside?" Alex asked.

"I'm pretty sure our doorknobs are tied together, so it's not going to help you any," Raynen replied, annoyance still thick in his voice from the Choosing Ceremony.

"Good to know," Alex told the Alpha. "I'll take care of it."

He made his way past the window and continued along the wall. Another set of heads poked out the windows to watch him.

The Academy had been built to house triple the number of werewolves currently inside. Alex reached the next set of windows belonging to one of the empty quarters. He pulled on the pane. It refused to give. He could see the little latch inside. Alex gritted his teeth and pulled harder. The latch began to give. Alex closed his eyes, focused all his strength on the frame, and jerked up. The window flew open so fast he almost fell off the ledge. He caught himself at the last moment and ducked inside.

Alex's heart stammered in his chest. He put a hand to it and waited for a moment for it to slow. When it did, he made his way through the empty room, out to the meeting room that echoed with his footsteps, and pulled open the main door. He jogged back up the hall to the set of occupied dormitory rooms. All of the packs except those in the last two quarters had already left for dinner. Alex hoped there was still food left.

A thick cord bound both doorknobs together. Alex untied it from the doors.

"Good to go," he called.

Jericho and Raynen opened the doors at the same time. Jericho laughed at the sight of the cord in Alex's hand. "At least we still have our doorknobs," the Alpha said.

"Do we have to stay across from you?" Raynen protested. "I don't need my pack getting hazed because of your stupid actions, Alex."

Alex was about to reply when Jericho speared Raynen with a look. "You mess with one of us, you mess with all of us," he replied in a tone that carried steel.

Raynen looked up at Amos and Don as they squeezed through the doorway behind their Alpha.

"We're good," Raynen muttered. He turned and barked, "Get out here." He stalked down the hallway without waiting for his pack to respond.

Jericho's pack waited respectfully until they were gone.

"Let's eat," Jericho said simply before walking down the hall.

The rest fell in line behind him. Cassie smiled at Alex. He

couldn't help a thrum of excitement that went through him at the thought that perhaps this term would be different from all the rest after all.

Chapter Three

Each pack sat at their own rectangular table spaced along the Great Hall. A spread of turkey, baked potatoes, honeyed ham, fresh rolls, stuffing, and cranberry sauce filled each table. Spiced eggnog and horchata made up the drink choices along with iced water with floating lemon slices.

"This is better than anything we eat at home!" Marky exclaimed.

Alex gave the boy a warm smile. The werewolf was one of the new seven year olds at the Academy for their first term. He had become a part of their pack by default because it was either Marky, a Fifth Year named Justice who glared daggers at Alex and would no doubt kill him in his sleep if chosen for Jericho's pack, or Brace, a werewolf Alex had scuffled with on a few occasions and chose not to put that on his pack.

Seeing Marky's expression as he took a bite of turkey convinced Alex that he had made the right decision. "You'll eat good every day you're here," Alex told him.

Marky's wide green gaze widened. "You mean the Strays eat like this all year long?"

A fierce rage swept through Alex. His hands clenched into fists. Trent opened his mouth to snap at the werewolf, but Alex took a calming breath and held up a hand. Jericho watched them both with interest. "Marky, we prefer to be called Lifers instead of Strays. Just because we're orphans doesn't mean we don't have a home. The Academy is our home." Alex's heart clenched away from the term, but he forced himself to continue, "If you want to make friends here, don't use the term Stray again, okay?"

Marky nodded, his eyes even wider. "I'm s-sorry, Alex."

"It's alright," Alex reassured him. "This is your first year.

You're still learning the ropes."

"Me, too, apparently," Jericho said quietly when everyone else had returned to eating and talking. "For a second there, I thought you might actually attack him."

Alex hesitated, then nodded. "I almost did." He met the Alpha's gaze. "It's a touchy subject."

Jericho nodded. "I'll keep that in mind."

Alex felt eyes on him. He glanced over his shoulder to meet Boris' gaze. The leader of the Termers glared at him. Alex stifled a sigh and turned back to the table. Apparently, he had made more than a few enemies at the Choosing.

"You did a good job," Cassie whispered.

Alex smiled at her as she piled turkey between two rolls, smashed it down, and took a huge bite. Though Cassie was small, she put even more food away than Alex. She had a tendency to eat when nervous, so dining in the Great Hall actually helped to calm her fear of being around crowds.

"Thanks," Alex whispered back.

***

Alex loved the soft shush of the grass beneath his feet as he made his way to the statue. It looked even bigger under the midnight sky, a huge Alpha wolf ready to protect the Academy should it come under threat.

"No one would mess with you," Alex said aloud. He took a deep breath of the cool night air; his senses flooded with the crisp scent of the pines that circled the Academy walls, the tangle of moisture that hinted at rain, and the bare wisp of a small herd of deer that bounded away from the walls, probably being pursued by Rafe's pack.

"I wish you could smell this," Alex said with a touch of sorrow in his voice. "I know you'd love it."

He shoved his hands in his pockets and leaned against the statue's right foreleg. It was his favorite place at night. The lights were out in the Academy windows, stars winked down from their deep velvet blanket, and the wind, always the wind, circling, toying with his black hair that was getting a bit longer than he usually let it grow, and promising that a run beyond the walls would be amazing.

Alex was about to give into the urge to run when the front door to the Academy opened.

The form paused on the top step, then made its way to the statue.

The familiar scent made Alex's tight muscles loosen.

"I thought I'd find you here," Dean Jaze said amiably when he reached the statue.

Alex smiled. "Maybe I'm getting too predictable."

The dean chuckled. "You proved that wrong today."

Alex nodded. "That was a bit above the norm."

"A bit," Jaze conceded, smiling at the sarcasm. "I suppose the Lifers and Termers are getting along?"

"As good as can be expected. Someone tied our door shut," Alex said. At Jaze's raised eyebrows, Alex shrugged. "I untied it. No harm done."

Jaze's gaze said he guessed more than what Alex let on. "Be careful, Alex. Don't push yourself too hard. I know how much you want to be an Alpha."

Alex shook his head. He lowered his gaze and said quietly, "I don't want to be an Alpha. I want to be like my brother."

Jaze's eyes traveled from the young Gray to the statue of the black wolf behind him.

Heartbreak filled Alex's voice when he asked the question that had circled in his mind hundreds of times but he had never dared to ask. He made himself do so now. "Could you have saved him?"

Jaze let out a slow breath. He turned and leaned against the base of the statue next to Alex. He glanced at the young werewolf. "I can't tell you how many times I've asked myself that same question," he said. "How many times I've ran the scenario over and over again in my head." The dean closed his eyes. "If I had known he was going to sacrifice himself for me, I would have demanded to go up there beside him, and he knew that."

"And you would have died, too," Alex answered in a whisper.

Jaze nodded. "I would have fought side by side with my best friend and died beside him." He stifled a smile when he said, "And he would have been so angry at me for sacrificing myself, even if I pointed out that was exactly what he had done."

Alex fought to keep the pain at bay, forcing the memories away of the day his parents were killed. Jet had found them and taken them to a werewolf safe house called Two. It was there he and Cassie had been told about Jet's death. He hadn't broken down then; he had been strong for Cassie, holding her as she cried, lost inside herself at the thought of all of their loved ones gone.

At the Academy, he had to be strong for different reasons. While Cassie found consolation in the woods and in the peace that reigned when the terms were no longer in session, Alex was constantly on guard, fighting for his spot among the packs, hoping someday to prove Jet proud, to be a brother worthy of the one who had died to make the Academy happen.

"I think he deserves to be here instead of me," Alex said quietly.

Jaze looked at him. He was quiet for several minutes. Alex appreciated the way the dean never talked down to him or acted like his opinion didn't matter. Jaze and Nikki were all Alex and Cassie had when they were brought to the Academy. Jaze had become a father figure to the twins, helping them through the heartache as he survived it himself.

"I can't tell you how many times I've thought that myself," Jaze admitted into the silence. "He had gone through so much in his life. To see what he had become in the time I knew him made me realize what it truly meant to love and to sacrifice, to trust and to be loyal."

Jaze looked at Alex as if debating how much he should tell the boy. He turned his gaze to the stars twinkling above, watching their world with impassive eyes, dwarfed by the moon that hung low as if caught in the trees. "He told me to kill him once," Jaze said softly.

Alex turned in surprise and looked at the dean. Jaze's dark brown eyes were filled with tears. "He did?" Alex asked.

Jaze nodded. "It was the day my mom died. I had been taken prisoner by someone who was supposed to be my ally.

He had Jet and other werewolves tied up. My mother was to be killed if I didn't murder the werewolves in front of national television to prove that werewolves were a threat to the world. Jet looked me in the eyes and told me to kill him so I could save my mom and Nikki."

Jaze swallowed and fell silent.

"What did you do?" Alex asked in a voice just above a whisper.

Jaze let out a shuddering breath. "There wasn't really a choice. I realized that, looking at your brother who was chained. It was something I had promised him he would never go through again. I loved your brother with all my heart. He was my brother, too. We had fought and bled beside each other." He let out a slow breath. "They weren't going to let my mom go, and she never would have chosen her life above the five werewolves chained against the wall. I freed them, and Jet helped me get them home. One of the werewolves married Mouse."

"Lyra," Alex breathed. The realization struck him hard. He rubbed a hand across his face to chase away the tears. "You had to sacrifice your mom to save Jet?"

Jaze nodded, his gaze on the trees that swayed with the gentle night breeze. "There really wasn't a choice, but Jet had been willing to lay down his life just the same, even if it was in vain. He loved my mom and he would have gladly died if it meant her freedom."

"But it wouldn't have," Alex said. A knot tightened in his stomach. "It was a catch twenty-two."

"It was," Jaze agreed quietly. "Most of what we were living through before the Academy was created turned out to be. We thought we had friends, but they turned against us, attempting to wipe us out because they feared we were stronger."

"Shouldn't the weak unite with the strong?" Alex asked, thinking of the way the strongest wolves in a pack protected those who were weaker.

A light appeared in Jaze's eyes. "Yes. That's why we built this place, to teach werewolves how to fit in and how to help the world instead of being a threat to it."

"Even though the world is a threat to werewolves?" Alex asked.

A small smile touched Jaze's lips. "Yes."

Alex was quiet for several minutes, then said, "I think Jet would be proud of what you've done."

Jaze studied the younger werewolf. "You think so?"

Alex nodded. "I know it."

Jaze smiled and looked up at the stars again. "I sure hope so." He glanced at Alex. "There's something I want to tell you."

Curiosity glittered in Alex's dark blue gaze. "What?"

"Nikki's pregnant."

Alex's eyes widened.

"I don't want you or Cassie to be worried about being forgotten when the baby's born," Jaze hurried to say. "You'll always be a part of our family and we'll always be there for you. So don't worry—"

Alex surprised Jaze by giving him a tight hug. "I'm happy for you," Alex said. "You guys are going to be great parents."

Jaze smiled down at him and ruffled the young werewolf's black hair. "Thanks for the vote of confidence. We have a lot to learn."

Alex stepped back and tipped his head toward the Academy. "I know a great place to learn it."

Jaze laughed. "Come on," he said. "Let's try to catch some sleep before chaos breaks out in the morning."

"Good idea," Alex agreed.

He walked beside Jaze back to the Academy. The statue watched over them, its black wolf form chasing away the fears of the night.

Chapter Four

Dean Jaze stood as breakfast wound down. "Today is your first day of classes," he began, addressing the werewolves who had gathered at their pack tables in the Great Hall. "Due to the great increase in students, we have set up this year different than the terms before. Instead of one pack per classroom, we will have two packs at a time. You will be rotated so that you don't share all classes with the same packs. First Termers, follow your Alphas." He smiled at Jericho. "Alphas, if you don't know where to go, follow the Sixth Years."

At Jaze's invitation, Professor Nikki stood. She held up a piece of paper. Happiness flooded Alex when her hand strayed subconsciously to her stomach. She seemed to catch herself and took it away again, but she and Jaze exchanged a warm smile.

Alex leaned over to Cassie. "Nikki's pregnant," he whispered.

Cassie's eyes widened. She looked from Nikki back to Alex. "Really?" At Alex's nod, she let out a gasp of excitement. Everyone looked at her. A blush ran across Cassie's face and she sank down in her chair. When the students looked away again, she whispered, "That makes me so happy!"

"I know," Alex replied, grinning at his sister. He followed her gaze back to Nikki.

The professor read from the page. "Packs Torin and Drake will meet in room twelve. Packs Raynen and Shannon will begin with Rafe and Colleen outside the wall."

Raynen gave a loud groan.

Nikki ignored him and continued, "Packs Maliki and Kelli are to meet in the gymnasium. Packs Jessilyn and Miguel will proceed to room two, and Packs Boris and Jericho are to meet in the training facilities. After your class concludes, your professor will instruct you where to go next."

Jericho gave Alex a surprised look. "What sort of training?"

"The only kind befitting a werewolf," Alex replied with a grin.

He led the way down the hall toward his favorite class. Maybe things were looking up after all. Beginning the day with training was just what he needed.

He was almost there when someone ran into him.

"Out of my way, twerp," Boris spat.

Alex turned to see Trent sprawled on the ground with the Alpha standing above him. Jericho, Don, and Amos hadn't reached the turn in the hall yet and so were unaware of their pack mate's danger. Alex took a step forward.

"Alex, no," Cassie pleaded, grabbing his hand.

Boris' gaze tightened. "Yeah, Alex, no," he mimicked, mocking Cassie's worried tone. "Stay back like a sissy and watch me teach your pack mate some manners." He grabbed the front of Trent's shirt and picked him up so they were nose to nose. "Like getting out of the way when an Alpha comes along."

"Leave him alone." The words came out of Alex's mouth before he realized he had spoken. His hands clenched into fists and he took another step forward despite Cassie's vicelike grip.

"What did you say?" Boris growled. He exchanged a glance with Sid, his Second. "Did you hear that?"

Sid nodded. "I heard it." A vicious gleam sparkled in Sid's eyes at the potential fight.

Boris dropped Trent and stepped over him to face Alex. "Do we have a problem, Stray?" Boris demanded.

Alex held perfectly still. Everything inside of him called for him to attack, yet Boris was an Alpha. Alex's jaw clenched. Instinct demanded that he back down. The Alpha was stronger, faster, and werewolf law dictated that a Gray should never challenge an Alpha. But the Alpha was challenging him.

"Did you hear me, Stray?" Boris growled in a tone that said he was seconds away from attacking.

Alex let out a slow breath and bowed his head, showing the deference he hated. "I don't have a problem, Boris," he said quietly.

"What was that?" Boris shouted.

"I don't have a problem," Alex replied through clenched teeth.

Boris watched him for another minute before nodding. "Good." He pushed past Alex. Alex leaned against the wall as the rest of Pack Boris walked by. The girl, Kalia, trailed last. She studied Alex as she passed. He refused to meet her gaze. He had to show deference to Boris, but there was nothing that dictated he owed her anything.

The rage rushed through him, barely contained. He wanted to tear something apart, anything.

"Alex?" Cassie asked quietly.

Alex shoved past her into the training room. He walked blindly to the wooden dummies in the corner and pulled out a practice sword.

He had training in the room for the last six years. Dray and Chet had helped him turn his helpless frustration at losing everyone he cared about into honing his fighting skills. It let him vent his rage and prevented him from hurting others or himself in the process.

Now, though, all he saw was red. He swung the sword so hard it snapped in two when it connected with the dummy.

He let out a roar, picked the dummy up despite the sand in the bottom that was supposed to weigh it down, and threw it across the room. He slammed a two-fisted punch into the next dummy; it rocked back under the blow. When it tipped forward again, he chopped the neck followed by an elbow to the back. The dummy hit the practice mat with a resounding thud.

Alex rolled over it, punched the next dummy in the groin, spun on his heel and jumped, kicking it in the back of the head. When it fell to the ground, he picked up the broken remains of the sword, and with another yell of anger, drove the broken pieces into the dummy's back.

Alex breathed hard, staring at the wrecked remains of his wrath. When he glanced up, he met Boris' gaze first. The werewolf stared at him, amazed at what the Gray had done. Alex looked down at the dummy again. No Gray should have been able to drive a wooden sword through the wooden dummy.

Alex's heart stuttered. He stumbled and would have fallen when a hand grabbed his arm. He met the light blue eyes of Boris' sister Kalia. She stared at him for a moment, and he swore, for a split second, that her eyes changed from blue to gold, then back again.

"Let him go," Cassie demanded.

She ducked under Alex's arm and led him to the wall. He sank against it and avoided everyone's gazes as his sister rushed to get him a drink of water. By the time she got back, he was feeling better.

"You alright?" Cassie asked quietly.

He nodded. He looked up to see Jericho walking over with a confused expression on his face. He was saved an explanation by Professor Dray's entrance.

"Welcome to combat training," the professor announced.

He glanced around the room, noting the condition of the dummies. His gaze met Alex's, and the corners of his eyes tightened in an understanding smile. He nodded. "I guess you've had an introductory lesson. Let's see if we can hone your skills a bit."

Alex was grateful the werewolf didn't question him about the mess. Dray was one of the few professors who was a Gray. He understood about Alex's difficulty giving in to authority.

At Professor Dray's instructions, everyone pulled a cloth practice dummy to the middle of the huge mat. Alex joined them. Dray proceeded to instruct them on the proper way to strike the bag with an elbow for maximum impact.

"This is stupid," Boris muttered from the other side of the room. "If someone messes with me, I'll just tear his head off."

Dray held up a hand. Everyone paused in what they were doing.

"You'll just tear his head off?" Dray questioned.

"Yeah," Boris replied. "Then he wouldn't be a problem anymore."

Dray nodded. "I see," he said musingly. "So while the world is terrified of werewolves to the point where we were wiped out to near extinction, your plan if someone gets on your bad side is to tear his head off?"

Boris' voice was a little quieter when he replied, "Yeah."

Dray nodded again. Alex fought back a smile. He and the instructor had undergone pretty much the same conversation when Alex was looking for ways to deal with his anger against the world.

"My job here is to teach you how to control your anger, and how to defend yourselves in ways that won't kill or severely maim the humans you might go up against. I'm giving you an outlet for your strength and your frustrations so that you can deal with the world on a normal level. If you come out of the Academy and never have a fight in your life, then I've done my job."

"Like that's going to happen," Sid whispered loudly to Boris.

Dray speared him with a look. "And if you do get in a fight, if you can survive it without killing anyone and without drawing attention to yourself, then I have also done my job."

Several members of Jericho's pack nodded. Boris' look less sure of Dray's statements.

The door behind them flew open. "Who's ready to kill each other?" Professor Chet demanded.

Dray rolled his eyes at the dark-haired Alpha. "I was just emphasizing the fact that combat training is for self-control."

"And for beating the crap out of each other," Chet replied with a grin. "I just got clearance from Jaze." He paused when Dray cleared his throat. "Alright, *Dean* Jaze," he continued with some annoyance. "We're going to start practice bouts in the ring."

Alex glanced at the boxing ring that had sat unused on the other end of the training room for as long as he had been there. The thought of actually fighting other werewolves sent a thrum of excitement through him. It had to be much better than shadow boxing and punching dummies. He took a step toward the ring.

"Don't you think we should teach them some control first?" Dray asked.

Chet waved the question away. "They'll learn in the ring." He smiled and popped his knuckles. "Who's first?"

Alex was about to raise his hand when Cassie grabbed his arm. She shook her head quickly, her eyes begging him not to be stupid after he had already pushed his heart too far.

"Alright, I'll call on someone. Ears, Bucky, step into the ring."

Everyone looked at Pip whose big ears were hard to miss. The Second Termer stared at Jericho and swallowed nervously; the sound was heard throughout the training room.

"Go ahead," Jericho urged.

Tomas from Pack Boris was already in the ring. He smiled, showing the big front teeth Chet had pointed out. The Termer was the same size as Pip, but bounced around on the balls of his feet excitedly. He swung his hands back and forth, slapping his shoulders.

"Let's get some gear on," Dray recommended. He tossed a pair of gloves to Chet for Tomas.

"You just keep making this less and less interesting," Chet grumbled as he strapped them on.

Dray wrapped the large gloves on Pip's hands. They dwarfed the little werewolf and looked ridiculous. "Just keep your hands up and protect your head," Dray advised. He gave Chet a worried look. It was obvious he didn't approve of the situation.

Chet shrugged. "What? Jaze agreed that it would be a great way for the students to learn self-control and to help each other hone their moves."

"Did you forget to mention that we haven't had a chance to teach them moves yet because this is the first year we've had these lesson plans?" Dray pointed out.

Chet shrugged again. "Possibly." He turned his attention to the waiting werewolves. "Now fight!"

Tomas threw two punches before Pip even had his hands up. The little werewolf rocked back on his heels. Alex took a step closer. Cassie followed, her expression anxious.

"Put your hands up," Dray repeated. "Protect your head."

Pip raised his hands, and Tomas immediately punched his stomach. Pip looked like he was about to cry.

"Chet," Dray said.

"Wait for it," Chet urged.

Pip lowered a hand to his stomach and Tomas hit his head again. Alex saw tears in Pip's eyes. He was about to reach for the ropes when Jericho shook his head. Alex paused, surprised by the unspoken command from the Alpha. He followed Jericho's gaze back to the ring.

Tomas hit Pip in the kidneys. Pip attempted a desperate swipe at the other Termer's head, but Tomas ducked and landed a punch on Pip's chin. Something snapped. Alex saw the moment Pip changed from scared and cowering to something else. He threw his hands down hard enough to force the gloves off and dove at Tomas. He phased as he did so, tearing his clothes and slamming against Tomas' chest in the form of a gray-coated wolf.

Even though the mass of the wolf and of the boy were the same, the wolven form and the muscles coiled beneath his fur gave him an impact that echoed through the room. Tomas landed on his back with the wolf snarling on his chest.

"Enough," Jericho said quietly.

Pip closed his mouth as if he had just realized what was happening. He looked down and his eyes widened. He stepped off of Tomas and backed away.

Chet clapped. He ducked under the ropes and crossed to Tomas. "Well done," he said.

Jericho gave Chet a searching look as the Alpha held up the rope for Pip to climb under.

"There's a change of clothes in the locker room," Dray said, pointing to a door. "Help him find them, then come back."

Jericho did as he was told while Chet helped Tomas up.

"You threw some good punches there," he told the boy.

"Uh, thanks," Tomas answered. He climbed over the ropes and made his way back to Boris. The Alpha gave a single nod of approval. A smile spread across Tomas' face. The rest of his pack commented on his fighting style, patting his back and congratulating him.

"Was there a point to this?" Dray asked Chet quietly.

Chet nodded and raised his voice to the class. There was a hard edge to it when he asked, "Did you see what just happened?"

Everyone immediately sobered at his tone.

Chet waited. Alex had been around the werewolf enough to know that he would wait until someone gave an answer.

He raised a hand. Chet tipped his head. "Yes, Alex?"

"Everyone has a break point," Alex stated.

Chet nodded. "Exactly." His voice still carried a bite. "And if you reach that breaking point in public, what happens?"

"You'll be shot," Boris said.

Chet pretended like he didn't hear the Alpha. Boris let out a loud sigh and raised his hand. At Chet's indication, he repeated, "You'll be shot."

Jericho and Pip walked back into the room. Chet gave each a short nod before he continued, "Yes. If you lose control like Ears just did—"

"Pip," Dray corrected.

Chet continued as if he hadn't heard him, "Then you're dead. Your goal in combat training this year is going to be extending your snapping point. If you can't control yourself here, you aren't going to do it out there. Let's get busy. Now, who's going to fight Boris?"

Chapter Five

Everyone was black and blue by the time someone tolled the gong three times, indicating the conclusion of class.

"I'm going to enjoy combat training," Boris said in the hallway.

Alex stood near Jericho. The Alpha bristled. Even though Dray had warned the werewolves to go light on each other, neither Alpha had pulled their punches. By the end, all of the werewolves were slamming their opponents as they ran through the punches and blocks Dray showed them. Alex was grateful werewolves healed quickly; even so, if every day was like that, they would all be one big bruise before it was over.

He rubbed a particularly sore bruise on his arm from blocking a kick Sid was supposed to land on his shin, but had aimed for his groin. It was a good thing Alex had fast reflexes. That might have been his snapping point after all that had happened.

"I'm not sure I approve of Chet's training techniques," Cassie said quietly, rubbing her arms. Boris' team was severely lacking in any weaker members, so Cassie had been forced to train against Brace, who had it out for Alex already and didn't mind showing his aggression against Alex's twin. Chet had finally stepped in and Dray finished training with Cassie.

"Maybe they'll let us train with our own pack members next time," Alex said. He wanted to give her hope that it would get better, but part of him needed to pit his strength against Sid again. The hatred in Boris' Second gave him something to match. He didn't hate Sid, but there were a few punches that made it a close thing.

"Dray says we have wilderness education next," Jericho said, catching up to them. "Where's that?"

Alex and Cassie exchanged an excited look. "We'll show you," Alex said. He took off running down the hall with Cassie at his side. The rest of the pack fell in quickly behind them.

Alex pushed open one of the rear doors to the Academy and stepped into the sunlight. He took in a deep breath of fresh summer air as they jogged across the clearing.

"Do you have to run everywhere?" Don protested, panting. "I'm built for strength, not running."

"That's gonna change," Alex called over his shoulder.

Cassie reached the gate first and quickly unlatched it. Everyone piled through. Alex began to pull off his shirt. He glanced around and realized that everyone was just watching him. He grinned. "Time to phase. Come on!"

Faces lit up around him at the command. Everyone stepped behind bushes and trees to pull off their clothes before they phased.

Alex willed the change to come. It took only a matter of seconds, but he enjoyed the way his arms and legs shifted, changing size and musculature. His ears lengthened and grew pointed, shifting to higher on his skull. His nose and mouth elongated and formed into a muzzle. Dark gray fur ran down his back and up his arms. He stretched, then shook, settling the fur around his shoulders. It had been far too long since he had been in wolf form.

A howl called through the trees. It was a command to gather. Alex gave a wolfish grin and stepped out from behind his tree. The other members of his pack joined him. Jericho had the thick black fur of an Alpha. The rest of the male members of the pack were various shades of gray, while the females were cream-colored. Alpha females were pure white, but there were no female Alphas on Pack Jericho.

Cassie bumped her shoulder against Alex's. The smile in

her eyes said she felt as happy to be a wolf as Alex did. Jericho looked at Alex. He tipped his head toward the origin of the howl. Jericho gave a bark of command and started to run.

The werewolves fell in behind their Alpha. Alex's paws ate up the ground in a steady thrum. The heady scent of loam and pine needles flooded him with joy. He was at home beneath the trees, one with the pack around him that matched the cadence of their Alpha. The next howl that sounded filled him with such elation he had to lift his voice with it. Soon, the howls of fifteen wolves mingled with Rafe and Colleen's voices. More howls rose to meet them; the other pack wasn't far behind.

They reached a clearing above the Academy that was flooded with sunlight. Alex blinked, willing his eyes to adjust after the shadows of the trees. Instinct warned him. He bent his knees and allowed himself to be bowled over, then rolled back to his paws prepared to defend himself.

His eyes adjusted to the older wolf with a dark gray coat. Rafe gave a huff of amusement. Alex answered with a toothy grin. He realized with a start that Jericho was right behind him, his hackles lifted and legs straight as if he was ready to defend Alex should he appear to need it. Alex bumped Rafe's shoulder with his own, showing their camaraderie. Jericho gave a snort, his gaze uncertain. A familiar scent touched Alex's nose.

"Glad to see everyone's getting along," Colleen said, stepping into the clearing.

She smiled as the other pack, which turned out to be Shannon and Shaylee's. The packs nodded at each other amiably, but kept to themselves as they waited for what was next.

"Welcome to wilderness education," Colleen told the

group. "Today is going to be more about fun and pack camaraderie than education, but hey, we'll learn as we go." She smiled at Rafe. The wolf sat near her feet and surveyed the group. "Your job today is to follow Rafe and his wild wolf pack; see how they interact, how they play, how they hunt."

She gave a little, amused laugh. "Each of your packs has fifteen members; throw in Rafe's pack, and we've got just under forty wolves roaming the woods. Good thing we're in Rafe's forest. You won't get shot if you stay within the boundaries."

She stepped behind a tree and came out in her wolf form. Colleen was the only black and cream colored wolf Alex had ever seen. Her violet eyes stood out in sharp contrast. Rafe touched her nose with his. He turned and ran into the woods. Colleen gave a sharp bark and followed. Jericho and Shannon fell in with the rest of the werewolves close behind.

Alex had never run with so many wolves. Those who grew up around the forest ghosted on near silent paws, while the city werewolves and others who hadn't had the freedom to run could be heard stepping on the leaves, sticks, and brush those who knew the value of silence avoided. Alex fought back a smile as Jericho quickly picked up the way Rafe and Colleen ran. He was quick at learning, and had proven to be a good leader so far. Alex was proud to be his Second.

Rafe's wolf pack joined them. The wild wolves ran within and around the werewolf packs. Alex could see the uncertainty some of the werewolves felt at running with truly wild wolves, but he had grown up with them near, and knew he could trust their instincts. They vanished again, running ahead to find a game trail.

A few minutes later, a howl sounded. Heat ran through Alex's blood. Rafe's wolves had found a scent. He caught up to the smell. The sharp, musky scent of a buck filled his nose. He surged ahead, careful to stay just behind Jericho, but anxious to watch the wolves at work. Jericho glanced back and saw how close Alex was. He leaped forward, willing to play along.

Rafe's pack backed the buck against a slab of rock. It was an older animal, and limped heavily on its front leg. A closer look showed that the leg had been injured and healed wrong. The animal wouldn't survive the coming winter. It lowered its head and swiped at the wolves with huge antlers. Adrenaline rushed through Alex. He wanted to be there with them, helping them to pull down the animal as he had done in the past.

He glanced at Jericho. Pack protocol dictated that he didn't participate unless his Alpha did, but the emotions from the earlier run-in with Boris were still fuming in the back of his mind. He needed to let it out somehow.

To his surprise, Jericho tipped his head toward the buck. Alex stared at him. Jericho gave what passed as a smile for a wolf and nodded his head at the buck again, granting Alex permission to go. The rest of the pack watched with uncertainty. Shannon and Shaylee exchanged glances and didn't move from their position.

Alex looked at his sister. Cassie's gaze was on the buck. She had helped the pack hunt enough times that he could see the want to participate in her eyes, but she held back. Alex snorted. She shook her head without looking at him. Alex blew out a breath and leaped forward.

Rafe jumped at the buck's head. One of the wild wolves bit a foreleg. The buck swept its head to the side, attempting to dislodge the animal with its antlers. Colleen grabbed an antler in her jaws. The weight of the wolf pulled the animal forward. Alex leaped at the animal the same time Rafe did.

Each latched onto a side of the buck's neck. As they pulled it down, a wolf disemboweled the animal. Rafe grabbed its throat and freed the buck's lifeblood. The wolves stepped back as it thrashed once, then grew still.

Alex's heart pounded loudly in his ears. Pride filled him at what he had helped the pack accomplish. Usually the pack went after smaller game; he had never helped them pull down a full grown buck before. The sense of accomplishment chased away the frustration and rage he had felt toward Boris. He panted and looked over his shoulder.

The other werewolves were watching them with wide eyes. If ever a wolf showed a look of horror, it was reflected on Shannon and Shaylee's faces. Even Jericho seemed a bit pensive as he watched Alex. Shannon and Shaylee turned away. The rest of their pack followed. To Alex's surprise, Cassie was the next to leave. She held his gaze for a second, then turned and padded away with her tail low. Von and Amos followed, with Pip, Trent, and the rest behind. Eventually, even Jericho joined them.

Alex was torn between joining the pack for the feast and following his Alpha. It was a part of pack bonding to share in the meal, but Alex's pack was gone. He followed the trail of the others beneath the trees. It was with a much different feeling that he shifted and pulled on his clothes. He found the two packs waiting for him near the gate.

"What was that?" Shannon demanded.

"Take it easy," Jericho warned her.

"What about the poor deer?" Shaylee seconded.

Alex stared at her. "You're sad about the deer?" he asked.

"Everyone's sad about the deer," Terith replied quietly. The young werewolf pulled on one of her blond curls and refused to look at him.

Alex studied them all, his chest tight. "The wolves had to

eat."

"We didn't have to be there," Shannon said.

"But you're wolves," Alex replied. He glanced at Cassie, confused. His twin sister stood at the edge of the group and looked at her toes.

"We're werewolves," Shannon said. "It's different." She waved toward the Academy. "We have lunch waiting for us, not some sad elk that's now getting eaten because of you."

"It was a deer, not an elk," Pip said next to Alex.

Alex stared, surprised at the young werewolf's courage.

Shannon clenched her hands into fists and took a step forward.

Jericho stepped in front of Alex and Pip. "There were other wolves hunting besides Alex, real wolves. They needed to eat."

Shannon shook her head. "He didn't need to join them. Control your Second, Jericho." She stormed away with the rest of her pack close behind.

Jericho was silent for several seconds. He glanced back at Alex. "We'll talk later," he said quietly.

Alex nodded.

Jericho led his pack through the gate for lunch. Cassie was the last to follow him.

"Cass?" Alex called quietly, his voice desperate.

She turned at the gate. "I wanted to join you, Alex, but you saw the way everyone watched the wolves." Tears showed in her dark blue eyes. "I didn't know what to do. I finally feel like I fit in somewhere. If I had helped with the buck, they wouldn't be speaking to me now."

Alex's heart threatened to break. He nodded. "I understand. It's alright." He mustered a weak smile. "I'm glad you're fitting in."

She gave him a hug. "I'm so sorry."

He patted her back. "It's alright. Go join the others. I'll be there in a bit."

"I'll save you a seat," his sister said.

He nodded and she slipped through the gate.

When she was out of sight, Alex let out a slow breath and leaned against the thick iron bars. He glanced up and was surprised to see Rafe walking silently through the trees in his human form. Rafe was the only instructor at the Academy who lived in the forest full time. Colleen had once told Alex that her mate was wild at heart. He loved the forest far more than walls and doors, and she agreed. Spending time in the forest had helped her learn how to control her phasing. She said she suspected it was Rafe more than the forest.

The golden-eyed werewolf studied him silently. "They were a bit harsh in their judgment," he said softly after a minute.

Alex nodded. Tears burned at the corners of his eyes, but he refused to let them fall. "I don't understand."

Rafe tipped his head toward the trees. "Walk with me."

Alex fell in beside the instructor. As hard as he tried, he could never step as silently as the wild werewolf. He felt clumsy even though his own tread had made his other pack mates sound like elephants.

Rafe stopped on little rise above were the wolves were feasting. Colleen sat near them in her human form. Two wolf pups fought over a small twig she held.

The wolves had done a good job on the buck. Bones showed in the noon light and their eating had slowed.

"When you look down there, what do you see?" Rafe asked.

"A pack that's fed and happy," Alex replied.

Rafe nodded. "Your pack mates see a deer that used to run free within this forest and is now lying slaughtered on the grass."

"But it was lame," Alex pointed out. "It wouldn't have survived winter."

"You and I know that," Rafe conceded. "But you have something they don't."

"What is that?" Alex asked, wondering if it was good or bad.

"You're in touch with your instincts," Rafe explained. "My fear with these new generations of werewolves is that they are only in touch with their human side. A werewolf is made of both human and animal. It is important to know both parts equally. You do."

Warmth filled Alex's chest at the compliment.

Rafe gave him a sideways look. "But your friends are more heart than practical right now, and that is also a good thing."

Alex glanced at him. "Why is that good?"

Rafe pulled a twig from an aspen tree and sank to a crouch on the ground. Alex followed his example and sat with his back against another tree. The werewolf was silent for several more minutes. When he finally spoke, his golden eyes were clouded as though he saw the images he described.

"You and I both witnessed the deaths of our parents. They were murdered in front of us." Rafe's brow creased, his gaze distant. "That sort of thing changes the way a person views death."

A shudder ran down Alex's spine. He saw his parents as they sat in the living room playing a card game while Alex and Cassie fought with toy lions on the floor. A fire glowed in the fireplace. Snow fell outside, its soft shush audible between his mom's laughter and dad's warm chuckles. Alex heard a footstep. He glanced up.

His mom and dad were already looking at the front door.

His dad's eyes widened. "Children, run," he said.

But the door burst open before anyone could move. Alex held Cassie; they huddled in the corner. She buried her face against him as the man with the mismatched eyes drew a knife across his dad's throat. The blood looked unnaturally bright as it poured down the blue checkered pattern of his dad's favorite shirt. His mother was next. A tear trailed slowly down her cheek. Alex's attention stayed on the tear, even as her eyes closed.

"Watching something so brutal alters the way death looks," Rafe continued quietly. He glanced at Alex. "It makes the way the buck died feel more normal, natural."

"Beautiful," Alex concluded softly.

"Because he died to feed others?" Rafe asked.

"Because he died for a reason," Alex replied.

Rafe nodded and stood. "The innocence of your classmates is a good thing. They might not understand you, but be patient with them. You've been through things they haven't experienced, which can make them uncomfortable." He tipped his head toward the Academy. "Come out here whenever the walls start to close in on you," he offered.

"Thanks," Alex replied. He watched the wild werewolf disappear back through the trees. One second Rafe was there, then Alex blinked and he was gone. Alex stood and made his way back to the school.

He let his hands trail on the bark of the trees, enjoying the way some were rough and pulled at the skin of his fingers, while others were smooth like a rock in a stream. The birds sang with the carefree notes of robins, sparrows, and starlings that had plenty to eat and warm sunlight on their wings. Alex knew there was a big difference between the bugs and nuts the birds enjoyed versus the deer the wolves had brought down, but in his mind, they had both fulfilled their purpose.

There was peace to the thought; he only wished the others could feel it.

Chapter Six

Alex smiled at the sight of the plate Cassie had already dished up for him. The others were already eating, and barely noticed his entrance. Alex sat down beside his sister and she gave him an apologetic smile.

"I really am sorry," she said quietly.

He shook his head. "I talked to Rafe and he explained things. It's okay."

"Are you sure?" she asked, her gaze worried.

He nodded. "Thank you for dishing me up some food."

"I was worried Amos and Don would eat it all," she replied.

Jericho chuckled from across the table. "It's not Amos and Don you need to worry about," he said. He pointed at Pip's plate.

The little werewolf had piled spaghetti, meatballs, salad, and rolls so high that the meatballs kept spilling off onto the table. The Second Year ate them as fast as they fell.

"What?" Pip asked with his mouth as full as a chipmunk's when he realized everyone was looking at him.

Alex laughed and shook his head. He took a bite of the spaghetti.

"Better than moose?" Shaylee called from across the room.

"It was a deer," Pip corrected, spitting food onto the table.

"Ew, Pip, gross," Terith complained. She shoved the pieces back to him with her napkin.

"Whatever," Shaylee replied. "We know you prefer something with hooves."

Alex ignored her, concentrating on his food to get it cleared as fast as possible.

"Why aren't the professors here?" Jericho asked.

Alex and Cassie exchanged a look. Several other Lifers at the table fought back smiles.

"There's a tradition," Alex answered.

"Every year," Trent said.

"What tradition?" Jericho questioned with a worried expression.

A roll flew across the room and landed in Torin's spaghetti, splashing sauce all over him. Torin's face reddened. The Lifer Alpha picked up his entire plate and threw it back at Boris. The Termer Alpha ducked; the plate flew past him and hit Kalia square in the face, covering her in spaghetti.

"Duck!" Amos yelled in his deep voice. Everyone at their table obeyed. A platter of lettuce flew over followed by a bowl of dressing. It splattered across the table.

"This is the tradition?" Jericho asked. "This is ridiculous!"

"Yeah," Trent said, scratching his buzzed head, "But the professors have found that the food fight creates camaraderie within the packs as they defend each other. They decided long ago that it was easier to stay out of it than try to break it up, and that the benefits outweighed the negatives." He paused. "Kind of like that deer Alex helped to bring down."

Everyone looked at Alex. He gave a little shrug of his shoulders as a bowl full of rolls slid under the table. He picked one up and handed it to Jericho.

The Alpha looked at his pack like they were crazy. He shook his head, and the hint of a smile crossed his face. "Pack Jericho?" he asked.

All fourteen other members of the pack grabbed rolls. "Pack Jericho," they replied.

"Get them!" Jericho commanded.

Pack Jericho swarmed from beneath the table and pegged the other tables with rolls. An answering hail of meatballs, dressing, and strands of spaghetti flew through the air. The pack dove under the table again.

"Well that wasn't a good plan," Jericho said, his chest heaving.

"What about the wolves?" Alex asked.

Everyone watched him carefully, wondering what he was getting at.

"Remember how they hunted?" Cassie pressed, catching on.

Terith nodded excitedly. "Strength in numbers," she said.

Jericho smiled as everyone warmed to the idea. He picked up a handful of rolls and meatballs and tucked them in his arm. Everyone followed their Alpha's actions.

"Ready?" Jericho asked.

"Ready," Alex replied.

"Let's hunt," Jericho said.

He jumped from beneath the table and the rest of Pack Jericho followed. They kept to his heels, pegging werewolves left and right as they tried to take down the pack's leader. Pack Jericho ran in a tight pack around the room, throwing meatballs and rolls, and pausing to resupply when the pack was low.

"We give up!" Shannon and Shaylee finally said, holding up their hands as Pack Jericho swarmed the table their pack was hiding beneath.

Alex couldn't help laughing. No one had ever given up during the food fight. Jericho gave him a thumb's-up and they ran to the next table, ready to peg those hiding beneath with reformed meatballs and handfuls of spaghetti.

"We're done," Boris shouted. Lettuce was caught in his hair. Alex spotted Kalia behind him still covered in spaghetti. She looked ready to phase into a wolf and tear someone's throat out.

"Come on," Jericho said. They followed him. Table after table gave in to the merciless onslaught from Pack Jericho.

They were almost to the last table. Pack Torin still waited. Alex wondered if they would give in like the other packs. Jericho was about to call out the command to attack when a single meatball flew through the air. It sped toward Jericho at a force only an Alpha could have managed.

"Jericho!" Alex shouted. Everything slowed. He leaped. Would he make it in time?

Jericho turned; his eyes widened. The meatball that was intended for his face slammed into Alex's chest. Alex fell to the floor gasping for air. Everyone froze.

Alex gulped in a huge breath, then the laugh he had been holding in burst from him. All around the room, answering laughter erupted. Jericho fell to his knees beside his Second gasping with laughter.

"I've never seen anything so hilarious," the Alpha proclaimed.

Alex sat up and attempted to wipe the meatball mess from his shirt while he grinned. "I couldn't let my Alpha take the bullet," he replied.

Cassie smiled at her brother. "That was awesome," she said, pulling spaghetti from her curly brown hair.

"That was ridiculous," Terith stated, but the grin on her face said she had enjoyed it.

"Way to be dramatic," Trent said, slapping Alex on the back.

Amos grabbed Alex by an arm and lifted him to his feet.

"Thanks, big guy," Alex replied.

"You funny," Amos said, giving a deep chuckle. "You make me laugh."

"He made all of us laugh," Jericho agreed.

The packs climbed from beneath their tables. Everyone

looked around at the mess.

"Well," Alex said. "Guess we better get cleaning."

"You mean you clean up, too?" Jericho said.

"Not like we can leave this for the professors," Pip replied. He grabbed several brooms from the corner where they had obviously been placed on purpose.

Alex took one and began sweeping. The other packs joined in, marking the conclusion of the first lunch of the term.

***

The students went back to their quarters to change.

"Awesome job, Second," Jericho said. "Way to go beyond the line of duty."

"Anytime," Alex replied. He stepped into his room and froze.

The scent of blood filled his nose. He flipped on the light, and grimaced at the carnage. Someone had taken a chicken and smeared the blood all over his bed and the floor. The following word was written in blood on the wall: Dinner.

"I just wanted to ask. . . ." Jericho's voice died away when he saw what Alex was looking at. "Any chance that's syrup?" he asked, though it was obvious by his expression that he could smell the blood.

"It's alright," Alex said. "I'll take care of it." He took a step forward.

Jericho grabbed Alex's arm. "No, Alex. We'll take care of it," the Alpha said. He called over his shoulder, "Pack Jericho, to Alex's room."

Within seconds, every member of the pack was staring at the blood. Cassie's eyes filled with tears. Alex shook his head, telling her not to cry. She took a calming breath and nodded, but her dark blue eyes still glittered brightly.

Jericho's voice carried steel when he told the pack, "Someone came into our quarters and violated the room of one of our pack members. Are we going to stand for this?"

The fierce 'No' that answered rang through Alex's heart. He had never had a pack member defend him before, let alone the Alpha. Alex watched numbly as everyone got to work scrubbing his room. He carried his blankets to the wash basket and was bringing a clean change back when Professor Kaynan opened the door to Pack Jericho's quarters.

Kaynan's nose wrinkled at the scent of blood. "Is everything okay?" he asked.

Alex nodded. "Just a bit of hazing. No one got hurt."

"Are you sure, Alex?" Kaynan pressed, his red eyes searching the meeting room.

"I'm sure," Alex replied. "Are we late for class?"

Kaynan nodded. "About ten minutes late. Grace is waiting to teach you guys English, then you have Mouse and Lyra for Biology. Pack Maliki is already down there."

"We'll hurry," Alex promised, amazed he must have missed the bell with everything else that was going on.

Kaynan hesitated, but Alex gave him a reassuring smile. Kaynan nodded and left the room.

"A bit of hazing?" Jericho said, entering the meeting room.

Alex shrugged. "A bit."

"If that's a bit, I don't want to know what a lot of hazing is," Jericho replied with a shake of his head.

"Someone's still holding a grudge against your hunt," Trent told Alex.

Nobody had to say who had done the dirty work. Though Shannon and Shaylee had been the most vocal about it, they must have told Boris. His scent was mixed with the blood in Alex's room. The Termers were holding true to the Academy tradition of hating Lifers. They were banning together. Alex realized it didn't matter if he was a Lifer underneath an Alpha who was a Termer; the target was still on his back.

Alex led the way to the classrooms. Jericho was content to follow, learning the hallways of the Academy. Alex liked the Alpha's quiet ways. He had been under a few Alphas who insisted on pushing their leadership on everyone, making sure each knew who was in charge. Jericho accepted that he was one of the newest members of the Academy, and it didn't seem to bother him to ask Alex for advice. Alex's views on what made a leader were changing.

"Welcome to English," Grace said from the front of the classroom. Her long dark brown hair swayed around her waist as she turned to smile at them with sightless blue eyes.

Alex took a seat and smiled at her even though she couldn't see him. Grace had lost her eyesight due to experiments during the same time Kaynan was made into a werewolf. Somehow, that linked them. Grace could see when Kaynan was in wolf form beside her. She taught without needing to see, however, and was one of Alex's favorite teachers.

"We thought it would be interesting to begin the term learning about 'The Call of the Wild'," Grace said. Several students in the class laughed. She held up the book. "Prepare to be educated by Jack London. This story was originally published in serial form in a magazine, with one portion being released at a time. We'll follow the same format as we read."

Alex glanced at Cassie. His sister was already ten pages into the book. He sighed and opened his own. Reading wasn't his favorite thing, but he would humor Professor Grace and attempt it.

***

Professor Lyra looked just like her husband in that she was small and skinny with big glasses, but Lyra also had long blonde hair pulled back in two braids. She wore a lab coat and smelled faintly of cleaning agents. Her room was the cleanest in the entire school.

Biology began with Professor Lyra showing the muscle breakdown of a deer on the screen. Everyone in Alex's pack moaned. Alex stifled a laugh.

"We just saw that," Terith complained.

Professor Mouse adjusted his glasses and gave her a surprised look. "If I'm not mistaken, this is the first time I've taught animal musculature," he began.

Von spoke up with a finger in his nose, "Professor Rafe's wolves killed a deer while we were in wilderness education."

Trent nodded. "It was a first-hand encounter with the deer's musculature," he said.

Mouse fought back a smile at the students' dismayed tones. The professor glanced at Pack Raynen's side of the classroom. "Did you happen to have a similar experience?" he asked.

Raynen shook his head. "The deer was pretty much eaten when it was our turn. We saw mostly bones."

"Lucky," Terith said quietly.

Mouse glanced at Lyra. "Wish I could have been there," she stated.

Terith shook her head and let out a loud sigh. "You're all sick."

Mouse chuckled. "Well, since you've already seen this up close, you'll know the answers to the questions I'm about to ask." He pointed with a laser pen to the hind leg. "What is the name of this muscle?"

"The rump roast?" Pip replied.

Several members of Raynen's pack laughed, but Jericho's wasn't amused. Alex shot him a grin, surprised at the small Second Year's bravery. It he wasn't careful, the Termer was going to be hazed next.

Mouse rolled his eyes. "Very funny, Pip. We're going to go with the biceps femoris muscle. Can anyone tell me why this is important?"

Chapter Seven

By the time the pack was dismissed, Alex's page was filled with notes. He shut his notebook and followed the others into the hallway.

"What next?" Pip asked.

Jericho gave him a stern look as Pack Raynen walked by. "Are you trying to get on the other packs' bad side?" he asked.

Pip ducked his head as protocol dictated and scuffed his toe on the ground. "No. I'm sorry."

Jericho couldn't keep his stern expression long. "I'm just trying to protect you," he told the younger werewolf. "You might want to keep that mouth in check if you don't want to become the center of attention around here, especially with the kind of attention our pack has been attracting."

"Okay," Pip agreed. He glanced at Alex. Alex was surprised to see the boy's search for approval. He couldn't keep a stern expression, and when he smiled, Pip grinned back and followed at his side to history.

Alex grimaced at the sight of Torin's pack already seated on one side of the room. The Lifer Alpha looked just as excited to see Pack Jericho walk in.

"Great, the rejects," he muttered.

Several members of his pack laughed.

"Hope you enjoy Pack Loser, Amos," Sid, Torin's Second, said.

"It's good," Amos replied.

"It's good," Sid mimicked, imitating the werewolf's slow speech.

Amos looked at Jericho.

"Ignore him," the Alpha commanded. Amos nodded and looked away from the laughing pack.

"Good morning, Professor Thorson," Cassie said as soon as he entered the room.

"Good morning, Miss Cassie." The smile the human professor gave her warmed Alex's heart.

Cassie and the elderly professor had become fast friends during their first years at the Academy. Professor Thorson was learning how to work with werewolves, and Cassie hadn't opened up to anyone besides Alex since their parents were killed. Given Cassie's keen interest in history, and Professor Thorson's ability to teach facts all day without referring to a book, it was a friendship forged the moment she had stepped into his classroom as a First Year.

"In this class, we're going to begin with werewolf mythology and how it ties into the fears we encounter today," the professor began.

Torin sat up. "How is that history? Werewolf mythology isn't made up of facts."

"Are you sitting here today?" Professor Thorson asked.

"Does it look like I'm sitting here today?" Torin retorted in an obstinate tone.

"Yes, it does," the professor answered simply, obviously used to stubborn students. "And you are a werewolf. Because werewolves are born, and not made through bites and other methods of spreading lycanthropy as some myths detail, werewolves have a past just like humans. Therefore, werewolf mythology must contain some facts, otherwise you appeared from nowhere."

"Poof," Pip called out.

The look Torin shot the Second Year was filled with threat.

Professor Thorson held up a hand. "Alright. Let me prove it to you. Open the books in front of you to page thirty. There are many accounts of ancient gods changing mortals into wolves. In fact, one of the oldest known written works on earth is called "The Epic of Gilgamesh", in which the goddess Ishtar turns a man into a wolf."

He smiled and sat on the edge of his desk. "In the human world, Lycanthropy is defined as a mental disorder in which the patient believes that he or she is a wolf." Several students laughed. The professor continued, "However, we know a lycanthrope is a werewolf; the word comes from the Greek lykos, meaning wolf, and the Greek anthropos, meaning man. This word can be found throughout history, and in some of the oldest accounts of mythology."

He indicated the page he had instructed them to turn to. "In ancient Greece mythology, the King Lycaon of Acadia attempted to feed human meat to a visitor, who turned out to be none other than the god Jupiter. Jupiter transformed Lycaon in to a wolf. Lycaon's name and the word Lycanthropy come from the root of the Greek word lykos, meaning wolf. So you see, the myths are connected."

"So the Greeks believed in werewolves?" Torin asked. There was a hint of interest in the bored tone he tried to maintain.

"Very much so," Professor Thorson replied. "Many civilizations have their own werewolf stories. Did you ever hear the story of Romulus and Remus?"

"I have," Cassie said.

Alex smiled. It was unusual for his sister to speak up in class.

At the professor's nod, Cassie recited, "Romulus and Remus are a part of Roman mythology. Their mother, Rhea Silvia, conceived twins by the god Mars. When the twins were born, they were thrown into a river by Rhea Silvia's jealous uncle Amulius. The twins were saved by a wolf who raised them. Remus was later killed, and Romulus founded a great city, and named it after himself."

"Rome," Pip said, his eyes wide.

Professor Thorson nodded. "Very good. The she-wolf who suckled the twins became an iconic symbol for the city and the legend."

"But they weren't directly werewolves," Torin pointed out.

"True," Professor Thorson conceded. He smoothed a hand down his thin white hair. "Don't forget that I am new to werewolf lore myself. I had to do research to teach this class." He smiled at Cassie. "It isn't often that I've had to do research in order to teach." He pointed to his head. "It's all in here. That's why I'm going bald. All the knowledge I've learned has taken up too much room so my hair can't grow."

Alex chuckled. Torin rolled his eyes.

Professor Thorson held out a hand. "It used to be thought that people became werewolves by putting on a piece of clothing such as a belt made from wolf skin. Germany, Belgium, and the Netherlands have such legends. If it was that easy, I think everyone would do it." He became sober. "But in Europe, tales of werewolves began to increase. People began to fear for their lives and for their livestock. A man named Peter Stubbe was one of the first captured werewolves. Unfortunately, he was tried and convicted of murder, putting a very black mark on the werewolf name."

The students were becoming more interested with each story. Even Torin had forgotten to keep his bored expression and was sitting straight in his seat, intent on what the professor was saying.

Professor Thorson leaned forward with an arm on his knee. "It's those kinds of acts that forced werewolves to go into hiding. Many civilizations have their own tales of werewolves. There are legends of skin-walkers among the

Native Americans, Scottish and Irish folklore detail men and women turning into wolves and seals, and Ancient Egyptians worshiped and feared their wolf god Ap-uat. Throughout our history, tales of wolves flourish, but the werewolf race has been very good at hiding."

"Until now," Alex said quietly.

Professor Thorson nodded. "Until now. As you know, Jaze Carso, the founder of our Academy, revealed werewolves to the world six years ago in order to protect our race from the Extremists who attempted to wipe it out. It was our only option. However, our allies turned against us, and genocide of the werewolf race was almost successful. You've been forced to go into hiding once again."

"History repeats itself," Cassie said.

The professor's gaze was sad. "Yes, it does. But maybe this time we can find a way to solve the werewolf problem."

"What problem is that?" Terith asked.

The professor adjusted his glasses and leaned forward. "You are such fearsome creatures that every time you are found out, society tries to annihilate you."

Smiles showed on all of the faces at his scary storyteller tone.

"That is a problem," Jericho said.

Professor Thorson nodded. "It's a problem for your generation to solve."

"What if we just take all power?" Torin asked.

"Yeah," Sid echoed. "What if we take over completely?"

The professor watched everyone with an interested expression. At his silence, Torin pressed, "Well?"

"You tell me," the professor invited.

"We become exactly what society fears," Cassie said. She fell silent when everyone turned to look at her. At Professor Thorson's encouraging nod, she continued in a quieter voice,

"They fear us because we're the more dominant species."

"Then let's dominate," Torin said. Cheers went up from his pack.

"But we don't have numbers," Cassie said, her voice slightly shaky at addressing an Alpha. "They would wipe us out completely."

"Let them try," Torin said with a snort.

"They did," Pip replied.

Torin glared at him.

"Cassie's right," the professor said. "So what options do you have?"

"We could hide ourselves forever," Terith suggested.

"Or prove that we want to live in peace," Alex said.

Professor Thorson nodded. "That is exactly what Jaze tried to do, but his efforts were negated by allies who turned out to be the enemy. They gave the world more reasons to fear werewolves than your race had to refute them."

"So we work on those reasons," Alex guessed.

"And keep yourselves hidden until society is better able to accept you," the professor agreed.

***

"To physical education with Professor Vance," Jericho repeated the instructions Professor Thorson had given him.

"Just Vance," Alex corrected.

"Isn't he a professor?" Jericho asked, confused.

Alex nodded. "Yeah, but he hates the title. I'd call him just Vance if you don't want to be stuck running laps. He's been pressing the dean to let him form a football team; he already runs class like we're on one."

"Good to know," Jericho replied.

When they reached the gym, Alex stifled a groan at the sight of Pack Boris already stretching on the floor.

"Again?" Trent complained under his breath. "Haven't we been tortured enough?"

"No," Vance replied. The instructor was a huge werewolf, the biggest Alex had ever seen. He towered above any teacher at the Academy and seemed more like a bear than a wolf. His dark blonde hair was cut short in a buzz cut, and he sounded like a drill sergeant straight from the movies. Alex hadn't had many classes with Vance yet, but knew the instructor had a short fuse. When he asked Jaze about it, the dean said Vance had lost his love, Nora, during the attempted genocide. Since then, he hadn't been especially happy around anyone, and who could blame him?

"You haven't been tortured enough. That's why you have P.E. with me," Vance continued. He motioned toward two doors. "The locker rooms are back there. Find the clothes, get changed, and be back here in less than two minutes."

"Two minutes?" Pip protested. "How's that even possible?"

Vance gave him a flat look. "I'm counting."

Pip turned white and everyone rushed to the locker

rooms.

"I knew our last class wasn't going to be an easy one," Trent whined as he pulled on the unflattering green shorts and white shirt.

Alex was relieved that at least the gym clothes smelled like they had been laundered. He pulled them on as quickly as he could.

"Phys Ed with Vance," Boris said, stepping around the corner already dressed in his gym clothes. "How scary. Are you going to call your mommy? Oh wait, I forget. You don't have a mommy, Stray."

Trent dropped his gaze and didn't answer.

Boris shoved the boy into a locker. Jericho was suddenly there. "Leave him alone, Boris."

Boris looked Jericho up and down. Standing toe to toe, Alex was surprised to see that they appeared to be an even match. Boris had always seemed so big before, yet despite Jericho's unassuming manner, if the other Alpha attacked, he would definitely put up a good fight.

A whistle blew outside the locker room. "Boys, get out here. You got beat by a bunch of girls."

The Alphas turned away from each other and rushed out of the room with their packs on their heels. The girls stood dressed in the same green and white clothes, and looked like they enjoyed them even less.

"Hope girls beating boys isn't a habit you're forming," Vance said. "Let's find out." He pulled out a cart filled with kick balls. "Dodge ball. Whoever loses has to run ten laps."

"Ten?" Pip protested.

"Twenty," Vance corrected.

Everyone glared at Pip.

"Mom said no throw things at girls," Amos said with confusion on his large face.

"Then make her regret sending you to the Academy," Vance replied. He dumped out the cart of balls and walked away.

"Pleasant," Jericho whispered, picking up a ball.

Chapter Eight

By the time Alex collapsed on his bed, he couldn't imagine every day going like the one he had just had. He threw an arm over his eyes and blew out a short breath. Just then, a howl broke through the air. Alex's heart raced in answer.

"What does that mean?" Jericho called from his room.

"Night games!" excited voices replied.

Alex jumped out of bed and pulled on his clothes.

"Everyone's happy about night games?" Jericho asked doubtfully, leaning against Alex's door frame as he pulled on a shirt.

"You'll see," Alex replied. "Trust me."

Jericho's eyebrows lifted.

"Have I ever steered you wrong?" Alex asked.

"It's the first day," Jericho pointed out.

Alex shrugged. "I'd like to keep a winning record."

Jericho smiled. "Fine. I trust you. Let's go."

Pack Jericho rushed out the door to find the other werewolves running down the stairs. They joined in the chaos, stampeding with the mass to the front of the Academy. Someone had already turned off the regular lights, bathing the courtyard and surrounding grass in darkness.

Boris and Torin stood on opposite sides of the courtyard. Lifers and Termers rushed to the alphas. Pack Jericho hesitated in the middle.

"Choose a side," Boris called out.

"Yeah, and not the losing side," Torin replied.

"You mean it's a battle?" Jericho asked.

Alex nodded. "Termers versus Lifers. Except our pack is split. That hasn't happened before."

"I don't think splitting up would be a good idea," Jericho

said.

Alex agreed. He thought quickly. "Let's play wolf tag," he called out.

The Alphas looked at each other. It was a game the students used to play when the Academy was first formed, but night games had since evolved into more team-oriented games like steal the flag.

"That's a sissy game," Boris argued.

"Are you admitting you're too sissy to play, then?" Torin asked.

Alex felt a rush of gratitude for the Lifer Alpha whose side he was usually on.

Boris grimaced. "Wolf tag. Fine. You're on. I'll be the first wolf."

Everyone started to run.

"What's the goal?" Jericho asked, sprinting beside Alex.

"If you're touched, you have to phase, then you're one of the wolves and you join in the chase. Last one in human form wins, then it flips," Alex explained.

"Easy enough," Jericho replied. He glanced over his shoulder. "Uh-oh."

Alex's heart pounded at the sight of a huge black Alpha chasing them down. Jericho took off one way while Alex ran around the statue. He glanced back to see the Alpha follow Jericho, and ran hard into someone hiding behind Jet's statue.

He rolled on the grass and ended up on his back gasping for air. He chuckled as he rose onto one elbow to see who he had hit.

"Sorry about that. I think Boris was going to—" He paused at the sight of Boris' sister glaring at him.

Kalia stood back up and brushed the grass off the knees of her pants. "Boris was going to what?" she demanded.

"Uh, tag me?" Alex said as more of a question than a

statement.

"Kill you, more like," Kalia grumbled.

"Probably," Alex agreed. "Night games are sort of open territory."

Kalia blew out a frustrated breath and leaned against the statue with her arms folded.

Alex fought down a rush of anger at how casually she treated the statue. "What are you doing back here?" he asked.

Kalia looked like she was going to brush him off, then she hesitated. She glared up at the starlit sky and admitted, "I don't exactly belong here."

Alex let out a humorless laugh. "None of us belong here. It's just where we're stuck."

She glanced at him. "But you're a Lifer. This is your home."

Alex avoided her gaze. "Is it? Or is this where they stuck us because they didn't know what to do with the genocide *Strays*?" He spat out the last word.

She didn't have an answer.

Alex felt bad for the way he had responded. "Sorry. I don't normally vent on total strangers," he paused. "Or anyone, for that matter. Let's start over. Hi, my name is Alex Davies."

"I'm Kalia James." He was surprised when a slight smile crossed Kalia's face. It was the first he had seen. "I can't imagine being stuck here."

He smiled. "It's not really that bad. I kind-of like it." He met her gaze. "So why don't you belong here?"

She hesitated as if debating whether to trust him. She studied his face as if she searched for something in particular. Her head tipped slightly to one side, and something lightened in her icy blue eyes. "I'm not a werewolf."

Alex lifted an eyebrow skeptically. "Yet here you are."

She nodded. "Yes, here I am. Ironic, isn't it?"

"Is it?" he pressed.

She let out a breath, allowing true loss to touch her face. "I'm not supposed to be here. I never phased like Boris did. I'm not a werewolf."

"Then why are you here?" Alex asked. Werewolves usually phased for the first time when they turned seven. It wasn't uncommon for parents to send their seven and eight years olds so that if they phased, they would be at a safe place to do so, but Alex hadn't heard of someone Kalia's age being sent even though she hadn't yet phased.

Kalia grimaced. "My eyes."

Alex found himself searching them. They were a pale icy blue that hid her true emotions well. Her eyes flicked to his and dropped his gaze. "What about them?"

Kalia ground the toe of her shoe into the grass. "When I get mad, they turn gold, so people tell me. My parents thought it meant I was going to phase."

"They might be right," Alex said, though he had never heard of such a thing.

"I'm not like Boris," Kalia protested. The aversion with which she said her brother's name surprised Alex. She must have read it in his expression, because she dropped her gaze again. "I'm not a werewolf," she repeated, saying the last word with some difficulty.

"We're not that bad," Alex replied quietly, feeling slightly insulted by the disgust in her tone.

"I know," Kalia protested. "I just don't— Alex!"

A whisper of paws heralded the wolf rushing toward them faster than Alex could react. The animal barreled into him from behind and sent him flying through the grass. He rolled as he landed, and came up on his feet ready to fight. He realized with a start that it was just students playing wolf tag.

"I guess. . . I guess I'd better go," Alex said.

Kalia nodded, her face silhouetted by the moon that had risen above the statue.

Alex shook his head and pulled off his shirt as he hurried around the other side of the statue. He phased with her words repeating themselves over and over in his mind. 'I'm not like Boris. I'm not a werewolf.' Her disgust ate at him. The way she had said the word 'werewolf' made it sound like something dirty, something lower than garbage. The fact that he was one of them filled him with dislike for her.

He gritted his teeth and ran after the fleeing werewolves who were still in human form. He found Cassie hiding in her usual place within the bushes that lined the walls. The bushes had been planted a short distance away from the wall, but as they grew, the branches reached out to touch the cold stone, forming a tunnel beneath that the twins liked to hide within.

"Alex!" Cassie exclaimed on seeing his dark gray wolf form. "I haven't been found yet."

Alex snorted and gave her a wolfish grin.

"What do you want?" she asked.

He ducked his head. Her eyes lit up. She climbed onto his back, her smaller form fitting easily. She tangled her hands in his thick fur. "Let's ride!" she said like she used to when they were eight and used to play by themselves behind the Academy, pretending that it was a castle and she the princess.

Alex took off beneath the bushes and rounded the Academy in time to hear Boris proclaim, "Kalia is the last still standing in human form."

"No, I'm not," Kalia protested, pointing at Cassie. "She is!"

One hundred and fifty werewolves looked at Alex and Cassie. Alex felt Cassie's hands tighten in his fur. He gave a wolfish grin and answered with a bark of defiance.

"Tag them!" Boris commanded.

Alex spun and took off through the grounds. He had the advantage in that he had explored every inch of the Academy's lands as it was being expanded. He leaped across the small stream that went behind the greenhouse, dove beneath the apple trees in the orchard, and darted across Professor Dray and Gem's garden.

He cleared the small fence that separated the flower beds and charged around the front of the school again. Alex climbed the steps just as the other werewolves were rounding the corner of the school. He stared down at them in triumph, his chest heaving as he fought for breath.

Kalia was nowhere in sight. The truth dawned in Boris' eyes. Cassie was the last human. The tables had turned.

The Termer Alpha gave a bark and began to run in the other direction. The other werewolves realized what was going on and ran as well.

"Let's get them!" Cassie yelled.

Alex leaped off the stairs and loped across the lawn with Cassie still on his back. She reached out and touched a gray wolf. The wolf slowed and turned back to find his clothes so he could phase and hunt the rest of the werewolves with them. Cassie touched another.

Soon, dozens of werewolves in human form were rushing around them. Alex herded the werewolves in wolf form toward them like wolves did in the wild, rushing their prey to those who waited refreshed and ready to catch it. The wolves scattered when those in human form jumped out from the Academy's shadows and touched as many as they could reach. A dozen more joined their ranks. Soon, only Boris, Torin, Jericho, and Raynen remained in hiding. The Alphas were showing off their true strengths.

Alex phased near his clothes and hurriedly pulled them on.

He jogged to the steps to find the other werewolves waiting. "We can't find them," Pip said.

"They've got to be here somewhere," Alex replied. "Have you searched the greenhouse?"

"Yes, as well as the storage sheds. They're nowhere," Terith protested.

"Did you check the tunnels?" Alex asked Cassie.

She nodded. "Every one of them."

Alex looked around. He had personally checked pretty much the entire distance around the Academy. There were only two other options. "Either they're in the Academy, or they're in the forest."

"We can't go in the forest," Trent said, his voice tight.

"The Academy is off limits," Pip replied. "They'd have to be in the forest. We should look."

"But it's night," Terith protested. "That's a bad idea."

"Rafe's wolves keep the forest safe," Alex pointed out. "If the Alphas were inside the walls, we would have found them by now."

"They wouldn't give up without a fight," Sid agreed. "They're out there somewhere."

"What do we do?" Parker, Boris' Second asked.

Alex smiled. "We find them."

Chapter Nine

Alex ran beneath the trees. He wanted to phase to wolf form and follow their trail, but that would have been cheating. The sound of the others following him died away as he ducked under boles and jumped over fallen trees. He loved the forest even more at night with the sounds of the crickets and other night insects creating a tapestry of sound that wove beneath the trees. An owl called above. Alex grinned and ran on.

Cassie was just as comfortable within the midnight forest as he was. He didn't have to worry about her getting lost or being afraid. She had even led him home a time or two when he was too stubborn to follow his own trail. He would be the first to find the others. The thought urged him on.

A scream tore through the air. Alex's heart skipped a beat at the sound of fear in Cassie's voice. He turned in the direction of the sound and phased, leaving his clothes in tatters beneath the trees.

Alex ran faster than he ever had in his life. He leaped a lightning struck tree, darted around a grove of aspens, and jumped the stream without slowing. His heart thundered in his ears in time to the beat of his paws on the earth. Her scent grew stronger. The smell of strangers flooded his nose. They were everywhere.

Alex burst through the trees. A gunshot ran out. Fire tore through Alex's hind leg as he skidded to a stop in front of Cassie. His sister cowered in human form against an evergreen's trunk. A growl tore from his chest as he faced her attackers.

"Drogan said you wouldn't be far behind," a man dressed in black said. He levered the gun so that it was aimed at Alex's head. "Shall we see if I can kill two birds with one stone?"

A black form darted behind the man. Yells rang out along with growls as wolves appeared from all directions.

"There're too many of them!" the first man shouted. "Regroup at the road!"

The men ran. Alex's first instinct was to chase them and pull them down like wolves on the hunt, but Cassie cried behind him, and the pain in his leg was breathtaking.

The other werewolves fell back as the men retreated. They circled around Alex and Cassie, protecting them. Alex sniffed Cassie all over, making sure she hadn't been hurt.

"Alex," she said, her voice quivering. She threw her arms around his neck and held him as she cried. Alex wanted to hold her tight and tell her everything was alright, but he was afraid of how much phasing would hurt with the bullet in his leg.

"What happened?" Torin demanded, appearing through the trees in human form.

"We heard a scream and a gun shot," Boris said, following close behind.

Kalia appeared behind her brother. Her eyes widened at the sight of Alex and Cassie in the middle of the wolves. Several of them slipped away to find their clothes and phase.

"They attacked me," Cassie said. "They appeared out of nowhere. I didn't even smell them." Her voice shook. "They were going to shoot me when Alex appeared."

"You were shot?" Jericho asked, appearing again through the trees in his human form. His shirt was still only halfway pulled down as he ran to them. He dropped to his knees beside the siblings.

Blood ran down Alex's leg. Pain stole in a numbing path from the wound. It was getting harder to breathe.

Dean Jaze appeared with many of the other professors

close behind. It was obvious by their state of apparel they had all dropped whatever they were doing, which was probably sleeping, and ran straight from the Academy. "Is everyone alright?" Jaze asked. His head turned at the smell of blood.

"Alex got shot," Cassie said with tears streaming down her cheeks.

Jaze checked Alex quickly. Gasps sounded from the students who had phased back to human form when Jaze's hand came away bloody. "Don't phase," Jaze told Alex. "It'll only make the damage worse."

Jaze met Kaynan's gaze. "Bullet wound. We have to assume it's silver. Get the medical ward ready."

"Silver?" Pip replied, his voice tight.

"I've got him," Vance said as he knelt beside the dean.

Alex felt the humiliation of being picked up in the huge Alpha's arms.

"Meet us at the school," Jaze told Kaynan. "Tell Nikki and Lyra to be ready."

Kaynan phased into his wolf form. His deep red fur and red eyes made him look like a creature out of a nightmare. He vanished before most of the students were even sure what they had seen.

"Vance, Chet, and Dray, get Alex and Cassie back to the Academy. Mouse, stay with me; we need to make sure everyone makes it back inside safely."

Professor Mouse nodded, his eyes huge behind his big glasses.

Jaze met Rafe's gaze. The wild werewolf's eyes glinted gold in the moonlight. "We need to find out where they came from and how they got past the wolves. Rafe, you and Colleen check the perimeter and the scents going in and out. I want to make sure this forest is clear."

"Got it," Colleen answered.

Pain surged through Alex's leg. A whine escaped his gritted teeth at the burning sensation.

Vance and Jaze exchanged a look. "Hurry," Jaze said.

Vance took off running through the trees. Alex struggled to look back and saw Chet pick up Cassie as easily as if she was a rabbit. Dray shifted and loped past them, checking the groves for unfamiliar scents.

Alex's thoughts numbed. The pounding of Vance's legs as they ran through the forest pulsed within him, sending his thoughts into a whirlwind as his blood system worked the silver from the bullet through his body.

"Stay with me, Alex," Vance growled in a low voice without slowing. His shirt was loose, having been barely fastened when Cassie's scream reached the Academy. Alex realized dazedly that the black whip scars that covered the Alpha's arms also tattered his chest in cruel black streaks. He wondered where they came from and if they hurt.

The gate creaked as it was thrown open. Vance ran across the yard and into the Academy.

"Lyra, Nikki," he called; the sound of his deep voice echoed up the stairs and through the hallways.

A door opened on the opposite end of the hallway from the student classrooms. "We're ready," Nikki replied. "Bring him in."

Vance entered the room and set Alex on a rolling bed with white sheets.

"Check the perimeter of the school." Nikki's voice was muffled to Alex's ears. "Make sure we don't have a security breech."

"Got it," Vance replied.

"And have Mouse check the cameras when he gets back," Lyra called before the door closed.

"How you doing, Alex?" Nikki asked, her voice kind as

she checked his leg.

Alex winced at the pressure. He clenched his teeth and shut his eyes.

"Is it silver?" Lyra asked.

"There's only one way to find out," Nikki replied. She leaned closer to Alex. He heard Lyra wheeling a cart of supplies over. They chinked together gently. "This is going to hurt just a bit," Nikki said. "We need to get the bullet out."

Alex nodded. He exhaled as something was injected into his leg.

"It'd be easier if he phased," Lyra said. "You wouldn't have to worry about fur."

"Yes, but phasing with a wound pulls at the muscles and could make it worse," Nikki replied. "I'd rather have him wait. We'll work with what we have."

Two more injections followed. The muscles around the wound began to ease, but Alex's lungs felt tight.

"He's having a hard time breathing," Lyra said.

"Give him the oxygen. His body's reacting too quickly to the silver," Nikki replied. "Hold on, Alex."

He felt pressure as she worked on his leg. Lyra slipped an oxygen mask over his nose.

"Take deep breaths," she instructed, her voice gentle. "It'll be over soon."

Alex tried to ignore the sensation of Nikki digging for the bullet. He took a deep breath, then another. He had to fight the pressure in his lungs. His heart stuttered. He willed it to calm. It stuttered again.

"His eyes are rolling back," Lyra said. "His pulse is weakening."

"Almost there," Nikki replied. "Just one more push and. . . got it!"

There was a metallic clink as the bullet was set on a tray.

"It's silver," Nikki noted. "They're designed to splinter. He might have some in his bloodstream. Alex?" she called.

He couldn't get his eyes to open. His heart gave another stutter, and darkness swarmed his thoughts.

STRAYS

***

Alex awoke to the sound of steady beeping. His head felt like it had been wrapped in cotton. He forced his eyes open. He was in a room he didn't recognize. The lighting was dim, and though there were other beds, his contained the only occupant. He squinted up at the monitor near his head. It showed a rhythm of jagged spikes. He focused inward; a slight smiled touched his mouth. The spikes were his heartbeat. It appeared to be stable.

He tried to remember what had happened. Memories of running through the forest came to him. He had been searching for the Alphas, and had left the rest of the werewolves far behind. Cassie knew the woods. He didn't have to worry about her.

The sound of her scream echoed through his mind. His heart gave a stutter and the monitor's beeping was thrown off for a moment before it regained its steady rhythm. He had run as fast as he could. The images slowed.

He entered the clearing and saw Cassie backed against a large tree trunk. Moonlight reflected off of many guns. The man in front was pulling the trigger. Alex leaped in front of Cassie. The gun fired. His leg gave an answering throb. He turned, placing himself in front of Cassie. He could hear her sobbing behind him. Her terror tore through his heart.

Alex met the gaze of the man wearing black. He half-expected to see the man with the mismatched eyes that had killed his parents, but this man's eyes were brown and cold. The only emotion in them was humor at the siblings cowering in front of him. He spoke, his words harsh and grating. His gun lifted, aiming at Alex's head. If the bullet went through, it would hit Cassie as well. His finger tightened on the trigger. Alex didn't know what to do to protect Cassie.

There wasn't time to react. If he leaped at the man, she could be shot by the other guns.

Howls reached him, the sounds of his pack as they charged through the underbrush to protect him and Cassie. They were a true pack, putting their life on the line for their members the same way he had seen Rafe's pack do in the wild. The thought made his heart calm. He took a slow breath and let out the tension that filled him at the thought of Cassie in danger. They had protected her when he couldn't. She was safe.

Chapter Ten

Alex looked around the room. He found the camera in the corner of the ceiling and held up a thumb's-up. A few seconds later, the door opened.

"You gave us quite the scare," Dean Jaze said, entering. He smiled down at Alex. "It was a bit of touch and go there."

Alex tried to find a comfortable position, but his leg throbbed. He looked down at it, surprised that it hadn't healed.

"Wounds from silver bullets take a lot longer to heal," Jaze said, following his gaze.

"You know this from experience?" Alex guessed.

Jaze nodded. He leaned against the counter. "At least Nikki has her nursing degree. Professor Thorson removed a bullet from my side with only a pair of pliers and a bottle of whiskey."

"The history teacher?" Alex asked, amazed.

Jaze chuckled. "How do you think we met?" He pulled up his shirt and showed Alex the scar. There were other scars as well, but Alex knew better than to ask about them.

"Do I have to stay here?" Alex looked around. "It's nice, but. . . ."

Jaze smiled. "Not at all. If you're feeling up to it, I know there's a pack waiting up there that hasn't slept yet because they're too concerned about you." He held out a hand.

Alex took it and pulled himself slowly to a sitting position. He was amazed at how weak he felt.

"Take your time," Jaze warned. "Nikki suspects that some silver got in your bloodstream, which was causing your heart to beat irregularly."

Alex chose not to tell the dean that his heart had beat that way ever since his family was killed. He stood slowly. His legs wobbled, but Jaze kept him steady.

"You want a crutch?" the dean asked, pointing to one that had been propped in the corner.

The wolf's instinct to never show weakness made Alex shake his head. Jaze smiled as if he guessed exactly why Alex refused.

"It's okay to take time to heal," the dean said.

"I'm already healing," Alex replied tightly as he tested his weight on his leg. The wound about halfway up his thigh ached and he could feel the pull of the muscles that had been damaged by the bullet.

"You could stay here, or I could carry you," Jaze offered. At Alex's dismayed look, he chuckled. "We'll just go slow."

Alex limped with his arm over Jaze's shoulder. By the time they reached the door, he had broken out in a sweat. He gritted his teeth and refused to say anything, but Jaze shifted his grip, holding more of Alex's weight.

"Your pack showed bravery attacking those men," Jaze said in an effort to distract Alex from the pain.

Alex nodded. "They did." His voice caught in his throat as he stepped. He took a steeling breath and continued, "I didn't expect that."

"We didn't expect any of it," the dean replied. He tried to stifle the hint of frustration in his voice, but Alex heard it. "Here we are trying to protect werewolves, and the Extremists come attacking at our front door."

"They wanted me and Cassie," Alex said.

Jaze paused and looked down at the young werewolf. "Are you sure?"

Alex nodded. "The man in front was holding the gun on Cassie as if he was waiting for me. When I appeared, he said, 'Drogan said you wouldn't be far behind.'"

"Good to know." The dean's tone said the information

surprised him. He helped Alex continue walking. When they reached the stairs, Jaze asked, "Did he say anything else?"

Alex grimaced at the pain of the first step. "Yeah," he replied tightly, "He said, 'Shall we see if I can kill two birds with one stone?' That's when Jericho attacked him. If the werewolves hadn't come, Cassie and I wouldn't be here right now."

Dark emotions rushed through Jaze's eyes. Alex could tell the dean was fighting to keep his anger in check. He had never seen Jaze so upset.

"Rafe has his pack running the perimeter. Dray and Chet are monitoring the road, and Mouse is setting up extra cameras," Jaze said aloud. "I need to ask Brock about the drone."

"Who's Brock?" Alex asked. The name sounded familiar but he couldn't remember where he had heard it.

Jaze looked as if he just remembered Alex was there. He shook his head. "Don't worry about it. You need to get some rest." He helped Alex to the top of the stairs and down the hall.

"It seems a lot further than I remember," Alex said, forcing his muscles to hold. His legs were shaking. He wondered how much the silver was affecting him, and how much was the rage that coursed through him at the thought of the danger Cassie had been in.

Jaze nodded. "Of course you guys had to have the last room," he joked. They paused at the door.

Alex grinned. "The pecking order doesn't take bullet wounds into consideration."

"It should," Jaze replied. He ducked from under Alex's arm. "Time to give your pack something to smile about." The dean turned the doorknob.

"Alex!"

Cassie's arms were around her brother's neck before he could even move. He was grateful for the door frame behind him that kept him up under her tight grip.

"I was so worried!" she said. "They wouldn't let me into the room, saying that they had to monitor you. I didn't know if that meant you were dying, even though they said they had taken out the bullet. I was just so worried."

"I'm alright," Alex tried to reassure her.

He glanced over the top of her head. Warmth flooded him at the relieved expressions on his pack members' faces. Everyone stood waiting for Cassie to let him go. Alex met Jericho's gaze. "Thank you," he said. "Thank all of you. You saved our lives."

Cassie stepped back, but kept a firm grip on Alex's hand to reassure herself that her brother was really there.

"That's what packs are for," Jericho replied. His gaze shifted to the dean. "Have you found any information on the attackers?"

"Some," Jaze replied. "Our students' security is our biggest focus. We'll get to the bottom of this."

"Let us know if there's anything we can do to help," Jericho said. He met Alex's gaze. "Our pack almost lost two members tonight. We'd like to get to the bottom of this."

Jaze nodded. Instead of being perturbed by the Alpha's persistence, there was a hint of humor in the dean's gaze that battled the anger Alex had seen on the stairs. "I'm glad Alex and Cassie have such a good pack," the dean told them all. "I'd recommend you get some sleep. We'll hold classes an hour later tomorrow so you can get the rest you need." He met Alex's gaze. "Don't think about going to class. You need to rest so that wound will fully heal."

Alex nodded. "Thank you, Jaze."

The dean stepped out of the door and shut it behind him.

Alex was immediately flooded with questions.

"Did the bullet hurt?" Trent asked.

"Was there a lot of blood?" Marky pressed.

Von had a finger in his nose when he asked, "Did you have to get stitches?"

Pip hung near the back of the room. He gave Alex a weak smile when the Second looked at him. "It hurt," Alex said, "But it's healing."

He took a step toward the couch, but his leg chose that moment to buckle.

"Easy," Jericho said, catching him before he could hit the ground. He practically carried Alex to the couch and helped him get settled.

"I'm fine," Alex protested quietly, his cheeks red.

Jericho met his gaze. "You're not fine, and until you are, you need to take it easy. You heard what the dean said. That bullet was silver. We all know the effects a silver bullet can have on a werewolf." The shadows in the Alpha's brown eyes let Alex know he understood the effects all too well. "Take it easy," Jericho insisted.

Alex nodded. The room fell quiet, all eyes trained on him. He shifted uncomfortably on the couch. "Uh, everyone should get some rest. I won't go anywhere."

"Promise?" Cassie asked. Her face was pale and drawn. It was obvious the night's terrors had taken a lot out of her.

Alex gave her a reassuring smile. "I promise. Go get some sleep. I'll be here when you wake up."

The other members of the pack obeyed. They were too exhausted to protest, and knew being late to combat training in the morning would come with a price, especially since they had been given an extra hour of sleep. It was well past midnight. Every hour of rest was going to count.

Cassie ran to her room and came back carrying the warm

red blanket Nikki had given her their first night at the Academy. It was her favorite possession. She set it carefully over her brother.

Her dark blue eyes searched his. "You sure you're okay?" she asked.

"I'm good," Alex told her, feigning a yawn. "With this blanket, I'll be asleep in no time."

She gave him a wide smile. It surprised Alex when she leaned down and kissed his forehead. His heart gave a painful throb. Their mother used to do that every time she tucked them into bed; no one had kissed his forehead for the last six years.

"Good night, Alex," Cassie whispered.

"Night, Cass," he replied.

She paused in the doorway one more time to reassure herself that he was safe. He listened to her tired footsteps as she made her way to her room. The door shut behind her with a quiet snick.

Alex let out a slow breath and looked around. The meeting room was warm and inviting. Pictures of mountain scenes were spread along the walls between the windows, and the lamps in each corner glowed softly on their lowest settings. It should have been cozy, and Alex knew he should have been exhausted.

Yet the memories of the attackers kept racing through his head every time he closed his eyes. He wanted to fight them, to protect Cassie, to keep the man in the middle from pulling the trigger. There were too many guns. He couldn't save anyone. Rest evaded him.

Eventually, Alex stood. The pain in his leg chased the other thoughts from his mind. He wanted to hit something, anything, yet there was nothing he could punch without damaging it.

Thoughts of the combat training room below toyed in the back of his mind. The rage in his veins cycled over and over until he felt like he would go crazy if he couldn't let some of it out.

He glanced down the hallway where Cassie slept. The sound of soft breathing and one person muttering in her sleep came to him. Alex limped toward door to their quarters. With each painful step, he reminded himself of the men who had threatened his sister. They would pay someday. He would make sure of it.

The anger fueled him as he limped down the stairs by leaning on the railing and easing his injured leg down one step at a time. When he reached the bottom, he felt like he had accomplished something.

After what felt like an hour later, Alex stood triumphantly in front of the combat training room. He pulled the door open and limped to the dummies in the corner. The image of the man with the gun floated in his mind, then shifted to the face of the man with the mismatched eyes. The man had watched while Alex and Cassie's mom and dad died, paralyzed by silver darts and then slain by his knife across their throats. He had then turned with a cold look on his face. Only the sound at the door had prevented him from killing the brother and sister at that moment.

Alex hit the dummy so hard it slammed backwards to the floor. He took a step forward to finish it, but his wounded leg gave out under the weight and he fell on top of the dummy.

"This is awkward," he muttered. He rolled and came up on his good knee, drove an elbow into the dummy's sternum, punched its stomach, and followed with a chop to the throat. He collapsed on his back fighting for breath.

"Really terrifying," a voice said from the other side of the room.

Adrenaline rushed through Alex's veins. He jumped up to a defensive crouch, his hands up and senses straining.

"Slow down, Rocky. I'm not going to attack you," Kalia said with a hint of apology in her voice. She stepped out of the shadows with her hands raised. "I figured you knew I was here, what with a werewolf's nose and all that."

Alex glanced at the fallen dummy. "That is not how I would have killed a dummy with someone watching."

"I hope not," she replied.

Alex willed his muscles to relax. His leg screamed at him for the movements, and as the adrenaline began to fade, he really regretted it.

"Uh, aren't you supposed to be in the medical ward or something?" Kalia asked, giving his leg a meaningful look.

Alex sat on the dummy and gingerly stretched out his leg. "For a bullet wound? They save the medical ward for more important things than that."

An unwilling smile crept across her face. "More important?"

"Yeah," Alex said. "Like decapitations and stuff."

"Oh," Kalia answered. "Right. Because there's a lot they can do about a decapitation."

Alex shrugged. "You never know."

"I hope I don't," Kalia replied.

Alex gave her a searching look. "I'm honing my skills as a lame warrior. Why are you here?"

"You are a lame warrior," Kalia said, crossing her arms even though another smile touched her face.

Alex rolled his eyes. "That was a setup and you didn't answer my question."

"I, uh, well. . . I couldn't sleep." Kalia's icy blue eyes studied the ground.

"Are you generally an insomniac?" Alex asked curiously.

She shook her head. She swallowed, then admitted, "I have a fear of guns."

A chill ran through Alex's body. He nodded, his voice quiet when he said, "That's understandable." Silence filled the space between them for a few minutes. Alex broke it by asking, "So why the training room?"

Kalia gave the dummy Alex was sitting on a pointed look. "I guess it's not the safest place. I just supposed that if I could, you know, defend myself, I might not be so afraid." Her last few words trailed off until they were barely audible.

For the first time, Alex saw past her stony countenance, icy blue gaze, and the tension he felt when she was around. Instead, he saw a girl his age who had been uprooted against her will and thrown into an Academy filled with a race of people she feared.

"You don't have the strength of a werewolf," he said quietly.

She shook her head and her white-blonde hair swished above her shoulders.

"You don't have to fear us," Alex said, willing her to believe it.

"I know," she replied with hesitancy in her voice. "It's just. . . I don't. . . ." She sighed and began again, "I don't fit in at home and I don't fit in here. What happens when they send me away?"

"They don't have to send you away," Alex told her.

"With you and Cassie being attacked, they're going to tighten down on security and my parents used to be Extremists." She covered her mouth and stared at him, amazed at what she had admitted.

"It's okay," Alex reassured her. "You don't have to worry so much. Lots of people used to be Extremists. I can't blame them for being afraid, and neither does Jaze. We just have to find a way to exist side by side in peace."

Kalia searched his eyes as if looking for something. "How can you say that when you and your sister almost got shot?" She motioned to his leg. "When you did get shot? How can you be so cavalier?"

Alex's mouth pulled up in a smile. "Cavalier?"

She rolled her eyes. "My mom's big into vocabulary. She says, 'You must talk like a lady to attract a true gentleman.'"

Alex snorted. "Seriously? What if you don't find a *gentleman* that can understand your vocabulary."

She laughed. "That's exactly what I told her!"

"And what'd she say?"

"To stop being so cavalier," Kalia replied.

Alex laughed. His leg began to ache. He moved off the dummy and eased his leg out straight.

"You really should be in the medical ward, shouldn't you?" Kalia asked with concern in her voice.

Alex shook his head. "Jaze cleared me. I'll heal good enough once my body gets rid of the silver."

"Jaze?" Kalia repeated.

Alex glanced at her. What she was asking suddenly occurred to him. "Oh, uh, Dean Jaze. Hard habit to break. We're kind-of like family."

Interest showed in Kalia's gaze. "How'd you become family with the dean?"

Alex wasn't sure how much he wanted to tell her. He settled onto his back on the mat and studied the white panel ceiling. "My parents were killed by Extremists when I was eight. We were brought to the Academy as orphans. Jaze and Nikki took care of us and the rest of the Strays," he said the word with a hint of bitterness that he tried to hide. "But they cared about Cassie and me because Jaze and my brother were really close."

Kalia's voice was quiet when she asked, "What happened to your brother?"

Alex was silent for a few minutes. His voice was almost steady when he said, "My brother was Jet."

Surprise filled Kalia's words. "You mean the statue of the werewolf who fought hundreds to save the werewolf race? I'm not a werewolf, and even I've heard of him."

Alex nodded without looking at her. The image of the black statue in front of the school filled his mind. Sadness brushed his thoughts. "Yes, that Jet." He had become a legend through the werewolves he had saved, a martyr to their cause, one of those who had sacrificed everything to save others. Yet to Alex, he was the big brother the young werewolf had never had enough time with. Sometimes Alex wished Jet wasn't a legend, because then Jet would still be alive.

"Your brother was brave," Kalia said softly.

Alex nodded, but didn't say the words that burned in his heart. He didn't tell her that stories couldn't hold someone when they hurt, and legends never soothed a broken heart. They couldn't teach you how to ride a bike or track in the woods; they couldn't take you to your first ballgame, or show you how to throw a football. Legends felt insubstantial when the brother left behind no longer had the one he used to look up to.

Alex pushed up from the floor. Kalia reached out a hand to help, but Alex let out a slow breath and willed his legs to hold. He felt a whisper of pride when they obeyed.

"I'd better go to bed. See you in the morning," Alex said.

"Goodnight, Alex," Kalia told him. "I'm glad you're okay."

Alex wasn't sure if he would go that far, but he nodded and left the room. When he reached the bottom of the stairs, he regretted the rashness of his decision to go down them in the first place. He clenched his hands into fists and worked his way slowly up them. By the time he collapsed on his bed, he had wondered for the thirtieth time if fighting the dummy had been worth it. He definitely felt like more of a dummy than the one he had slammed to the ground in the training room.

Chapter Eleven

"As you know, we've already questioned Cassie about what she saw. We just need to go over the details in case we missed anything," Jaze said, his tone kind.

Cassie sat next to Alex with her gaze on the table. He hated the terror that had filled her gaze when she recounted what had happened two nights ago. Alex looked at the professors and staff members who watched him. Nikki and Lyra gave him warm smiles. Mouse was busy fiddling with a small electronic device. Jaze gave him an encouraging nod, while there was true interest in Vance's expression. Alex couldn't forget the way the huge werewolf had carried him to the Academy as if the fate of the world rested on his life. He shifted uncomfortably in his seat.

"I think I told you everything," he said.

"The tiniest detail could help us," Chet pressed. "You sure you don't remember anything else?"

Alex let the memories flood over him, hoping for something that would help them. He finally shook his head, frustrated. "I was too worried about protecting Cassie to pay more attention to the men. I would know their scent if I saw them again, but that's about it."

The dean nodded. "Thank you, Alex. If you think of anything else, please let us know."

"I will," Alex promised.

He and Cassie rose. Together, they watched the professors walk out of the room. Several heads were bowed as they walked in twos and threes in deep discussion.

"Where do you think they're going?" Alex whispered to Cassie.

"I'm not sure," she replied. "Probably their offices."

"I'm going to follow them," Alex told her.

"Why would you— Alex!" Cassie said in a loud whisper.

Alex motioned for her to keep quiet as he limped around the table and paused at the door. The staff members were heading to the other end of the hallway away from the classrooms. The students never had a reason to go that way. It was made up of teachers' offices and a storage closet at the very end.

"See, I told you," Cassie whispered.

"Wait a sec." Alex's eyes widened when Professor Dray pulled open the door to the storage closet, glanced behind the other professors to make sure nobody was watching, and stepped inside. Chet followed, then the other professors. Soon, even Jaze was inside the closet. The door shut with an audible click.

"Did you see that?" Alex asked excitedly.

"All the professors are crammed in the storage closet, so?" Cassie replied.

Alex limped down the hall as quickly as he could manage. He threw open the storage room door. Disappointment flooded him when he saw that it was empty. He turned to show Cassie, but his bad leg faltered at the sudden movement and he fell against the back of the closet. Something popped, and then he was rolling down a flight of stairs. He covered his head as he rolled and hit the bottom with a loud thud.

Dazed, Alex blinked at the surprisingly well-lit room. Monitors, screens, diagrams, and digital readouts lined the walls from floor to ceiling. Red and yellow markers moved across city maps. Several people on rolling chairs watched the screens. They wore headsets and spoke into them. A few glanced down at the intruder before turning back to their work.

Alex's gaze shifted to the professors who glared down at him with disapproving looks.

"Alex, do you have anything to say for yourself?" Jaze asked.

"Uh, ouch," Alex replied, too stunned to question what he was seeing.

"Alex," Cassie called, running down the stairs. "Are you o—"

Cassie's mouth fell open when she reached the bottom step and turned the corner. "What is this?" she asked.

"It *was* a secret," Vance replied.

Lyra slapped his shoulder. "It's the headquarters of Jaze's werewolf security and protection database. We monitor werewolf activity all over the world."

Cassie's gaze flitted over the screens. Jaze stepped forward to help Alex to his feet. Alex was about to ask a question when Cassie let out a scream and buried her head against him.

"It's him, Alex. It's him. Don't let him find us. Don't let him know where we are," she said, her voice shaking.

Alex held her tight and quickly searched the monitors. A knot tightened in his stomach at a face shown on one.

"Are you alright, Cassie?" Nikki asked, hurrying quickly to her side.

"Can you take her out?" Alex asked.

Surprised, Nikki nodded. Alex moved his sister's tight grip to the dean's wife and watched them make their way slowly up the stairs. When the door shut, he turned to find everyone's gaze on him. He motioned toward the monitor.

"That's the man who killed our parents."

The professors looked at the screen. Jaze's brow was furrowed when he asked, "Are you sure?"

Alex nodded, feeling sick. "I would never forget."

"Who is that?" Lyra asked.

A skinny man with spikey brown hair turned in his chair.

He held a bag of potato chips and had paused mid-crunch. Recognition flooded Alex. He was taken back to a small house filled with werewolves and humans who were Jet's friends. They were there for Alex and Cassie's seventh birthday. It was the night they phased into wolves for the first time.

The man answered, "Drogan Carso; General Jared Carso's son. He's topped the werewolf's most wanted list just below his father for continuing with the genocide on the General's orders."

Jaze nodded. "Thank you, Brock."

"Anytime," Brock replied. He grinned and spun back around in his chair as he crunched on another chip.

"Wait," Alex said, his heart hammering in his ears. "Your uncle's son is the one who killed my parents, and now he's coming after us?"

Jaze nodded. "It appears that way."

"But why?" Alex asked. He felt lost, adrift. He had figured that his parents were killed by Extremists exacting revenge on all werewolves. The fact that the General's son was the one who had performed the murder made it personal.

"We've got to find out," Jaze replied. He gave Alex a serious look. "And we have to believe that he is seeking out you and Cassie to finish the job."

"Did he try to kill you after he murdered your parents?" Mouse asked. The professor's tone was gentle as he probed for information.

Alex nodded. His chest was tight when he answered, "He would have, but he was distracted."

"By what?" Vance demanded, his tone a bit harsh as his patience for the conversation ran thin.

"By Jet," Alex replied softly.

The professors looked at Jaze. The dean nodded, and

swallowed with some difficulty. "Jet brought Alex and Cassie to Two. He didn't mention Drogan, but we didn't know Drogan and Jared were connected at the time. Now that we know Drogan is Jared's son, we've been trying to track him down."

"But he disappeared off the grid," Brock concluded, spinning back around with a popcorn ball in his hand. "Until now, that is."

Alex looked at the man. He realized by the scent that Brock was human. "Until now?"

Brock ran a hand through his spikey hair. "Our sources spotted Drogan in Haroldsburg just before you and Cassie were attacked. With the information you've given us about the attack, we assume he's the one who sent the men."

"What? The whole 'Drogan said you wouldn't be far behind' tipped you off, did it?" Vance stated in irritation at the obvious.

"But why do it himself?" Nikki asked, ignoring Vance. "He didn't have to go to the city to order the attack. Why not just send his men?"

"Maybe he didn't trust that they'd get the job done," Vance answered. "And apparently he was right."

"Thank goodness," Lyra said, setting a hand on Alex's arm. "We're so glad you're okay."

Alex gave her a warm smile, aware that she was partially the reason he was still standing. "Thank you." He shifted his attention to Jaze. "So what do we do?"

Jaze's expression was firm. "*You* will go back to class when you are rested and do your studies with the rest of the school. *We* will work on Drogan location and find out what we can about the attack on you and Cassie." Alex opened his mouth to argue, but Jaze shook his head. He put a hand on Alex's shoulder. "I'm glad you're alright, but it was too close.

The last thing we need is students taking security into their own hands. I need you and Cassie to stay within the Academy walls for the next few days while we do what we can to increase security and ensure that our student population is protected. Will you do that?"

Alex didn't want to agree. After what he had seen and heard, he wanted to do everything he could to find Drogan and end the threat once and for all. Yet he was being asked to sit back and let others do it.

"Alex, you're in no shape to go running after shadows," Jaze said quietly. "Let us do our job and we'll find Drogan."

Alex nodded against his will. "Okay."

Jaze smiled at him. "I think you'd better get up to bed. Stairs weren't made to be rolled down, especially on a leg like that."

"Tell me about it," Alex replied. He was already dreading the climb back up to the storage closet. He kept his expression carefully calm as he limped to the first step.

"Take care of yourself, Alex," Brock called.

Alex waved a hand without looking back. He eased up the first step. A glanced over his shoulder showed that the professors were already in deep discussion again. He breathed out a sigh and slowly climbed up another step.

The door shut behind him and he leaned against it to catch his breath. He couldn't help overhearing the conversation below.

"We have got to find out why the General and Drogan want to kill Alex and Cassie," Jaze was saying.

"Isn't it enough that they're Jet's siblings?" Nikki asked.

"I don't think so. Why Alex and Cassie, and why now?" Jaze replied. "There must be more to it than we know if he's going so far out of his way to get to them. I need information on this fast."

"I'll get on it," Brock said.
Alex pushed away from the door and limped to the stairs.

***

Alex found Cassie curled in a ball on his bed. She was covered in the red blanket Nikki had given her, and the blanket shook with her sobs. Alex set a hand on her shoulder.

"Are you okay?" he asked, though it was obvious she wasn't.

Cassie sniffed and pulled the blanket down enough to look at her brother. "We've got to stop him, Alex."

"We do?" he asked, surprised at her train of thought.

"Yes." She sat up and pulled the blanket around her shoulders. "If we don't stop him, what's to keep him from doing to other parents what he did to ours?"

Alex sat on the bed next to her. He held up his arm and she scooted beneath it. "Jaze's team is working on it. He said he'll take care of it."

Cassie sniffed again. "It's not enough," she said. She used the corner of her blanket to dry her tears. "They probably have thousands of bad people on their list. We have one."

"Two," Alex corrected her gently.

She watched him with wide eyes. "What do you mean?"

Alex let out a slow breath as he debated what to tell her. "It turns out that the man with the mismatched eyes is named Drogan Carso."

A shudder ran down Cassie's spine as if giving the man a name made him more real. Her eyes flitted around the room as she thought. "You mean Carso, like Jaze?"

Alex nodded. "Like's Jaze's uncle, General Jared Carso. Drogan is his son."

Cassie rubbed her eyes, then she nodded slowly. "After all Jet did, it makes sense that he's trying to kill us. Jet helped free the werewolves he was planning to murder. Because of him, a lot of the students at the Academy and their families survived."

Alex gave his sister a searching look. "We're just kids. How are we supposed to make a difference?"

Cassie met his look with one of strength that surprised him. "We're not just kids, Alex. We're Jet's siblings. Take what he did and times it by two. That's what I want to do."

Cassie's words filled Alex with meaning. He hadn't realized until that moment that he had been searching desperately for some way to avenge his parents. He had always told himself the same words, that they were just kids, and that they had no way to stand up to someone with the entire Extremist force at his back. Yet Cassie was right. Look at all Jet had done. Jet's strength ran through their veins. They could do it.

"I have an idea," Alex said.

Chapter Twelve

"You sure this is a good idea?" Cassie asked.

"Definitely," Alex replied. He cupped his hands around his mouth and howled.

Lights flew on around the Academy. Alex stretched out his sore leg on the top step of the Academy courtyard and waited.

"You want to go after the General and Drogan, right?"

Cassie nodded.

"Then we're going to need an army," Alex told her.

Werewolves began to pour out of the school.

"Night games!" a few of the younger students yelled excitedly.

The Alphas followed at a more sedate pace. Alex caught their confused looks. It was customary for an Alpha to make the call for night games, yet all of the Alphas left the school together.

Jericho spotted Alex. "Shouldn't you be in bed or something?" the Alpha asked with a bemused smile on his face as if he guessed Alex was up to something.

"I probably should," Alex replied. He attempted to rise. The Alpha reached out a hand and helped Alex up. "Thanks," Alex told him quietly.

"Who called the night games?" Boris demanded. Kalia leaned against the building next to her brother. She had her arms crossed and looked disgruntled at the fact that Boris had required her to participate.

"I did," Alex said, limping forward to the curve of the steps. The werewolves milling below looked up in surprise. The Alphas crossed to him.

"Skipping protocol?" Boris asked, though he didn't look as angry as he first had.

"Good to see you up and about," Torin said, holding out a hand.

Alex shook it in surprise. "Thanks. Can I have a minute?"

Torin nodded. Alex shifted his gaze to Boris. The Termer Alpha finally nodded. "Go for it."

Alex glanced at Cassie. She waited near the school, her expression worried as if she wasn't sure what reception they would receive. He gave her a reassuring smile and turned to the crowd of students.

"As you know, Cassie and I were attacked in the forest a few nights ago," he began. Heads nodded at his words. He looked at the Alphas behind him. "What you don't know is that it was a planned attack."

Murmurs of surprise rushed through the students.

"Are you sure?" Torin asked.

Alex nodded. "Positive. Dean Jaze confirmed it." As much as he wanted to reveal Jaze's secret den for monitoring werewolves beneath the Academy, he felt it was better to keep it to himself for the moment, as well as the fact that Jaze was related to Drogan. The last thing he wanted was for the students to mistrust their dean. He figured leaving out Drogan's last name for now wouldn't be a bad idea. "Drogan is the man who killed my parents and attempted to kill Cassie and me a few nights ago. We need to stop him."

"How do you plan to do that?" Jericho asked quietly behind him.

Alex met the Alpha's gaze. "Drogan men got through the security at the school, so I plan to create my own."

"With night games?" Boris asked.

Several members of the Termer Alpha's pack laughed, but Alex found the other Alphas watching him carefully. He addressed them. "I plan to use night games to train the students." Talking ran through the crowd. He held up a hand.

"We're already divided into packs. Each pack has an Alpha and a Second. It will be the Alpha's job to see to the training of his pack members."

Boris' gaze darkened. "Are you telling us what to do?"

To Alex's surprise, Torin crossed to the Termer Alpha. He lowered his voice so only those on the steps could hear. "We were useless when those men attacked. I, for one, would like to know we aren't sitting ducks if they come back."

"How do we know they're coming back?" Boris demanded.

Torin met his gaze directly. "Did you like feeling as if our school and our packs were in danger? Because I didn't. Don't you think it'd be smart to be more prepared if there is a next time?"

Boris met Torin's glare. It was obvious the Alphas were on edge. Alex worried a fight would break out at any moment and destroy what he was trying to accomplish.

"I think it's a good idea."

Everyone looked at Kalia in surprise.

"You do?" Boris asked.

She nodded at her brother. "I do. Strength in numbers and all that. If you guys are united, they're less likely to get through. They failed last time, so they'll probably try again. It wouldn't hurt to be ready."

Her gaze flicked to Alex, then back to her brother. Alex was surprised to find Kalia on his side. She had declared her disgust for werewolves and admitted that her parents used to be Extremists. Maybe she was trying hard not to follow in their footsteps.

"Fine," Boris said. He blew out an angry breath. "But that doesn't change anything."

"What, that you're an idiot?" Torin asked.

Boris' hand clenched into a fist. Alex thought the Alpha

would hit Torin, but instead, he turned to face the crowd of students who waited eagerly below.

"We train," Boris declared. "Each pack is a subgroup. The Alphas will meet together separately for battle strategy, and then train you according to what we have decided. A call to night games is a call to train. Be prepared."

Boris met Alex's surprised gaze. He shrugged with a hint of self-consciousness. "My dad was in the army."

"Army brat," Torin replied.

Boris ignored him, his attention still on Alex. "So what's your plan, Jericho's Second?"

There was a moment of complete silence. Alex knew the question was much more than what had been asked. It was not his place to tell Alphas what to do, and he didn't know enough about battle strategy to do the job justice. He could either defend the position because it was his idea, or choose the path that would be best for the students' safety.

Alex swallowed his pride and met Boris' gaze. "It sounds like you're the one with the most experience. I concede to your leadership in regards to the training unless someone else can prove more knowledge on the matter."

It was clear the Alpha had expected anything but that. He stared down at Alex with shock on his face, then looked at the other Alphas. Small nods went around the circle. Everyone accepted Boris as the leader. A glimmer of pride touched the Termer Alpha's gaze. He said gruffly, "I accept." He looked at Alex and Alex was surprised to be addressed as an equal instead of a Gray. "So how do we find out information on Drogan's whereabouts?"

"I have that covered," Alex said.

Boris nodded without pressing him for more information. The Alpha turned to the others. "Let's begin by practicing sweeps through the yard. If the professors look out, it'll appear that we're playing Steal the Flag. Each Alpha needs to work on commands; use barks and yips in wolf form to break and bring back to formation, and make sure your pack follows. We fight together, or not at all."

Alex fought back a smile as the Alphas hurried down to their packs. Excitement filled everyone's faces. It looked as if he wasn't the only one frustrated by the attack. Having a way to fight back was also a chance to push away the fear. If everyone could keep the same goal, they might actually have a chance.

"Nice plan," Jericho said, pausing on the step. "Did you think to tell me before you brought out the entire school?"

Alex felt a hint of guilt. "I should have. I figured it would be best if everyone had a say." He lowered his gaze. "I'm not so good at the whole pack protocol thing."

"A bit of a loner like your brother, I hear," Jericho said. When Alex looked at him, there was humor on the Alpha's face. "The dean told me. He figured it would help me understand you." He nodded toward the statue. "I don't hear anybody complaining about what Jet accomplished."

Alex smiled. "Me, neither."

Jericho gave him a stern look. "I don't want you running on that leg, and that's an order from your Alpha. Take it easy this week. You can join in the next."

"Yes, sir," Alex replied with a hint of sarcasm.

Jericho rolled his eyes. "You're going to be trouble, aren't you?"

Alex shrugged. "Guess you'll have to wait and see."

Jericho looked at Cassie who hung back against the Academy wall. "I have no reason to leave your sister out of the training."

"Cass," Alex called.

She walked over slowly as if reluctant to hear what they

were talking about.

"Jericho needs you in training," Alex told her.

Her eyes lit up. "I thought you'd see us as a security threat and leave us out."

Jericho studied her. "Should I?"

She shook her head quickly. "Nope. I just have a tendency to overthink things." She ran down the stairs before he could change his mind. Terith smiled when Cassie joined the rest of Pack Jericho.

"She's a sharp one," Jericho noted.

Alex grinned. "You have no idea. Have fun, Captain."

Jericho chuckled as he ran down the stairs to lead his pack.

"I didn't see that coming."

Alex turned at Kalia's voice. He gave her a smile. "Thanks for the support."

She shrugged. "I think Boris was ready to kill you."

He nodded and leaned against the wall to ease the weight from his leg. "Yeah, me too. Why'd you do it?"

She was silent for a few moments. When she spoke, her voice was quiet. "My parents hid the fact that Boris was a werewolf from me for years. They sent him away here during the school year and said he was at the military academy. He was always so angry when he came home, and I realize now it was because he could never speak about what he was. He was always forced to hide it, to be ashamed of it." She smiled. "You gave him something today when you turned the training over to him."

The thought made Alex feel a bit better about his decision. He eased carefully down the wall so that he could sit with his leg out. "Yeah, but you stood up for me before you knew what I was going to do."

A small smirk showed on her face as she sat down beside

him. "Maybe I have my own form of rebellion."

Alex snorted. "So you were trying to cause dissension?"

She raised her eyebrows. "Now who's using big vocabulary words?"

He grinned. "Let's just say that being a Lifer at the Academy comes with its share of perks."

She laughed. "If that's a perk, I'm glad I'm not a Lifer."

He chuckled and rested his head against the brick wall. A pack of wolves rushed by in a tight formation. He recognized Drake leading them. Pack Jessilyn was close behind. "Looks like training is going well," he noted.

Pack Torin came loping by. Alex sat up when he saw Pack Boris rounding the opposite corner. They ran straight at each other.

"Oh, great," Kalia muttered.

Torin and Boris veered to either side at the last moment. Each Alpha snapped at the other while the packs broke through with growls and a few snarls.

"Guess you can't change everything," Kalia said.

"Who says I want to?" Alex replied.

Kalia laughed. "So you approve of dissension?"

Alex thought about it for a moment. "I do." At Kalia's look, he explained, "Packs in the wild defend their territories against other packs. It bands them together to fight for what they love."

Kalia gave a huff of surprise. "And I just thought you liked trouble."

He smiled. "I won't deny that trouble between the packs keeps their attention from me. I've managed to cause a few problems this term already."

"Yes, you have," she agreed.

Alex glanced at her. "Shouldn't you be running with Pack Boris?"

She shook her head. "What am I supposed to do? Bite at someone with my human teeth? Scary."

He stared at her. "You wish you were a werewolf."

Kalia appeared affronted. "I do not," she protested.

Alex nodded. "Yes, you do. You wish you were out there training with the rest of them. You want fur and fangs."

"I do not!" she replied with a laugh. "That's ridiculous. I hate werewolves."

"So that's why you're sitting here talking to one?"

She looked surprised, then embarrassed. "You're different than they are."

"I turn into a wolf, too," he pointed out.

"Not that," she said. "You're not another follower, even though being a Gray, I think you're supposed to be."

He fell silent.

She glanced at him. "I'm sorry."

He shook his head. "Don't be. You're right." He leaned forward with his elbow on his good leg and studied the cement at his feet. "I've never fit in here, no matter how hard I pretend. This is the first year I've actually been a Second. Usually, I'm picked last and spend my time wishing for summer when the Termers go home."

"And now?" Kalia asked.

He let out a sigh. "Now, I have a position, but I don't know how long Jericho's going to tolerate me. I have so many of my own ideas it's hard to follow somebody else, even when he is a good leader."

"Perhaps you can lead by following," Kalia suggested.

He gave her a quizzical look. "What does that mean?"

She laughed at his tone. "You already did it. Look." She gestured toward another wolf pack running by. This was led by Shannon and Shaylee. The white wolves led their Grays silently. The pack ghosted by on soft paws. "They're doing what you suggested, but you're not leading them."

"Yet their accomplishing what I set out to do," Alex concluded quietly.

She nodded. "Keep it up, and everyone will be answering to you without realizing it."

Alex gave a huff of approval. "I'd say I was smart, but I didn't realize that's what I was doing."

Kalia grinned and her icy blue eyes danced. "So your sister's the brains of the operation?"

"Don't tell her," Alex said. "It'll go to her head."

"Don't worry, I won't," Kalia promised.

Chapter Thirteen

Alex stood by the door in the closet a few days later. He tried to push against it, but it was locked from the inside. He found a knot hole near the middle of the door. He touched it. To his surprise, a little red light scanned his finger. The door refused to budge. He realized that falling through it the other day had been a fluke. Someone must have not shut it all the way after using the fingerprint scanner.

It was well past three o-clock in the morning. The packs had already gone to bed, and Alex hadn't heard any sounds from the instructors' wing when he walked by. He took a chance and tapped on the door.

No one answered.

Alex glanced around the supply closet. Above the shelves of paper towels and toilet cleaner, he spotted a small camera. Alex grinned and waved, giving his best innocent expression. He knocked on the door again while looking at the camera.

He heard footsteps up the stairs.

"I can't let you in here."

Alex smiled at Brock's voice. "Yes, you can."

"No, I can't," Brock answered. "This is a highly restricted area."

"Then why are you in there?"

Brock blew out an exasperated breath. "Because I work here."

"But you're not a werewolf," Alex pointed out.

"That really doesn't matter," Brock answered.

Alex leaned against the door. "Then we should work together. We'd be a good team."

"What makes you think I want to be on your team?"

"Because you were my brother's friend," Alex answered.

There was silence, then something beeped and the door

slid open. Brock stood in the way before Alex could go down the stairs. He held an apple in one hand that had two bites taken out of it. "What does that have to do with anything?" the spikey-haired human asked.

"It has to do with everything," Alex said quietly, his tone serious. "Drogan killed my parents. Jet would want them avenged, especially since they seem so intent on killing his siblings as well."

Brock hesitated. Alex could tell he had gotten to the man. "You really should let Jaze handle it," Brock finally said.

Alex jumped on the indecision in his voice. "I am, really. I just want to be better prepared if Drogan comes back, and so I need your help."

"Do you?" Brock asked dryly.

His tone caught Alex off guard. "What's that supposed to mean?"

Brock sighed and led the way back down the stairs. He took a bite of the apple as he walked. The crunch echoed down the staircase. Alex followed close behind. As soon as the werewolf passed, the door slid shut. He limped down the stairs after the human.

"It means that I've been watching your little night games exercises the past few nights. Everyone else passes it off as some new game you guys made up, but I can tell it's more than that."

Alex was glad to see that the room was empty. The wall of cameras from the Academy that lined the north side showed empty halls and a quiet forest. "What makes you say that?"

Brock sat down on his chair and spun around to face the werewolf. "Because they're the same exercises Jaze ran with the professors here when the Academy first opened."

Alex took the next seat. "Why did they stop?"

Brock shrugged. "We got more students, and Mouse's cameras were supposed to work better, and— why am I explaining anything to you?"

Alex smiled. "Because you're going to help us."

"What? Give your little werewolf army the information to track Drogan down so you can end the threat once and for all?" Brock's eyes widened at the expression on Alex's face. "That's exactly what you want to do, isn't it?"

"Yes, except that finding Drogan doesn't end the threat, because the General will still be out there."

Brock's eyes narrowed. "And you think that by finding the son, you can flush out the father."

Alex leaned forward in his chair. "Just like they used Cassie to flush me out. Blood is strong. We can use that against them."

"What's this *we* business? You heard Jaze. Let them handle it," Brock protested.

"I can't do that," Alex replied. He sat back in his chair and folded his arms. "They killed my parents and threatened my sister. That's enough to make anyone see red. I'm trying to handle it the right way."

"You can't expect a bunch of students to act like an army," Brock argued.

"You're right," Alex agreed. Brock's mouth fell open. Alex continued, "But I can expect a bunch of werewolves to act like a pack. That's all I'm doing, using instinct to my advantage."

Brock's eyebrows pulled together. "You really do know what you're doing."

"I know a little extra security couldn't hurt this place," Alex replied. He gestured at the cameras. "It looks like you have it all covered, but I just want to be careful. Cassie's safety is my greatest concern. No little girl should have to wake with night terrors each night because she was there when her parents were murdered."

"You're the same age she is," Brock said quietly.

Alex leaned his head in his hand, his gaze on the floor. "On the outside, yes, but not on the inside. I held Cassie against me so she wouldn't see them die, but I couldn't let Drogan's men be the last thing my parents saw. They knew I loved them, because I didn't look away. I wasn't strong enough to save my parents, but when my mom mouthed that she loved me before Drogan cut her throat, I said it back, and she knew I meant it." Alex let out a shuddering breath and looked at Brock. "I am Cassie's protector. I never want her to go through something like that. If I can find Drogan and the General, she'll never have to."

Brock sat back in his chair. He ran a hand down his face as if the things Alex had told him bothered him deep inside. His foot tapped on the floor as he thought. He glanced at the pile of junk food sitting next to his workplace, reached for a donut, then shook his head and sat back. He finally made up his mind. "I'll help you," he said. "What do you need?"

Alex's face lightened. "Jaze mentioned that Drogan was in Haroldsburg when Cassie and I were attacked. I just need to know if he appears there again, that's all."

"Alright," Brock agreed. "I'll let you know."

Alex stood. "Thanks." He shook Brock's hand, then headed for the stairs. He paused with his foot on the step. "Hey, any chance I can get clearance for down here?"

"No way," Brock replied sternly.

Alex chuckled as he made his way up the steps. "I had to ask."

The door at the top beeped, then opened. Alex stepped through into the storage closet.

***

"You're turning into a regular insomniac," Jericho noted when Alex opened the door.

Alex was surprised to see the Alpha still awake. "Same to you, apparently."

Jericho smiled. "Boris asked us to come up with some training regimens for tomorrow night. I thought I'd work here because Lyra caught me diagraming on the back of my notebook during Biology."

"That's what the commotion was about," Alex said with a laugh. He limped to the chair across from the Alpha and sat down. "I thought she was giving you a hard time for an answer in your homework."

"That, too," Jericho admitted. "The question asked me to describe an atom. I said I don't trust them because they make up everything."

Alex chuckled. "And she didn't like that answer?"

He shook his head. "She said I needed to assert myself more."

"She has a point," Alex replied. At Jericho's look, he laughed. "Lighten up. You're the one planning battle strategies past midnight. It'd help to have a sense of humor."

"I'm not so sure about that," Jericho said. He passed the paper to Alex. "What do you think?"

Alex took the paper, surprised that the Alpha wanted his opinion. He looked it over. "It's good," he said.

"Don't try to protect my feelings," Jericho replied dryly.

Alex grinned. "It's great. I think Boris was right to ask you." He studied the paper closer. "What do you think of sending the Seconds left instead of right?"

"It'll create a net with the enemy in the middle," Jericho said musingly. He accepted the paper back. "Good idea." He erased a few lines and drew new paths for the Seconds to follow. He nodded. "I think that's what was missing. I knew it was something, but I couldn't put my finger on it."

"I'm heading to bed," Alex said, rising. "Battle planning is too deep for this kind of night."

"I agree." Jericho stood as well. "Night, Alex."

"Goodnight," Alex replied, limping sleepily to his room.

Chapter Fourteen

It was obvious everyone could feel the full moon coming. Nobody could sit still in their seats.

"By the end of June, the French surrendered to the Germans, but Britain won the Battle of Britain, fending off air attacks and eliminating German's chance of gaining foothold. In Operation Barbarossa. . . ." Professor Thorson looked around the room. "Is anyone listening?"

"Something about Twinkies?" Torin guessed. His pack broke into laughter.

Professor Thorson gave a self-suffering sigh and leaned against his desk. "If I didn't know the full moon was tonight, I would have guessed it by the pack of wild animals in my classroom."

Alex grinned. "You can't blame us, Professor. We don't have a choice."

Professor Thorson nodded. "Yes, but I do have a choice. My choice is to let you guys go before I either recite myself blue in the face despite the fact that no one is listening, or I go crazy enough with your wiggling to join your packs under the moon."

"Uh, you're not a werewolf," Pip commented, sitting on his history book as though he was hatching an egg.

Professor Thorson gave the Second Year a flat look. "Yes; thank you, Pip, for pointing out the obvious. Be gone, the lot of you. Come back tomorrow with your instincts eased and a reestablished ability to sit still for an hour."

"We never had that ability," Trent muttered.

Everyone put their books back on the shelf and hurried from the room. Alex was about to leave when he noticed Cassie holding back. He leaned against the cold door frame to see what she was up to.

Professor Thorson was busy erasing the whiteboard and humming to himself. He glanced over his shoulder and appeared surprised that there was still a student left.

"May I help you, Cassie?"

She nodded, her brown curls bouncing on her shoulders. "Yes, Professor. I have a question."

"Ask away," the professor replied. "I don't have another class until three ten, and I'll probably just have to send them away as well. There's plenty of time for your question."

Cassie perched on the front of a desk and balanced her history book on her knees. "Now that the world knows about werewolves, will they rewrite the books?" she asked.

Professor Thorson's eyebrows rose. "Why would they do that?"

She set a hand on her book. "If history is a true accounting of what actually happened, won't they need to include the history of the new race they just found out exists?"

The professor gave her a kind smile. He folded his bony arms over his book, trapping it against his chest. "That is the question, isn't it?"

Cassie nodded.

"They're afraid," Professor Thorson said, his tone gentle. "So afraid that they tried to wipe you out. The same thing has been done to wild wolves in most parts of the world. If they are eliminated, they don't need to be thought of again. The farmers and ranchers go on without thinking of the animals that were destroyed, because their life is easier that way."

He studied the book he held in silence for a few minutes before he said, "I don't think they'll ever enter your race in their history books. I'm sorry, Cassie."

Alex was surprised to hear that the professor really meant it. Alex cleared his throat. "That's okay. We don't want to be in some stupid book anyway," he said, trying to chase the pain from Cassie's face.

"But we should matter," she said, looking at him over her shoulder.

Alex nodded. "We do matter, and someday maybe it'll be different, right Professor Thorson?"

The professor nodded. "Right, Alex. Maybe we'll rewrite the books ourselves."

Cassie's face brightened. "That's what I'll do when I grow up!"

Professor Thorson patted her shoulder. "I'm sure you will. Now you'd better catch up to the rest of your pack before they get into too much trouble."

Alex walked beside Cassie up the hall. He could tell the conversation still bothered her. "It's alright, Cass. We don't need some book to tell us we exist."

Cassie nodded. "Yes, but someday they'll be proud that we exist. They'll want us in the books."

"Yes, they will," Alex promised. "Don't worry. Someday, werewolves will be seen as good guys instead of monsters."

Cassie's grin warmed him as they made their way to P.E. It was a few minutes before Pack Boris joined them.

"We all know class isn't going to happen today," Vance said as soon as Pack Jericho and Pack Boris had somewhat settled down. "Don't bother getting dressed. I know better than to try to teach on a full moon."

"He teaches?" Trent asked his sister in an undertone.

Terith elbowed him in the ribs.

"Jaze, well, Dean Jaze to you," Vance said, "Is going to address the students in the courtyard just before sunset. You might as well head there."

One class cut short and the other one being cancelled entirely put all the students in a great mood, especially when they got to skip wearing the ugly gym shorts. The students crowded together through the door.

"Head outside to go around," Vance yelled after them. "I don't need to be scolded for my students destroying the halls."

Jericho pushed open a side door and herded his pack outside. Boris ignored Vance and thundered with his pack through the school.

"Is it that hard to listen?" Pip asked, looking after them.

"It's his pack, his responsibility," Jericho reminded the Second Year. "Let's go."

Pack Jericho ran around the side of the school and reached the courtyard in time to see Nikki scolding Pack Boris as they walked outside.

Pip started laughing. Boris glared over Nikki's head at Pack Jericho. Jericho slapped Pip on the back hard enough to steal his breath. Pip began to cough instead of laugh.

"Live and learn," Jericho told him quietly.

The students milled in the courtyard. As more packs began to join them, a few students started games, stalling until night. It felt like the minutes dragged by until sunset.

Finally, Dean Jaze stepped out onto the stairs. "Students, welcome to the first full moon at the Academy!" Jaze called.

Cheers went up from the mass of waiting packs. Everyone milled anxiously, prey to the moon even though the sun hadn't yet set. Alex clenched and unclenched his fists, eager to phase.

"The full moon games are a way for us to keep you busy when everyone is in wolf form and liable to cause mischief." Laughter rose at his words. He continued, "For those of you who have never participated in the full moon games before, stick with your packs. In fact, that's the rule of the night. You cannot reach a checkpoint without your pack, or it doesn't count," Jaze explained.

Nikki leaned closer to him. "You should probably explain what a checkpoint is."

Jaze grinned. "Oh, yes. It's been a full year since I've had to explain this. Pardon me if I'm rusty." A few staff members laughed. Jaze gestured to the back of the Academy. "The full moon games test the limit of your abilities as a wolf. We always have a game the first full moon of each term. You have to reach one checkpoint before going to the next, and as I said before, you have to achieve them as a pack. The games for the first full moon of the school year vary. Tonight's will be about using your five senses. I'll only give you one hint, and that is to follow your nose to the first checkpoint. The next clue will be given to you by the human waiting there."

He smiled at the professors behind him. "I'd like to thank our human staff members who volunteer for every first full moon game for the sake of running the games while the rest of us are, well, unable to speak."

Chuckles rose.

"Your goal is to collect as many of the senses medals as you can. The pack with the most medals wins a steak dinner," Jaze concluded.

Laughter came from the watching students.

"Why is that so funny?" Jericho whispered to Alex.

Alex grinned. "Because we just had a steak dinner."

"But we want all the medals, right?"

Alex nodded. "Definitely. The most one team has gotten during the full moon is three. Usually they offer five, but nobody's ever gotten all five."

Jericho smiled. "Then we'll get five."

The rest of the pack nodded with answering grins on their faces.

"Five?" Pip squeaked. "Are you sure?"

"Five senses," Jericho said. He pointed at the Second Year's big ears. "We're going to need those for sonar."

Everyone laughed, and pride showed on Pip's face. "I can track anything by sound. Just you wait."

"Oh, I'm counting on it," Jericho answered.

A rustle ran through the crowd. Everyone's eyes turned to the horizon. The first rays of moonlight showed above the wall. Alex felt the urge to phase as it pulsed across his skin.

"We'll see you out there," Jaze told the werewolves.

A flood of students ran up the steps. Jaze, Nikki, Mouse, and Lyra held open the doors. Mouse stood behind them so he wouldn't be flattened by the mad rush of students. One hundred and fifty-two feet pounding up the stairs made the halls echo as everyone raced to their rooms.

"Happy hunting," Jericho called over his shoulder, disappearing into his room.

"Same to you," Alex replied. He pushed his door shut, but was careful not to close it all the way. Every full moon, someone made that mistake and got trapped inside, unable to participate in the games.

Alex pulled of his shirt and pants. His heart raced. He closed his eyes and willed his heartbeat to slow. He thought of the moonlight, of the way it tingled on his skin. An answering shudder ran across his arms and down his legs. He smiled and gave into it.

Phasing didn't hurt. It felt like stretching sore muscles at first, as though the bones and sinews had been in one place for too long and needed to be reminded where to go. Alex relished the feeling of his joints shifting, of his nose and mouth elongating into a muzzle that drew in each breath filled with scents his brain quickly categorized.

Colors faded and were taken over by grays and blacks so sharp the contrast was beautiful. The shadows in his room thrown by the curtains waving gently over the open windows danced as if they were alive. The carpet felt too soft beneath Alex's paws; he longed to run across forest loam and down game trails.

Howls arose within the Academy. Alex could hear his pack mates rushing to Pack Jericho's meeting room. The sound of paws across the carpet and the eager huffing of the wolves made him grin. It was going to be a night to remember.

Alex nosed his door open. Several of his pack members were already waiting by the door to the hall. Happiness filled Alex at the sight of Cassie standing there next to Terith. She was small compared to the other girl; both female wolves were cream-colored, but Cassie had her same dark blue eyes. She met Alex's gaze and wagged her tail. He opened his mouth in a wolfish grin and let his tongue hang out the side. His sister rolled her eyes, reminding him that letting someone know how stupid they looked crossed to wolf form.

Jericho rose onto his hind legs and pawed at the door handle that was a lever instead of a knob for just that reason. The door swung open to reveal the commotion of dozens of werewolves running for the stairs. Jericho gave a bark of command his pack recognized from the night games training sessions. They weren't to get caught up in the fray. They would stay together, an organized team amidst the chaos. Jericho took off and the pack flowed behind him in tight formation.

There was a traffic jam of wolves on the stairs. Apparently someone had tripped, and then others, so that the lower stairs looked like a pile of paws, legs, ears, and muzzles. The other wolves were fighting to get through. Boris was near the front of the mess with Torin not far behind. Both black Alphas looked entirely displeased at the state of things.

Jericho gave a lower bark. All of Pack Jericho looked at him, wondering if he was crazy. Alex fought back a smile because smiles didn't translate well on a wolf face and he didn't want to start a fight by showing his fangs by accident. The bark Jericho had given was one that indicated they should take the high route. It was a command he usually reserved for traveling creek beds and indicating the pack should take the shoulder. The pack exchanged glances. Jericho met Alex's gaze. Alex gave a minute nod. Jericho barked again and jumped.

All of Pack Jericho followed. They leaped on wolves' backs, sides, haunches, whatever was pointing toward the ceiling as they made their way down the stairs. It felt like they were traveling down a living staircase, which was the truth. The werewolves below them rebelled against their passage by snapping at their paws and stomachs, but Pack Jericho reached the bottom unscathed just as Boris was able to extract himself from the fray.

Boris looked at Pack Jericho, then back up the stairs. Alex swore he saw humor in the Termer Alpha's gaze when he looked back at them. Jericho gave a yip and the pack followed him out the door.

Chapter Fifteen

"First pack, huh? I thought the others would be close behind," Nikki commented. She pushed open the gate. "Follow your noses. Bring me one of what you find and I'll give you the clue for the next hunt."

Jericho took off into the night.

Alex was filled with joy. He could think of nothing better than the soft forest soil beneath his feet, his sister and the rest of his pack around him, and the scent of evergreens and meadow grass filling his nose. They followed the trail that didn't belong in the forest. It was pungent and sharp.

Alex's human mind recognized it as lemon, while his wolf one was repulsed by the scent. Someone was playing a joke on the wolves because canines hated the scent of lemon, yet they had to follow it. He made a mental note to thank Nikki when they got back, and tried to breathe with his mouth open to keep the scent from filling his nose.

The barks and howls of wolves announced that others had untangled themselves from the stairs and had begun the hunt. Pack Jericho had a good lead. Nothing would keep them from winning the first medal. The scent was getting stronger.

Another scent caught Alex so quickly he was thrown off track. He paused, testing the air. It was strong, but old. He couldn't get it out of his mind. Without realizing it, Alex trotted to the east, following the trail that brought fear to his mind.

He drew up at the sight of the meadow where he had protected Cassie from being shot. The scents of Drogan's men still lingered on the plants and soil despite the few weeks in between. The scene played over in his head, the man pointing a gun at Cassie, his grating voice, the sight of guns in unwavering hands, the smell of hatred. He couldn't save Cassie; the bullet burned in his leg. He wanted to attack them, to protect his sister the way he hadn't been able to protect his mom and dad.

Alex's heart thundered in his ears. It was the first time he had visited the meadow since it had happened. The helpless fury he had felt at that moment surfaced, blinding him to all other thoughts. He wanted to fight back. He wanted to make the men pay who had scared his sister so badly. He wanted to avenge his parents' death. He needed to find them.

A shoulder bumped his. He looked up at Jericho. The look the Alpha gave him wasn't of frustration; it was of understanding. Jericho glanced around the meadow. The huff he gave said that he knew what had brought Alex there. He tipped his head to the side and gave a small bark, waving his tail.

Alex remembered the hunt. He had gotten distracted. He was going to make his team lose. He gritted his teeth and nodded. Jericho took off. Alex ran behind the Alpha, leaving the meadow far behind. Within seconds, they reached Pack Jericho waiting anxiously on the trail. It was obvious by the sound that at least one of the other packs was ahead of them. Cassie threw Alex a questioning look. He dropped his gaze, ashamed of what he had done and what he had probably cost them.

At Jericho's command, everyone fell in. They ran even faster than before. Alex's heart dropped when they reached the meadow just as Pack Torin and Pack Maliki left. Justice, the last wolf picked for Torin's pack, was carrying something in his mouth as they ran. Alex followed Jericho to the center of the meadow and grimaced at the sight of a pile of lemons there.

They were losing time. Alex grabbed a lemon in his

mouth. The surprise on Jericho's face was almost comical. Alex snorted. Jericho barked and they ran back into the forest.

They reached the Academy gate just as the other two packs took off again. Alex breathed a sigh of disappointment at the sight of the silver medal hanging on a ribbon around Torin's neck. The wolf snapped at him as they passed. Alex jumped out of the way and deposited the lemon at Nikki's feet. The tart taste lingered on his tongue. He couldn't get it to leave.

"Sorry about that, Alex," Nikki said with a warm smile.

Professor Thorson gave him an apologetic look. "Vance put us up to it. You'll have to thank him for it later."

They could hear another wolf pack closing in.

"Your next sense is sound. Follow the sound and bring us what you find," Nikki said.

Pip surged to the front as Pack Jericho took off. His big ears looked comical even for a wolf, but he put them to good use. He honed in on the small tinkling of a bell and led them forward. Alex could hear the faint sound, but Pip's course didn't falter. He led them straight toward it instead of the roundabout way they could tell some of the packs had taken to locate the source. Pip kept his ears locked on the sound.

They passed Pack Maliki fumbling through a thick aspen grove a few paces away. Alex realized that aspen groves were everywhere. It was only Pip's careful guidance that kept them on a clear path. A few short seconds later, they leaped a stream and reached the bells hanging on a branch. Pack Torin was nowhere in sight.

Alex reared on his hind legs and grabbed a bell in his mouth. They ran back toward the gate in time to pass Pack Shannon who appeared to be backtracking. Shaylee held the lemon in her mouth, but didn't look pleased about it. They fell in behind Pack Jericho and followed them back to the gate.

"Well done!" Nikki said. She placed a ribbon bearing a medal around Jericho's neck as Professor Thorson gave Pack Shannon directions for the bell challenge. "Now you get to use your sight. Follow the ribbons on the trees to the next item."

Alex glanced behind him. Ribbons had been tied about halfway up the first two trees he could see. They were too high to have been in an ordinary wolf's line of sight. They had to run with their eyes up instead of surveying the path as they usually did. It was a very unnatural way to run.

To all of their surprise, Amos, the huge Gray, bounded on ahead. He didn't care if he ran into trees or bushes, he merely plowed his way through with his eyes on the ribbons. The pack rush around him, pushing him out of the way with their shoulders if he was about to run into a boulder or trunk. Amos let himself be swayed, but loped with his gaze locked on the ribbons, guiding them as they dashed beneath the trees.

They reached the meadow and found a big tub filled with water. Beneath the water were eleven painted rocks. Don, the other big Gray, dunked his head in the water. He came up with a rock in his teeth and water streaming from his nose and mouth. He and Amos exchanged a proud look. Jericho gave a bark and they were off again.

"This time, it's touch," Professor Thorson explained. "Go to the gate on the other side of the school. When you feel a patch of ground that is softer than the others, dig. Bring us what you find."

Pack Torin reached the gate just as Pack Jericho left. They loped around the school at top speed. When they reached the main gate, Jericho barked and they all spread out.

Pack Torin reached the gate and started to search. Cassie was the first to find the soft ground. She began to dig; Pack Jericho gathered around. Within seconds, she unveiled a little bag. She grabbed it in her teeth and they took off. A few seconds later, they heard a yip of excitement from Torin's pack. They had found their bag.

As soon as the third medal was around Jericho's neck, Professor Thorson gave them the final instructions. "Taste is your last challenge. Go to the stream where it runs beneath the fence. There are five bowls of water. Bring whatever is in the water that tastes like soap."

"Soap?" Nikki asked, taking a rock from Pack Drake and a bell from Pack Raynen.

"Another of Vance's influences," Alex heard Professor Thorson say as they ran along the gate.

They reached the bowls of water. Different colors of apples were floating in each of them. Jericho and Alex immediately ran to the first two bowls. Cassie took the third, with Trent and Terith close behind.

Alex's bowl tasted sweet. Jericho's expression said his was particularly nasty. Terith gave a bark and grabbed an apple from her bowl. They loped back along the gate.

"It's yellow!" Nikki exclaimed. "Well done!" She slipped the fourth medal around Jericho's neck. "You must have a pretty disciplined pack to have made it that fast."

Pack Boris and Pack Torin almost bowled Pack Jericho over in their haste to reach Nikki first. The disappointment on both of their faces when they realized Pack Jericho was already there was almost laughable. Pack Jericho trotted to the trees a few paces away and sat there catching their breath while the other packs turned in their items.

It took a while for the other packs to catch up. Pack Maliki and Pack Drake were trailing way behind. The rest of the packs joined Jericho's beneath the trees to rest. Alex was disappointed Pack Jericho hadn't earned five medals like their goal. He knew it was his fault. If he hadn't been distracted with the scent of Drogan's men and the memories that flooded him, his Alpha would be carrying five medals. He tried to console himself with the thought that four was more than any pack had ever gotten on a full moon, but it didn't make him feel better.

Something made the fur rise on the back of Alex's neck. He looked to the left. A lone brown wolf stood beneath the trees. He recognized the wolf as being from Rafe's pack. The animal watched them with searching golden eyes. At Alex's attention, the wolf took a few steps into the forest. Alex rose uncertainly.

Jericho gave a questioning whine. Alex tipped his head toward the wolf. Something bade him to follow it. He paced forward, then looked back at his pack. Jericho watched him, his gaze curious. The rest of the pack began to notice their silent exchange. Jericho gave a soft huff. Several of them rose and followed. The rest quickly fell in behind their Alpha.

The other packs looked from Alex to Rafe's wolf. Alex could see the curiosity on their faces, but Boris and Torin were busy scuffling over something. Alex let Jericho pass, then followed his Alpha.

Rafe's wolf began to run as soon as he realized the other wolves were following. Jericho dipped his head. The other members of Pack Jericho fell into a run behind their leader. They leaped the stream, loped down an empty wash, and made it to the other side in time to see Rafe's wolf vanish beneath the trees. Disappointment flooded through Alex. He had led his pack on a wild goose chase.

Jericho gave Alex a look filled with humor. The other wolves appeared a bit less inclined to see the situation as funny, but before everyone could get too disgruntled, the wolf returned. Alex was surprised to see Rafe in wolf form following behind. The werewolf's golden eyes seemed to glow in the light of the moon. He lowered his head and dropped something to the ground. A closer look showed it to be a ball.

Alex snorted. It had to be another of Vance's tricks. Other members of the pack began to turn away. Alex was about to follow, but Jericho waited. At Alex's puzzled look, Jericho took a step forward. Rafe pushed the ball with his nose toward the pack. Jericho crossed to Rafe and picked it up. Alex blinked; Rafe and the wolf disappeared. He couldn't hear their paws on the forest floor. Rafe was an enigma.

Jericho gave Alex what appeared to be a slight shoulder shrug which Alex didn't even know was possible as a wolf. The Alpha trotted past him to the front of the pack. Everyone fell in behind and loped back to the gates, worried they had missed something.

"Here they are," Nikki said. Jericho walked up to her and dropped the ball at her feet. It would have been hilarious, a huge Alpha wolf bringing what appeared to be a tennis ball to the dean's wife, yet Nikki's gaze said otherwise. "They did it," she said.

Professor Thorson nodded, his expression pleased. "It appears that way."

Nikki pulled a string on the ball, unthreading it as all of the wolves watched. The ball opened. Something glinted in the middle. Alex's heart slowed at the sight of another medal. Jericho glanced at him. Pride surged through Alex as his Alpha stepped forward to have the medal placed around his neck. The metal chinked against the others he already wore.

Alex felt like laughing. He had cost his team one medal, then gotten them another. His blunder had been repaid.

"No one has ever followed the wolf before," Nikki informed the watching werewolves. "The sixth sense of a wolf is instinct. We've had Rafe's pack waiting for someone to follow their instincts and earn the medal ever since our first full moon games started." She smiled at Pack Jericho. "Now we'll have to come up with another one. Keep your eyes open next year!"

With that, the packs were dismissed to run or do whatever they would like until the moon set. Pack Jericho roamed the Academy grounds. Alex was content to be within the walls where he didn't have to worry about Cassie. She pranced happily beside him, her pride in her brother evident on her face. She nipped at his leg, then took off running. Soon, all of Pack Jericho was involved in an extensive game of tag. It wasn't long before the other packs joined in.

Chapter Sixteen

Alex's leg began to ache. It had been a while since it had bothered him, but with all the running, jumping, tackling, and chasing down the challenges, he had definitely pushed it too far. He climbed to the top step and settled on his stomach to watch the games below. A familiar scent touched his nose; he turned his head and spotted Kalia leaning against the wall.

"Wore yourself out?" she asked. She paused a minute, then smiled and said, "The strong, silent type, huh?"

Alex watched her, wondering why she was out at night when she wasn't a werewolf and hadn't been exactly silent about her dislike of the race.

"I can't sleep," Kalia said, coming to sit across the steps from him. "I figured watching the wolves run around would be boring enough to make me tired." She hesitated, then gestured toward the moon that hung just above the treetops. "But I think that's the reason I can't sleep."

As Alex watched, her icy blue eyes turned golden for the briefest second as she looked at the full orb that bathed the courtyard in gentle light. The color change had been so fast he wasn't even sure he had seen it.

Kalia shook her head, unaware. "Whatever's going on, it's annoying being stuck in the middle. I wish my body would just figure it out so either my parents can fear and despise me, or I could go home. As it is, I'm not sure how Christmas break will go." She glanced at Alex. "You're a great listener," she said mockingly.

Alex snorted softly with humor. She studied him, and he watched as emotions filled her eyes. He recognized them as sorrow and regret.

"I guess you don't go anywhere for the break, do you?" she asked quietly. "I shouldn't really complain about my family. Everyone knows what happened to Jet's parents. He protected you, didn't he?"

Alex's stomach clenched. In his mind, he saw that night again, his parents dead, Drogan's mismatched eyes watching the twin werewolves as he sliced their mother's throat. He let their mother fall to the ground and took a step forward. The lamplight glinted off the knife he held. The dark red sheen of blood looked fake, like it had been dipped in molasses. Alex willed himself to believe it.

Sights and sounds become unnaturally harsh to Alex's senses as he held Cassie. He would protect her with his life against the man with the mismatched eyes. At eight years old, he was willing to die if it meant she would live. Drogan took another step; Alex rose slowly. Cassie clung to his arm. Alex pushed her gently behind him. Her sobs filled the air.

Drogan's eyes narrowed at Alex's defiance. He lifted the knife. A soft footstep sounded on the porch. Two thumps followed as bodies fell. Drogan froze. The door burst open, and Jet was there.

"I'm sorry," Kalia whispered. "I shouldn't have brought it up."

The memories cleared enough for Alex to realize she had scooted next to him. Something was smoothing the fur on the top of his head. He realized with a twist of amazement and humor that she was actually petting him.

He gave her a look of surprise.

She paused with her hand in the air. "Uh, yeah," she said with embarrassment. "This is a bit awkward. I, uh, have a dog at home. I guess I, uh, well, I'll be going." She stood and hurried into the school.

Alex watched her with a huff of humor. He had definitely never had anyone pet him before. He tried to imagine her doing the same thing while he was in human form. The thought made him laugh inside.

A slight tingle ran down his limbs. He glanced up to see that the moon had vanished completely behind the trees. The power of the moonlight was gone. They could phase back.

He stretched slowly and was bombarded by werewolves running up the stairs in wolf form. As great as being a wolf was, it was the early hours of the morning and everyone was eager to catch some sleep. They reached the doors, and Alex realized that Kalia had shut the door that was normally propped open for the wolves.

"I've got it!" Pip yelled.

The Second Year had phased and was running completely naked up the stairs. Everyone let out groans and shielded their eyes from the sight as he pulled open the door and propped it with the doorstop left there for that reason. Pip phased again and gave a wolfish grin, his huge ears comical with the look of pride on his face at what he had accomplished.

Boris shook his massive head and padded past the werewolf into the Academy. The other wolves joined him. The hustle to get down the stairs had been replaced by a sedate climb back up as exhausted werewolves made their way to their quarters. Alex reached his room and phased, then pulled on the cotton pants he slept in. He walked back to the meeting room and collapsed on one of the couches. Several of the pack were already there, sprawled on the couches and the thickly carpeted floor.

Cassie fell onto the couch next to Alex and laughed. "You had to follow Rafe's wolf."

Alex grinned. "It felt like the thing to do at the time."

"Maybe you are a wild wolf," Trent said. Everyone laughed.

Jericho came back in carrying the five medals. The pack

sobered as he hung them on the wolf statue that sat on the mantelpiece. The statue fell from the weight. He caught it with his fast reflexes and grinned. "Guess we got too many."

Answering grins spread around the room.

The Alpha hung them on the corner of a picture of wolves lounging on a mountain shelf overlooking a snow-covered valley. When he turned back around, there was pride on Jericho's face. "Well done, Pack Jericho."

Applause went up. Pack mates slapped each other on the shoulders, and the girls smiled at everyone.

"I thought we lost it," Jericho continued. He looked at Alex.

Alex's heart fell. "I almost lost it for you," he apologized quietly.

Jericho shook his head. "I know what happened back there. You aren't to blame." His eyes creased. "Besides, you made up for it with this," he said, pointing to the fifth medal. It hung on a red ribbon that made it stand out from the white ribbons on the others. "Well done." The Alpha leaned against the mantle and crossed his arms, viewing his pack with respect.

"Awesome job," Trent said.

"You followed your instincts," Pip exclaimed.

"Yes," Jericho said, smiling at Alex. "I've learned never to doubt Alex's instincts." He gave Pip a surprised look, "And never to doubt your hearing, apparently."

Everyone laughed. Alex patted the little werewolf's shoulder. "You said you would lead us on the sound challenge."

"And I did!" Pip exclaimed. He pointed to his ears. "They're like sonar!"

Jericho chuckled. "From now on, Pip will now be known as Sonar."

"Sonar," Pip repeated. His smile was so big it looked like his face could barely contain it. "I like that!"

"And you, Amos, nobody could run like that with their eyes on the trees. You didn't even look down!" Jericho said.

Amos gave a deep chuckle. "I hit tree," he replied, his words slow. The grin on his face made everyone laugh.

"Then we figured out how to protect you." Jericho replied. "I'm sure the professors have never seen anything like that."

Amos laughed. "You little wolves pushing me around. It was fun."

Everyone laughed again.

"Cassie's got the soft paws," Marky pointed out.

"That's right," Jericho said with a smile at Alex's sister. "You found the place to dig. Pack Torin was right behind us. And poor Terith had to drink soap."

"It was nasty," she replied, making a face. "And the taste of an apple in wolf form isn't much better."

"Try the lemon," Alex said.

"That's right!" Jericho exclaimed. "I forgot you had to carry that."

"I had to make up for my mistake somehow," Alex replied, his cheeks burning slightly at all the laughter. "But it was horrible."

"I think that's why Pack Shannon fell so far behind," Von pointed out with a finger in his nose. "They couldn't decide who had to carry the lemon."

Everyone gave weary laughs.

"Alright, Pack Jericho. Get to bed. We've got another day of school in the morning," Jericho reminded them.

"Can't we tell the dean we slept in?" Trent whined.

"I don't know where the professors went when the full moon rose, but I can guarantee Chet and Dray will be there ready for combat training, and I don't want to spend the morning scrubbing mats if we're late," Jericho replied. "Get some sleep."

Everyone rose and stumbled to their rooms. Alex was about to follow, but something in Jericho's comment stuck in his mind.

"I wonder where the professors disappeared to," Alex mused aloud outside his door.

"Don't know," Jericho replied, walking into his own darkened room. Alex heard him sprawl on the bed. "But I'm getting some sleep. You should probably do the same."

The sound of Jericho's snores arose before Alex could even make up his mind. He fought back a smile and crossed the meeting room to the hall door. He was tired, but instincts told him to investigate. After following Rafe's wolf, he wasn't going to ignore those instincts.

"Where are you going?"

He glanced back at Cassie's voice. "There's something I need to check out."

"I'm coming with you," she said; though she looked exhausted, her firm tone gave him no chance to argue.

Alex gave his obvious exhausted sister a chance to go to bed. "I'm not sure I'll find anything."

She smiled and rubbed the sleep from her eyes. "I've know better than to sleep when you have a hunch."

"Fine," Alex replied, glad to have her company. School this year had been so different. They didn't have as much time together as they usually did. He valued the time he could have with her.

They walked quietly down the stairs. The Academy was completely silent. The twins' footsteps echoed along the wooden hall as they made their way to the closet.

"You're going back down there?" Cassie whispered.

"I'm just wondering why none of the other professors were at the full moon games. Last year they even participated," Alex explained. "I'm worried something's up."

Alex stepped inside, waited for Cassie to follow, then pulled the door shut behind them. He reached for the back door. It was locked. He knocked on it. The sound seemed unusually loud in the enclosed space.

Silence filled the closet. Alex looked up at the camera. He gave a little wave and knocked again.

"Who are you waving at?" Cassie asked.

"You'll see."

A few seconds later, he could hear footsteps below. The door opened a few inches. "What do you want?" Brock asked, his voice tired.

"We were just wondering if the professors were below," Alex replied.

Brock shook his head, his messy hair visible in the shadows. "No one here but me."

That spiked Alex's curiosity. He pushed the door open, giving Brock no choice but to step back.

"You're not supposed to be in here," Brock said, waving the piece of pizza he carried in protest.

Cassie agreed. "We probably shouldn't go down there," she said, worry clear in her voice.

Alex jogged down the stairs. "I'm not going to hurt anything. I swear. I won't even touch. See." He held his hands in the air like he was under arrest. "No touch."

"This is top secret," Brock replied with Cassie close behind.

"We won't tell," Alex answered with what he hoped was a winning smile.

Brock gave a frustrated sigh and collapsed back on his chair. "I don't have the brain power to argue with you both right now. There are more important things going on." He took a bite of his pizza and scooted back to the screens he had been monitoring.

Chapter Seventeen

Alex's eyes widened at the sight of a dozen camera views spread out on the screens. One showed Jaze riding in the back of what appeared to be a van without seats. He wore a headband with a camera on it, black clothes, and gloves. There was a small silver wolf paw print medallion around his neck. His camera showed about twelve other werewolves crammed together in the same van.

"What are they doing?" Alex asked.

"They're on a mission. Quiet," Brock replied, his eyes on the screen.

Alex pulled two rolling chairs over. Cassie took a seat next to him.

"This is it," a familiar voice said. Jaze's camera panned to show Mouse in the driver's seat.

"We're going in," Jaze said. "You got us, Brock?"

Brock set his pizza down and touched his earpiece. "Got you. Be careful."

"We're always careful," Jaze replied. The other cameras showed a grin on his face. Alex felt himself smiling back.

"Yeah, I'll believe that when I see it," Brock said, rolling his eyes. He took a bite of a huge sandwich that sat next to the pizza as he watched the monitors.

Alex followed his gaze to another screen that showed what appeared to be a house layout. Red lights flashed and moved. There was a single red light in the middle of the house that others were milling around.

"Whose house is that?" Cassie asked in a whisper.

Brock glanced back at them. "We tracked Drogan to it. They're holding someone inside. Jaze's team is investigating."

Alex felt Cassie tense beside him. He leaned forward, his own muscles tightening.

Brock recited what he saw on the house monitor. "There are four bogies on the front porch, three behind, and two waiting in the trees. They're rotating shifts every ten minutes. If you want silence, you'll have to take them all out."

"Got it," Jaze replied. He motioned to his team. "Let's move."

Alex watched as the van door was pulled open and the members of Jaze's team swarmed out. Alex's gaze locked on Jaze's monitor as his team split to either side, leaving him and another werewolf to take the porch.

Jaze nodded at his companion; Alex was surprised to see it was Kaynan. The red-eyed werewolf kept to the shadows as he crept noiselessly to the far side of the porch and out of sight. Jaze waited next to the porch for a minute. Brock watched everyone on the monitor. The red dots took up places near those that had been there before, then grew still.

Brock touched his earpiece. "Everyone's in place," he said quietly. "Go."

The red dots attacked. Not a sound was heard. Alex watched in shock as Jaze leaped the porch and slammed a fist into the first man's jaw, knocking him out cold. The Alpha caught the body and lowered it just as the second man on his side turned. Jaze spun and knocked his feet out, and made it back around in time to catch him in a headlock before he hit the ground. A few seconds in a sleeper hold had the man out beside his companion.

Jaze rose and Kaynan did the same, leaving two more bodies near the shadows. The glint of a blade showed in the gray predawn light before Kaynan fastened something around his wrist. Alex realized he had seen the wristband before. The professor always wore it. Alex had figured it was a gift from Grace; the fact that it was a weapon changed his whole view of the professor.

"That's our dean?" Cassie whispered in awe.

"And our professors," Alex replied. "I never would have believed it."

Brock grinned at them both. "There are a lot of secrets at this Academy. It's good to know who has your best interests at heart, isn't it?"

The twins nodded in amazement.

"Ready?" Jaze whispered over the intercom.

Brock checked the screen. The other red dots were still. "Ready," he replied.

Jaze's team surged toward the house. Kaynan tested the door knob; it was locked. A quick glance showed three more members of the werewolf team waiting on the stairs. Chet's dark eyes and black hair were easy to identify within the shadows. Dray waited next to him, his sun blond hair held back by another headband with a camera similar to Jaze's. The third member turned out to be Colleen. Chet moved to kick the door in, but Jaze motioned for him to wait. Colleen slipped something into Kaynan's hand.

"Old habits can come in useful," she whispered, her violet eyes flashing in the porch light.

Kaynan opened his hand and smiled at the small pieces of metal he found there. He knelt by the front door. In less than five seconds, Alex heard a click and the door opened with a slight creak.

"How's the back door?" Jaze asked.

Brock, Alex, and Cassie shifted their gazes to the other monitors. A camera showed Rafe on one side of the door with Vance on the other. Vance put a hand to the doorknob. It was obvious that it was locked as well. Vance gave the knob a sharp turn. The door opened.

"Good," Vance replied.

"Keep low, stay silent," Jaze whispered. "Let's try to do

this without a shot fired. We don't know who they have and don't want to put whoever it is in jeopardy. Mouse, you got the lights?"

At that moment, the power in the house cut completely. Commotion could be heard inside. The cameras switched to night vision.

"Move in," Jaze commanded.

Both teams opened their doors and stepped inside. Jaze flowed silently to the left through a small dining room. Kaynan followed close behind. Dray and Colleen took the right.

Three men waited in the kitchen. Jaze reached one, punched him in the kidney and slammed an elbow into his ear. As the man fell, Jaze was at the second who was just turning with his mouth opening to give an alarm. Jaze silence him with a straight punch to his throat followed by a blow to the stomach. When the man doubled over, Jaze elbowed him in the back. The man fell to the floor and the Alpha still him with a fist to the side of the head.

He stepped over the man Kaynan had already brought down.

"There are four men upstairs, but the majority are in the basement," Brock informed them. For once, his sandwich and pizza sat forgotten next to the computer.

Vance's team ran up the stairs. Jaze motioned for Colleen to stay on the main floor in case backup arrived. He, Kaynan, Dray, and Chet hurried on silent feet down the stairs.

"The power company's sending a guy to check it out," one of the men in the basement said. He held out his phone, its glowing light casting the room in shadows.

"No need," Jaze replied in the darkness.

Everyone turned in surprised. The werewolves had them surrounded. Jaze crouched and knocked the feet out from beneath two men with a sweep of his leg. He silenced them both with two haymakers. Jaze rolled forward, hit a man in the groin, then rose and slammed the back of his elbow into another man's jaw. He spun and kicked the head of man who was grappling with Dray. Dray dropped him and turned to slam a two-fisted punch to the next man's chest.

A shot rang out. Jaze tackled the shooter against the wall. He slid a chop down the man's arm to knock his gun out of his grasp and followed it with a back-hand across the man's face. The man tried to punch him in the stomach. Jaze blocked the punch and popped an uppercut to the man's jaw that sent his head against the wall. He slid to the ground.

A quick check showed all of the men down.

"Is everyone alright?" Jaze asked.

"A shot was fired," Chet pointed out dryly. "Mission failed."

Jaze shook his head. "Lights on, Mouse," he said.

The power was immediately turned back on. A single door led from the room.

"Anyone else in there?" Jaze asked.

"Two people," Brock replied, looking at the screen.

"Careful," Kaynan warned.

Alex watched with abated breath as Chet reached for the doorknob at Jaze's nod. When the door opened, Jaze dove into the room, came up to his knees, and knocked the waiting man's gun away before he could fire. Jaze drove a fist into the man's groin followed by a punch to the stomach. The man doubled over. Jaze wrapped an arm around the man's neck and rolled, slamming the man's body to the ground.

"You get to have all the fun," Chet said from the door.

"That was awesome," Alex breathed, unable to tear his eyes from the screen.

Jaze rose without a word and walked to the cage in the

corner. A lone woman sat huddled on a dirty blanket with another thrown over her shoulders. Jaze touched the cage.

"We're going to get you out of here," he said gently. She looked up at him

Cassie's hand grabbed Alex's. His heart skipped a beat.

"It's Mom!" Cassie exclaimed. "That's Mom!"

Alex shook his head. "No, it can't be," he replied, though he stared at her sitting there. Her dark hair was shorter than his mother usually wore it, but the same light blue eyes looked straight at the camera, filled with loss and pain from her confinement. She had the same high cheekbones and the creases at the corners of her eyes that said smiling was a habit, though no smile lit her face. Only fear showed in her eyes at the werewolves that surrounded the cage.

"It can't be," Alex said again. Tears burned in his eyes and began to stream down his cheeks. "I saw her die. I watched her die, Cass. It can't be."

"But it's Mom," his sister replied, her voice tight and her gaze locked on the woman in Jaze's camera. Tears trickled down her cheeks. "It's Mom. It has to be."

Brock looked between them, stunned.

Alex shook his head, his voice broken. "She died, Cass. It can't be."

He watched as Vance broke the lock to the cage and Jaze stepped inside.

"I'm Jaze Carso," he said. "Do you know who I am?"

Her face showed a flicker of familiarity with the name. She nodded. "I know who you are," she said softly in a voice that was so like Alex's mother's that his heart clenched because he knew it couldn't be.

Jaze held out a hand and the woman took it. Jaze led her carefully from the cage.

Brock checked the screen. "The area's clear. Have a safe

trip back."

"Thanks, Brock," Jaze replied. He reached up and his camera turned off. The others soon followed.

"That was her," Cassie said. Sobs shook her shoulders. "She was on the camera. You saw her." Her voice was near hysterical.

"It couldn't have been," Alex replied, putting an arm around his sister's shoulders. He was so confused. The woman looked just like his mother, but her voice was slightly different. He had watched his mother die. Yet the woman's face looked so achingly like hers that he couldn't stop picturing it in his mind.

"Where are they taking her?" Cassie asked. The same confusion showed in her voice. Tears wouldn't stop rolling down her cheeks.

Brock set his sandwich down. He looked as though he knew he shouldn't tell them, but after what they had seen, he couldn't deny the twins. "To our closest safe house," he answered. "It's on the other side of the forest at the furthest end of the preserve."

"Can we go there?" Alex asked.

Brock shook his head. "It would be best if you wait for Jaze. I'm sure he'll have some answers for you." He looked around and ran a hand through his spikey hair. "He's going to be upset you were down here."

"Tell him I overpowered you," Alex replied.

Brock gave him an incredulous look. "And you forced me to open the door in the first place? I know better than that."

"Tell him I was crying," Cassie said.

They both looked at her. She tried to wipe the tears from her cheeks, but they wouldn't stop coming. "I bet he wouldn't be so upset."

Brock nodded. "Fine. I need you both to go to your

rooms. I'll wake you as soon as Jaze gets back."

"Thank you, Brock," Alex told him as he led his sister up the stairs. She clung to him, refusing to let go after what she had seen.

"Yeah," Brock replied, his tone showing he doubted whether he had made the right decision.

Alex and Cassie made it back to Pack Jericho's quarters. Cassie refused to go to her room, so Alex let her into his. She settled on his bed wrapped in her red blanket. Quiet sobs shook her small body. Alex held her close while he stared out the window, wondering with an aching heart about the woman they had seen on Jaze's camera.

Chapter Eighteen

Alex listened for the vehicles to return. He kept seeing his mother's face in his mind, watching the way the light had flickered out. He had to remind himself over and over again that the woman Jaze had rescued wasn't her. He wanted to believe so badly. He listened to his sister cry herself to sleep, and it broke his heart. He wanted to tell Cassie that he was wrong, that by some miracle their mother was still alive. Yet he knew deep down that it couldn't be true, and every time he reminded himself of that, it felt like a piece of him died.

He finally rose and, checking to make sure Cassie was sleeping soundly, he crept down the stairs. Early dawn light spilled in through the windows, lighting the halls that would soon be packed with students rushing to class. Alex couldn't find any joy in the thought of being with them. He had to know; nothing else mattered until his questions were answered.

He was surprised to hear voices from below when he stepped in the closet. He closed the door behind him and listened for a few seconds.

"We have no idea how they found her, or why he was holding her," Brock said.

"You have some idea," Vance replied.

"That's a discussion for a later date," Jaze answered.

At the sound of the dean's voice, Alex raised his hand to the door; all talking below ceased.

"Why is Alex up there?" he heard Jaze ask quietly.

"He was down here," Brock replied.

"What?" Vance demanded, his tone heated. "Why was a student down here?"

"What matters is what he saw," Jaze answered, his voice level. "Is that why he's here?"

Alex could picture Brock nodding. He felt bad for putting the human in the situation, but he needed to talk to Jaze, and Brock's honesty was the only thing that could get him through the door.

"He saw it all," Brock said, his voice showing the same exhaustion Alex felt. "He and Cassie both. They watched the rescue."

"Let him down," Jaze said.

Footsteps sounded on the stairs.

"He shouldn't be down here," Vance argued. "He of all werewolves. If Drogan was to capture him—"

"Then we have all failed," Jaze finished quietly.

Brock opened the door. He gave Alex a weak smile around a sucker that was in his mouth. "I figured you'd be here," he said.

Alex gave him a humorless smile in return. "I didn't want to miss the party. By the way, how'd everyone get here without me hearing? I was listening for cars."

"Let me keep at least some secrets," Brock replied.

Alex nodded in answer and followed Brock down the stairs. He paused at the sight of the werewolves who had been a part of Jaze's team sitting around an oval table.

"You're welcome here," Jaze said.

Vance's expression told otherwise, but Alex ignored him. He took the seat Jaze indicated.

Jaze studied him for a minute in silence. As much as he wanted to ask all the questions that had been swirling around in his mind for the past few hours, Alex held his tongue.

"What would you like to know?" the dean asked, his attention fully on Alex.

"He shouldn't know anything," Chet pointed out, though his tone was less harsh than Vance's.

Jaze met the Alpha's gaze. "You all know how this affects

Alex and Cassie." An affectionate smile touched the dean's lips when he saw the tired expressions on his team's faces. "Get some sleep, everyone. It's a school day in about," he checked the clock above Brock, "Two hours. Better make them count."

"Can't we just tell the students we slept in?" Kaynan asked, stifling a yawn.

Alex fought back a small smile at the same comment Trent had made, though Kaynan said it without the whine.

"I'm sure Grace could cover for you," Jaze replied with a chuckle.

"And leave my wife to those animals?" Kaynan asked, his tone aghast. He glanced at Alex and winked. "Not that we're much better."

Alex answered with a good-natured smile.

Kaynan rose and patted Alex on the shoulder as he walked past. A few of the others did the same before stumbling tiredly up the stairs. Alex wondered how many alarm clocks would be broken in the morning.

"Go ahead, Brock," Jaze said, dismissing the human.

"Are you sure?" Brock asked. "Someone's got to keep an eye on the monitors and with Mouse out repairing equipment. . . ."

Jaze nodded. "Go ahead. I've got things down here."

Brock gave him a grateful smile and gathered up a few bags of snacks for his trip up the stairs. "I'm wasting away without your mother's cooking," Brock said with a sorrowful sigh. "I'll catch some shuteye and be back in a couple of hours."

"Take what you need," Jaze said.

When the door closed above to leave only the two of them in the security room, Jaze sat back in his seat. Alex imagined he looked as tired as the dean, but he couldn't rest until he had some answers. Now that everyone was gone, Alex leaned forward with his elbows on his knees.

"Who is she?"

Jaze nodded at the question as if he had been anticipating it. There was a light of understanding in his eyes that was tempered by sadness. "I'm sorry you saw that. I wished I could have explained it first."

"We insisted on being down here." Alex rubbed his eyes with one hand. "I just don't understand what it was that we saw."

Jaze took in a slow breath. His gaze was searching as if he debated how much to tell the student. He let the breath out slowly. "You've been like a son to Nikki and I," he said.

Alex nodded, keeping silent.

"You've gone through so much." Jaze opened a hand. "I have, too," he said with a weary smile. "I suppose that's why I felt we could help you and Cassie. We wanted you to live a normal life."

Alex didn't know what the Alpha was getting at. He was anxious to have his question answered, but it felt like Jaze was stalling. Jaze never stalled as a matter of principle. He was always straight-forward and honest. The direction the conversation was taking confused Alex even more.

He couldn't hold it in any longer. "I just want to know who she is."

Jaze was silent for a few seconds. When he spoke, he gave Alex a sad smile. "She's your mother's twin sister."

Alex stared at the dean. He was filled with amazement and disappointment at the same time. The part of him that hoped Cassie's words were true, the part that wished his mother had somehow survived the night, faded to leave the gaping hole his parents' death had created in his heart. It hurt to let that hope go, even though he had known at the time how ridiculous a hope it had been.

Yet the other side was filled with relief. He had felt something when he saw the woman on the screen, even though he knew she wasn't his mother. Now he knew why. She was family, perhaps the only family Alex and Cassie had left.

Alex shook his head, thinking aloud, "I didn't know Mom had a twin sister."

The dean gave a gentle smile. "There are quite a few things you don't know." Before Alex could ask any more questions, Jaze held up a hand. "Those things will be cleared up in time, but now is not the opportunity to address them."

Alex nodded, as much as he wanted to ask. He had never questioned Jaze's words, and refused to start doing so.

"I will explain what I can," Jaze continued. "You know that Drogan has been looking for you and Cassie. We put that to revenge against what Jet did. He brought them down and pretty much single-handedly freed the werewolves General Jared Carso and his men gathered to destroy. Jet made them look foolish, and even though he died, I don't think they can forgive that."

"So why capture my mom's sister?" Alex asked.

Jaze's brow furrowed. "We can only figure that they meant to use her as bait. Whether you knew your mom had a twin or not, if you saw her, you would try to rescue her."

The truth of Jaze's words burned in Alex's chest. He knew how fatal such an action would be, but he would have tried.

"Is she alright?" Alex asked.

Jaze nodded. "She suffers from dehydration and minor wounds as a result of Drogan's captivity, but I think she'll be okay. She's in our safe house across the forest from here."

The need that burned in his chest to ascertain her safety

surprised Alex. "Can I see her?"

Jaze hesitated, then shook his head. "I don't think now would be a good time. There's a reason your mother kept her existence from you. If it was to protect her, we need to make sure both your safety and your aunt's is taken into consideration."

"I understand," Alex said softly.

His words surprised Jaze. "You do?"

Alex nodded. "I don't want her to end up like my mom. If not knowing us will keep her from that, then it's worth it."

Jaze's gaze softened. He set a hand on Alex's knee. "You have carried so much, and you're still so young. I lost my dad when I was seventeen, but I wasn't there." Memories flooded through the dean's eyes. Alex could tell he was seeing things that haunted him. "I couldn't imagine going through what you did at your age. When it's safe, I'll introduce you to her. Until then, we'll do everything we can to make her comfortable."

Alex nodded. Jaze's words and confidence meant the world to him. A yawn caught him by surprise.

Jaze smiled. "You better get to bed yourself."

"What about you?" Alex asked.

Jaze stretched. "Oh, I've got another few hours in me." He winked at Alex. "You don't have to worry about this old man."

Alex smiled as he stood. "Oh, come on. You're only what, forty?"

Jaze barked out a laugh in reply. "I'm younger than that, Alex."

"How old are you in dog years?" Alex asked.

Jaze pushed him toward the stairs. "Get to bed. I don't need your cheekiness."

Alex laughed and ran up the stairs. He paused at the top

and turned. "Jaze?"

Jaze looked up at him. "Yes?"

"Thank you for saving my aunt."

"You're welcome," Jaze replied. "We'll do everything we can for her."

Alex shut the door behind him and walked up the stairs to his room. A few of the early rising students said hello to him in the hallway. He mumbled barely audible answers before making his way to his room. He almost fell into an exhausted heap on the bed until he remembered that Cassie was beneath the red blanket on top. Alex let out a sigh, grabbed a pillow, and settled on the floor.

"It's not her, is it?"

The heartache in Cassie's voice made all of the emotions from the past few hours storm back. Tears burned in Alex's eyes.

"I thought you were asleep," he said, sitting up.

Cassie pulled the blanket down just enough to look at him. Her eyes were rimmed with red. "I knew it couldn't be her. But I hoped...." her voice fell away.

Alex opened his arms and Cassie came down to sit in his lap like she used to do when they first lost their mom and dad. He held her close and felt her shoulders shake as she began to cry. He wondered how many hours he had spent holding her and consoling her, trying to keep his sanity at the same time past the empty void that filled him at the thought that their parents were gone.

"It's okay," he whispered quietly into her hair. "You have me, Cass. I won't leave you alone."

She sniffed. "Do you remember the way she used to sing to us to wake us up in the morning?" she asked, her voice muffled.

Alex blinked quickly, willing the tears not to fall. "Yes,"

he said, his voice almost steady. "She sang, 'Zipadeedoodah', and it would always make us laugh."

"And if we pretended to still be sleeping," Cassie began.

"She would tickle us until we gave up," Alex replied. The tears began to slide down his cheeks. "She smelled like strawberries."

"And cookies," Cassie said. She gave a little giggle that ended in a hiccup. "She used to tell the best bedtime stories."

"She always checked for monsters under the bed, too," Alex said. The sorrow that filled his chest made his heart hurt. He remembered the million things his mother used to do that made their lives wonderful, the games they used to play, the things she would teach them how to cook.

"Do you remember making lemon bars?" Alex asked past the knot in his throat.

"She got mad at us for getting covered in powdered sugar," Cassie replied. Her laugh ended in a sob. "Then she chased us around and we had a big powdered sugar fight. In the end, the entire house was covered. Dad said he thought a sugar bomb had gone off."

"Yeah," Alex remembered with a smile despite his tears, "Then we all attacked him with the sugar. He looked like a giant snowman when we were done."

Cassie wiped her cheek with a corner of her red blanket. "Dad had the warmest hugs."

Alex nodded. "I used to think that nobody could hurt us with Dad around. He was so strong." His voice choked off.

"He used to play dollies with me," Cassie said. She cried as she spoke, "He did the voices and everything. He said every daddy needed to remember what it was like to be a child."

"I miss them so much," Alex admitted, saying the words he had refused to let himself speak for years because he was afraid of the pain they brought, and of admitting that they were never coming back. Seeing what he thought was his mom's face, then having that taken away again had brought the ache back so fresh and real he could barely breathe.

"I do, too," Cassie said. She leaned against Alex's arm. His sleeve was soaked with her tears. "Mom used to fall asleep on the couch waiting for Dad to come home for work."

"She said she couldn't sleep in the bed without him because it was too empty." Alex sniffed and rubbed his eyes. "I remember the first time Mom told me we had a brother. You were asleep, but when it was close to the full moon, I had a hard time sleeping. When Mom checked on us, she saw that I was awake. I asked her to tell me a story, and she told me about Jet."

He rested his head back. "She said that they loved him so much, but he was kidnapped when he was only a few days old. I was so sad thinking that we would never see our brother. Mom said she kept hoping he'd find his way home. She never gave up believing." He gave Cassie a small smile. "That's why she used to check on us every night, to make sure we were safe. She said we were the most important things in their lives, and they wanted to do all they could to let us know how much they loved us, because they knew what it was like to lose a child."

Cassie was silent for a few minutes. When she spoke again, Alex could hear the smile in her voice. "I remember when Jet came home. Mom and Dad were so happy. It felt like we were all together again, like something we hadn't known was missing had come back together."

"Like a puzzle piece," Alex said, remembering.

Cassie nodded. She sat back and looked at him. "Do you remember Mom and Dad smiling for days on end, and they would hug each other all the time for no reason?"

Alex smiled down at her. "I remember. It was like they were all the sudden young again. They wanted to play with us all the time, and whenever Jet was there, it felt like we had a whole pack."

"We did," Cassie said. "It was wonderful. There was so much love." Her smile faltered.

Alex shook his head. "Don't let it go, Cass. Don't forget." At her creased brow, he explained, "As long as you hold it in your heart, the love is always there. It never goes away. No matter what you do, Mom, Dad, and Jet will always love you. Never let it go, because as long as you keep it with you, they will always be with us."

"Do you still feel it?" Cassie asked, her eyes bright as she looked up at him.

Alex nodded. "I do." He swallowed, pushing down the emotions that filled his chest. "I always do," he said.

"Me, too," she said, giving him another smile as she wiped the tear tracks from her cheeks. "I promise I won't forget."

"Me, either," Alex replied. His heart gave a strong stutter and he leaned his head against the bedframe. "Mom never told us that we have an aunt," he said quietly.

"She's our aunt?" there was a hint of light in Cassie's respond.

Alex gave a tired nod. "She's mom's twin. That's how come she looks just like her." He heard the sadness in the sigh Cassie let out; he completely understood. He blew out a breath. "I'm sorry, Cass."

She nodded. "I knew it was too good to be true. I just hoped. . . ." She let the words die away.

"I know," Alex replied softly. "A part of me hoped, too, even though I knew it couldn't be true."

"Is she going to be okay?" Cassie asked softly.

Alex nodded. "Jaze said she'll be fine. She's been through a lot, but they're taking care of her. I'm going to go over there in the morning."

"But Jaze said—"

"I know," Alex replied, cutting her off. "I won't let her see me. I just want to be sure."

"You want to make sure she's safe," Cassie finished; an appreciative smile crossed her face.

"Yes," Alex answered. "But I don't want you coming with me. I worry too much when you're outside of the walls."

Cassie smiled. "You're sweet, Alex."

Alex shook his head. "Don't let anyone hear you say that," he told her in a mockingly stern voice.

She laughed and Alex was happy to hear it. "Okay, I won't," she said.

Chapter Nineteen

Alex waited until everyone had left to combat training before he slipped out the backdoor. He phased behind a tree and left his clothes where he could get to them when he returned. He glanced back once at the Academy before turning away to lope through the trees.

The forest was much bigger than he had anticipated. He had never tried to cross it completely. It wasn't until close to noon that he climbed a rise and saw a small cabin nestled below in a secluded valley surrounded by trees. Alex trotted down the slope. He slowed when he drew closer to the cabin. Wolves paced around the perimeter. Alex drew up far enough away and downwind so his scent wouldn't be carried to them. He sat and waited.

Alex wasn't quite sure what he was hoping for. He wished there was some sign that his aunt was alright, some way to tell that she was safe within the walls. He knew Jaze wouldn't place her anywhere she would be vulnerable to attack. The fact that another safe house existed made Alex happy. He figured at least some of the wolves outside the small cabin were in Jaze's rehabilitation program; he doubted so many would be required for security.

Alex's heart slowed when the backdoor opened and his aunt stepped out. He realized at that moment that he didn't know her name. She shielded her face from the sun as if it had been a long while since she had beheld such brightness. Alex found himself smiling, but the smile fell as he wondered why. He didn't know her. She wasn't his mother. Yet the fact that he watched his mother's twin sister in freedom after all they had all been through filled him with relief. He would have wanted the same for Cassie if something had happened to him.

Someone walked out the door after her. True warmth spread through Alex's heart at the sight of Gem, Dray's wife. Her pixie cut bright pink hair practically glowed in the noonday sun. She skipped out behind his aunt, her happiness palpable even at that distance.

Alex had never met anyone like Gem before he and his sister made it to the Academy. She had personally assigned to herself the goal of cheering up all of the orphans from the attempted werewolf genocide. At first, it was a trying process, but nobody could resist Gem's charms and smile. Eventually, she got all of the students to warm up to her. She usually taught math at the Academy, but this year she had been noticeably absent. A new assignment to the safe house to help with rehabilitation fit the cheerful werewolf like a glove.

Satisfied that his aunt was alright, Alex made his way back to the Academy. He had missed all of his morning classes, and probably lunch. When he reached the Academy and phased back to human form, he had no desire to mingle with the rest of the students. No matter how good Kaynan and Grace were at teaching, he just couldn't bring himself to sit through English. The sun shining on his shoulders was too great of a temptation to turn down.

Alex pulled on his clothes and walked to the front of the Academy. Jet's statue stood tall, the silver seven on its shoulder blazing in the sun as though it had been written there by lightning. Alex had wondered a thousand times what the seven meant, and why his brother had it. If it was silver, it would have never stopped hurting. He wondered if his brother had chosen the mark or if it had been given to him.

Alex sprawled out on the sun-warmed grass beside the statue. He closed his eyes, willing his body to soak up the warmth. He kept a hand on the huge stone that made up the base of the statue. His weary mind drifted away, lost in the feeling of the rough rock beneath his fingertips and the grass that brushed against the back of his neck.

STRAYS

***

"Do you like ice cream?" Alex saw his younger self ask Jet.

The older werewolf glanced down at him, his expression solemn. There was so much depth to the black-haired werewolf's deep blue eyes. Sometimes it looked as if he had seen the end of the world; other times, Alex could have sworn there was a shield over Jet's eyes, holding everything in so that the only emotion seen was the distance the Alpha kept between himself and everyone around him.

This shield vanished at the question. "I love ice cream," Jet replied. "I could eat it all day."

"Me, too," Alex replied.

It was one of the few memories Alex had of he and Jet alone together. The older werewolf visited as often as he could, but Alex knew he was busy saving other werewolves from whatever he had gone through. At that time, Alex knew Jet had experienced horrible things, but nobody told him exactly what. His young mind had been left to wonder, and then shudder away from those wonderings.

That day, Jet had stopped by for a surprise visit. The twins were supposed to be cleaning their room, but Alex had seen Jet wandering down the street as though wondering what to do with himself. Alex had seen the same searching, somewhat lost expression a few times on his brother's face. He figured it was his job to chase it away.

He had slipped out the back door and ran to catch up to Jet. He could never sneak up on the werewolf. Jet always knew he was coming no matter how quiet he was.

"Where you going?" he had asked.

Jet's hands clenched and unclenched. He glanced at Alex, then back down the road. It was a few minutes before he had answered with, "I'm not sure. The walls got too small."

Alex nodded. "I know what you mean. They're even smaller in our room, but probably because it's so messy in there. I'm supposed to be cleaning."

He was grateful his brother didn't send him back inside to finish the chore. Instead, they walked together in silence. That was when Alex had the idea about the ice cream. The gas station a few blocks away had the best ice cream around. It was one of their favorite family walking destinations on bright, sunny days like that one. He led Jet there and pulled out the few dollars he had saved up from his allowance. Alex had been saving the money to buy a yo-yo, but the chance to have ice cream with his big brother was a rare one. Toys could wait.

"What kind would you like?" the woman behind the counter had asked.

Jet looked at the many flavors with a concerned expression. His gaze kept darting from one to the next. At the woman's rapidly growing annoyance, Jet glanced out the door. Alex could tell he was losing his brother.

"Two scoops for both of us with mint chocolate chip," Alex said, setting his dollars and coins on the counter.

The woman gave the coins a disapproving look.

"It's three dollars and twenty-two cents, along with two dollar bills," Alex explained. "Sorry for the pennies. Mom said she would pay us a penny a weed that we pulled. My sister and I pulled a lot of weeds."

"Very well," the woman answered. She glanced at Jet again. Alex could tell his silence disturbed her. She shook her head and began counting the pennies one at a time.

"Mint chocolate chip is my favorite," Alex told Jet. He could tell the walls were feeling small for the werewolf again. It showed in the way his dark gaze kept seeking the sunlight beyond the glass door, and in his hands that opened and closed the way they always did when he was anxious about something. Alex hoped the woman would hurry.

"Do you want to meet me outside?" Alex asked quietly.

Jet looked down at him. This time, when their eyes met, Alex could tell Jet really saw him. A hint of a smile showed on his face and he crouched down so that they were eye level.

"I'm sorry I'm not the best company," Jet said. It was a lot of words coming from the quiet werewolf. "I've got a lot to learn about being a friend, or," he hesitated, then said, "A brother." The word made his smile deepen and touch his eyes. "But don't give up on me, Alex."

"I won't," Alex promised.

Alex accepted the ice cream the woman held out. To his surprise, she also gave him his money back. She glanced at Jet who hovered by the door. "Was he in the army?" she asked softly.

Alex realized she had overheard their conversation. He nodded, because he didn't know what else to say. She reached over and ruffled his hair. "Hang in there. He'll get better," she promised with a kind smile.

Alex thanked her and hurried to give Jet his ice cream. Jet pushed open the door as though he couldn't get out of the shop fast enough.

They walked a few more blocks, then sat in the shade of a giant oak tree to eat their ice cream. Jet ran his free hand over the grass. A look of relief crossed his face.

"What is it about grass that's so wonderful?" he asked.

Alex looked at him, wondering if it was a real question, or if the werewolf was just speaking his thoughts aloud. Jet was usually so quiet; speaking out loud without a purpose was unheard-of for him. Alex took the question seriously.

"The smell," he finally answered after pondering the

question for a while.

Jet leaned down and gave the grass a good sniff. He sat back with an appreciative look. "You're right. It's the smell."

Alex nodded, glad his brother approved of his assessment. "Sunlight, rain, spring, and life all rolled into a tiny little green blade."

"Hope," Jet said quietly. At Alex's look, his brother gave a real smile. "Hope lives in the smell. With grass beneath your hands, it's impossible not to feel hope." His face grew solemn. "I lived many years without hope. I know the feeling of it when it's there. Be wherever you feel hope."

Alex and Jet finished their ice cream cones in silence, but it was tempered with camaraderie, the scent of grass, and hope.

Alex woke up and smiled at the statue above him. Jet was right. After all that had happened, and all they had lost, he still felt hope whenever he laid on the grass.

Chapter Twenty

"Are you going to see her?" Cassie asked.

Alex nodded. "If I go now, no one will miss me." He had taken to visiting the safe house in the evenings before night games. It gave him fewer reasons to make up for skipping class, and he enjoyed his time in the woods. "She seems stronger. She was walking around the garden helping Gem pull weeds. You sure you don't want to go?"

Cassie shook her head. "I'm okay." She hesitated. "Did Jaze say when she'll be leaving the safe house?"

"I didn't ask," Alex replied. For some reason, the thought of his aunt leaving made his heart ache. He still hadn't talked to her, but watching her get stronger and seeing her smile with Gem made him feel almost like he had something of his mother back. He didn't want to lose that again.

He hadn't mentioned to Jaze that he went to see her. He was worried the dean would forbid it because he traveled so far, but he had to keep going.

"Be careful, okay?" Cassie said.

Alex nodded. "I will. Stay within the walls while I'm gone." It was the same thing he made her promise every night. He still worried about Drogan, though things seemed to have quieted down. Even Brock didn't have any news.

"I will," Cassie replied.

He heard his sister's soft sigh as he left Jericho Pack's quarters and shut the door behind him. He often asked Cassie if she wanted to go, but there was something that kept her back. He knew deep down that she feared seeing their aunt would make losing their mother feel that much more real. It was hard to see such a familiar face, yet know it belonged to a stranger. But Alex had to keep going. He wanted to reassure himself that she was alright.

"Are you leaving again?" Pip asked. He glanced up the stairs nervously. Alex wondered if Boris or Torin had been picking on the Second Year again. He made a mental note to mention it to Jericho.

"Yes, but I'll be back in time for games."

Pip glanced at his watch. "You sure? You're leaving a bit later than usual."

Vance had forced the werewolves to run extra laps in PE because Boris had gotten angry when Parker, his Second, couldn't throw the baseball fast enough and Pack Jericho scored. Boris had broken the bat in half, then threw it at Parker. Alex still wasn't sure why Pack Jericho had to suffer, but nobody argued with Vance. The extra laps had cost him some time.

"I might miss the beginning, but I'll be there," Alex promised.

He jogged down the back steps and crossed the dark lawn to the gate.

"Off on another of your mysterious runs?"

Alex turned at Kalia's voice. She was leaning against the fence eating an apple.

"I like the forest at night," Alex replied. "It's full of animals and sounds that aren't there during the day. You should try it sometime."

Kalia shook her head, her white-blond hair swishing across her shoulders. "My ears aren't as good as yours. I'd be afraid of getting eaten by something out there."

Alex opened the gate and smiled at her. "Wolves, a few mountain lions, and the occasional bear are the only things I've seen. I think you'd be alright."

She closed the gate behind him. "I'll stay here," she replied. She looked meaningfully at the bars. "Although this is a bit prisonish."

Alex shrugged. "Only if it's locked."

She smiled at that.

Alex hurried behind a tree and phased. He was already late. If he pushed it, he would be able to stay ten minutes before he turned around to catch the end of night games. The training was his idea. It would be bad form to miss it. He fell into the mile-eating lope of the wolf, and lost his thoughts in the shadows that toyed across his path.

She was always outside when he arrived. He didn't know if she had a penchant for the outdoors, or also felt like Jet had said that the walls were getting too small. Whatever it was, she was sitting on a small bench looking up at the stars. Alex smiled down at her from the shelter of the trees. Half of him thought of his mother, moonlight bathing her face as she searched for the secrets of the universe; the other half was just grateful to see the expression of peace on his aunt's face. She was finding herself again.

Alex stayed longer than he planned. By the time he headed back, he knew he would be lucky to catch the tail end of training. He ducked under branches and leaped windfalls as he pushed himself faster and faster toward the Academy. The smells and sights of the school were drawing closer when a sound caught his attention.

The steady thwap-thwap of a helicopter was rapidly approaching. Alex's heart began to thunder. A spotlight shone down through the trees. Alex darted to the left. The helicopter stayed with him. He ducked beneath a bole, then down a wash. He followed the riverbed in the hopes that the distance and the trees would thwart them.

Alex knew he was close to the Academy. He was about to dart back up the bank when something struck the dirt beneath his paws. The earth exploded in front of him, sending him backwards against the other side of the wash. He scrambled to his feet and blinked through the dusty haze. His nose was filled with dirt. He tried to peer through the dust to see. The air began to clear. Alex's stomach clenched. He was surrounded.

Men with guns stood on both sides of the wash. A single gunman stepped forward. He took off his black mask. The pit in Alex's stomach turned into a boulder at the mismatched eyes of Drogan Carso.

"Thought we'd given up?" Drogan asked.

In answer, Alex lifted his muzzled and let out a howl. It was a low note in a very specific key.

"Is that how you beg for mercy?" Drogan pressed. He leaned forward. "You know I don't speak wolf."

Howls suddenly rose into the air around them. One hundred and fifty wolf howls told the men that they were more than surrounded; they were history. The howls drew closer. The men began to press together.

"What is this?" Drogan demanded, his eyes wide.

Alex watched carefully. Drogan's gaze shifted for the briefest second to the dark woods around them. Alex leaped.

He grabbed Drogan's gun hand in his teeth and ground down, forcing the man to drop his gun. Drogan let out a yell of pain. Alex gave a jerk of his head that dropped Drogan to his knees. Alex carefully kept Drogan between himself and the men with guns who looked fearfully between their leader and the wolves that began to appear through the darkness.

"Don't shoot!" Drogan cried as blood streamed down his hand.

Alex spotted Jericho at the head of the giant wolf pack. Alex jerked his head to the side, making Drogan cry out again. Jericho dipped his head in answer and began to run clockwise. He leaped the wash, ran down the other bank, and leaped it again. The wolves fell in behind him, circling the attackers.

"What is going on?" one of the men demanded.

"They're demons," another said.

Alex could smell the scent of urine as a man wet his pants out of fear. "Why are there so many of them?"

Ropes dropped from the helicopter that hovered above. The men clipped onto them, looking more than eager to get out of the forest.

Alex couldn't stop thinking about the fear in Cassie's eyes when Drogan had pointed a gun at her in the grove. He wanted to release his hold on Drogan's hand and leap for his throat. He could end Drogan's life the way the wolves had brought down the buck. It would be fast, and the threat Drogan brought with him would be gone forever.

Alex ached to avenge his parents. He wanted more than anything to have them back and wake up to find that it had all been a terrible nightmare. Yet he knew that the man who had made it all a reality stood at his mercy. He loosened his grip on Drogan's hand, preparing to bite his throat.

A bullet struck the ground, followed by several more. Memories of the pain from the last bullet flooded through Alex. He let Drogan go and backed up to the shelter of the trees. Drogan scrambled to the rope and fumbled with his ruined hand as he tried to hook the clip. As soon as it was done, he waved frantically to the men above. He was pulled quickly up.

Alex's eyes stayed on the man as the helicopter flew past the trees. The taste of Drogan's blood lingered in his mouth. He had let his enemy go. Regret slammed into him like a fist. He took a step in the direction Drogan had gone.

Jericho appeared in front of him. The great black wolf barred his path. Alex gave a half-whine and tried to go around the Alpha. Jericho surprised him by growling. Alex couldn't ignore the command in the Alpha's voice. He dropped his head. When Jericho turned, he followed the black wolf back to the Academy. The rest of their pack fell in around them. Alex felt Cassie's presence to his left. He glanced at her. His sister's dark blue eyes were filled with worry.

They reached the Academy just as the professors were rushing across the lawn.

"What was that?" Vance demanded.

"We heard the helicopter and the howl," Dray said.

Relief filled Jaze's expression when he spotted Alex and Cassie.

He gave Alex a concerned look. "Go phase. Meet me in my office."

Alex nodded and padded through the door Nikki held open. The worry on her face matched the same look in Cassie's eyes. Alex ran up the stairs without seeing them. A hundred paws followed close behind. Alex phased in his room and pulled on some random clothes. He was about to head back downstairs when Cassie grabbed his arm.

"Are you okay?" she demanded.

Alex's attention jerked back to his sister at her tone.

"Did they hurt you?" she asked.

He shook his head. "N-no. I'm fine. Trust me."

"Trust you?" she repeated. "You almost got killed out there."

The reality of what had just happened started to hit Alex hard. He put a hand to his chest as his heart rebelled.

"Easy," Jericho said from behind him. He grabbed Alex's arm and led him to the couch. "Breathe."

"I heard the helicopter, then they were there. I couldn't get away," Alex told them, his voice tight as he thought back. "How did you know to come?"

"You called us," Jericho replied, watching Alex closely. "We were running training exercises. I think half the wolves thought it was part of the exercise."

Several pack members around them nodded.

"I know I did," Trent said. "I thought you were just running a simulation like they do during fire drills."

"No," Alex replied, shaking his head. "But that would be a good idea."

"You need to go see the dean," Jericho reminded him. "Leave the night games training planning to us."

Alex gave him a humorless smile. "Glad to see it's working."

Jericho nodded and held out a hand. "Yeah, but the point is hopefully not to use it."

Alex accepted the hand and let Jericho pull him up. He walked to the door.

"You sure you're okay?" the Alpha asked when they were out of earshot from the others.

Alex nodded. "I'm still in one piece, thanks to you guys."

"I'm coming with you," Cassie insisted, hurrying to the door.

Alex knew better than to argue. Besides, if his heart decided to act up again, he didn't want Jaze to find him sprawled at the bottom of the stairs. He nodded and Cassie followed him into the hallway. He shut the door, then leaned against it.

"We don't want to keep Jaze waiting," Cassie reminded him gently. "He needs to know what happened so we can figure out what to do."

Alex nodded numbly and followed her down the stairs. His twin sister kept looking over her shoulder to make sure he was alright. Her concern worried him and made him feel a bit better at the same time.

Chapter Twenty-one

Cassie and Alex paused at the door to Jaze's office. Nikki, Vance, and Dray were also there. The office was huge, but sparsely furnished besides the hundreds of books that lined the walls, a single desk, and cushioned chairs. Its simplicity belied the fact that a room filled with surveillance equipment, monitors, and information on every werewolf in existence was just beneath the floor.

"What was that?" Vance was arguing. "Did you see the students? They were organized, like an army."

"I'm sure it was just a coincidence," Jaze replied, though his tone said otherwise.

"We should have known," Vance continued.

Jaze held up a hand as soon as he saw the twins. "Come in," he welcomed.

Cassie and Alex crossed the wooden floor to the two empty chairs near the big desk. Nikki and Dray sat on chairs close to the big curtained window, while Vance paced in front of the fireplace.

Jaze sat down across the desk from the twins. He met Alex's gaze. "Tell me exactly what happened."

Alex hesitated. Telling meant letting the dean know that he had been checking on his aunt every day. He wondered if Jaze would forbid the runs.

"Everything," Jaze said in a tone that let Alex know he guessed more than Alex thought.

"I was visiting my aunt," Alex admitted.

"You've been seeing Meredith?" Nikki asked, amazed.

Hearing her name sent a rush of warmth through Alex. It fit her just as Mindi had fit his mother. "I've been watching her, making sure she's recovering okay," Alex admitted.

"Has she seen you?" Jaze asked curiously.

Alex shook his head. "I've been careful. I wanted to meet her, but not without your permission."

"I appreciate that," Jaze replied. The light of curiosity lingered in his gaze, but he pressed on. "Then what happened?"

"I was on my way home in wolf form as usual, when I heard the helicopter. I was almost to the Academy. I tried to run down a wash to lose them, but they shot some sort of a grenade into the dirt and it blew me back. I was surrounded before I had my wits back together." A shudder ran down Alex's spine as he remembered. "Drogan was there."

Cassie grabbed his hand. He gave her what he hoped was a reassuring smile.

"I howled for the wolves. When he tried to shoot me, I bit his gun hand."

"Well done," Dray said quietly.

Alex remembered the sound of the wolves howling, the way it echoed through the forest, cutting through even the beat of the helicopter's blades above.

"If it wasn't for the werewolves, I would have been shot," he admitted.

"Yeah," Vance cut in, his tone brusque. "What was that? They were organized."

Alex nodded. At Jaze's raised eyebrows, he explained, "We've been training. We used our night games time to run simulations and battle sequences."

Surprise filled Vance's face as though he had suspected something of the sort, but not quite what Alex was saying. "You mean you turned the students into your own private army?"

Alex shook his head quickly at the Alpha's tone. "No. Not like that. We just wanted to be able to protect ourselves. After the last attack on Cassie and me, we knew we needed to be more prepared."

"Night games as a training tool. It's brilliant," Dray said, giving Alex an approving smile.

"We should know that our students are training to be some sort of militia," Vance argued. "It's too dangerous."

"We don't have weapons," Alex told him. "We practice formations and run drills for particular scenarios. It's really just like hunting with Rafe's wolves. Everyone knows where they belong and what their job is. The packs are better that way."

There was a light of respect in Jaze's gaze when he nodded. "I have to agree. I've never seen the packs so united. There are still squabbles between the packs, but they are definitely tighter within. I figured we could attribute that to the new academic schedule."

Nikki smiled. "We could only hope."

Jaze leaned forward and put his elbows on the desk. "Someone must have tipped off Drogan. Who knows that you take these trips through the woods?"

"My pack knows, and several other students have noticed. I just tell them that I like to go for runs. There really haven't been any questions." Alex thought of leaving to go on his run. His blood ran cold. "Kalia knew I was going."

"Kalia Dickson?" Vance asked.

Alex nodded. "She was at the gate when I left. She was the last person I talked to before my run."

Darkness filled the huge werewolf's gaze. "If the Dicksons are working with Drogan, we need to get Boris and Kalia out of here immediately."

Jaze held up a hand. "We don't know for sure. Let's not be hasty." He turned back to Alex. "Was Kalia anywhere near when you and Cassie were attacked the first time?"

Alex thought about it. "She and I spoke at Jet's statue

while everyone was playing werewolf tag. She probably saw the packs take off into the forest to search for the Alphas." He felt sick. The girl he had trusted could possibly have been the one to betray him to his worst enemy. Could her icy blue eyes hide true animosity against him and his sister? Perhaps her efforts to talk had only been to get close enough for him to trust her. The fact that Boris was her brother definitely should have warned him.

Cassie gave Alex a searching look, worry in her wide eyes.

"We don't know anything," Jaze said softly, his gaze on both Alex and Cassie. "The last thing we need to do is jump to conclusions. No one has been found guilty yet, but we will investigate."

Nikki nodded. "Give everyone the benefit of the doubt until we find out who is behind the attacks, but perhaps we need to ensure that you two stay within the walls."

Alex's heart constricted.

"It's alright," Jaze said, interpreting his look. "Meredith will be safe. In fact, she's going to fill a position here next year."

"As a professor?" Alex asked, surprised.

Nikki nodded. "We told her about the Academy, and she's excited to help. I think the thought of something useful to do has assisted in her recovery."

Relief flooded Alex's thoughts. Perhaps he wouldn't lose his one connection to his mother after all.

"You two should go get some rest. I'm sure your pack's anxious to ensure you're okay," Jaze said.

Alex and Cassie rose.

"We're glad you're safe," Nikki said.

"Thank you," Alex told her. He put an arm around his sister's shoulders and walked with her out the door. As soon as they were alone in the hallway, Cassie buried her head against his shoulder.

"I was so afraid," she said. "I knew it was your howl, and that you wouldn't have done it if everything was alright. When I saw the helicopter, and those men. . . ." her voice choked off.

"I'm okay," Alex reassured her as she sobbed against his chest. "They didn't hurt me."

"They could have taken you away like Mom and Dad. Alex, I might never have seen you again." She looked up at him, her dark blue eyes filled with tears. "I would have been all alone."

He gave her a weak smile. "I will never leave you alone, Cass. I promise."

"They tried," she said.

He nodded. "And they failed, again. They're not going to get me, Cass. We have the students, and you heard what Jaze and Nikki said. They're searching for Drogan. They'll make sure we're safe."

She watched him, checking to see if he believed his own words. He gave her a true smile. "Everything is fine, Cass. Believe me."

Cassie drew in a shuddering breath and nodded. She wiped away her tears and followed him up the stairs. The rooms they passed were silent at the late hour. Alex was surprised when he pushed open the door to Pack Jericho's quarters to find their Alpha waiting for them on the couch.

"Everything alright?" he asked, rising on their entrance.

Alex nodded. "As good as can be expected." He gave Cassie a final hug. "Get some sleep, sis. I'll see you in the morning."

She nodded as a yawn escaped her. Alex watched his sister walk wearily to the girl's rooms and disappear down the hall.

He met Jericho's gaze again. "Will you keep an eye on her?"

Jericho didn't look at all surprised at the seriousness Alex's tone had taken now that his sister was out of earshot. "That bad, huh?"

Alex shook his head. "Things are fine, but I'm tired of getting shot at." Rage flooded through him, powerful and angry at all the things he hadn't been able to prevent. "I need this to stop. I can't keep Cassie safe if they can appear out of nowhere with a dozen guns ready to shoot us down. We need to find out who the snitch is, and I need to end this before it gets worse."

Jericho nodded. "Let me know what I can do."

"Just make sure she's safe," Alex repeated.

Jericho's brown eyes glittered. "Nothing will get in here. Trust me."

"I do," Alex replied. "Thank you."

He hurried back down the stairs. The door to the closet closed just as he reached the stairs. He hurried inside and knocked on the inner door. The footsteps on the stairs paused.

"Who is it?" he heard Jaze ask.

"It's Alex," Brock replied when Alex looked up at the camera.

Jaze's footsteps returned and the door opened.

"I figured we weren't done talking," the dean said, stepping back to let Alex pass.

None of the werewolves below looked surprised when they entered the room together. Alex walked straight to Brock. The human put down the candy bar he had been munching on and braced for whatever Alex was going to say.

"Did you know Drogan was in Haroldsburg?" Alex demanded.

Brock shook his head quickly.

"Whoa, now," Chet cut him off. "Take it easy, Alex."

"They dropped out of a chopper," Alex replied, trying to control his anger. "They had me surrounded in seconds, and I'm supposed to take it easy? If Cassie had been there, she might have been killed."

"It sounds like you were the one almost killed," Vance pointed out.

Alex clenched and unclenched his hands as he fought back the urge to hit something. A hand touched his shoulder. He spun, knocking it away as he crouched in a defensive position, ready to defend himself.

Jaze held up his hands. "Easy, Alex," he said quiet. "We aren't your enemies."

Alex's heart thundered in his chest. It skipped a beat, making his breath catch. He leaned against the wall, burying his face in his hands. "I can't do this," he said. "I can't sit here and wait for Drogan to take us out. It's like I'm sitting on a time bomb, not knowing when it's going to explode."

Jaze put a hand on his shoulder. "Alex, you need to calm down."

Alex shook his head. "I can't. I'm tired of living on edge."

"Believe me," Jaze said softly. "All of us have been there. We know what you're going through."

Alex looked up at the dean. The werewolves around the table behind him nodded. Kaynan's red gaze was stark as if he remembered it all too well. There was steel in Dray's expression as though he knew just what it took from Alex to be attacked and helpless.

"Use me as bait," Alex said. Determination filled his voice as the idea fleshed out in his mind. "We'll flush Drogan into the open, then you can take him out."

"That's too dangerous," Jaze said, shaking his head. "We

won't let you put your life on the line like that."

"It's already on the line," Alex pointed out. "It's driving me crazy to know that Cassie is a target and I may not be able to protect her. At least this way we'll have some control."

At Jaze's silence, Vance spoke up. "He has a point," the huge werewolf said. He looked at Alex. "But using you as a target?" He shook his head. "We can't guarantee your safety. It's a no."

Everyone looked surprised by the werewolf's concern.

"You don't have a choice," Alex argued. "I'm not losing Cassie the way I lost everyone else." His throat tightened. "And I won't risk leaving her here alone, either." He met their gazes, his own determined. "I'm telling Kalia we're going to Haroldsburg and she can spread the news to Drogan so he can come after Cassie and me, only Cassie will stay here where she's safe."

Jaze held up a hand. "Don't be hasty. The only way to get to Drogan is to make sure we have our bases covered. Jumping in without a plan is only going to get you killed."

"Will you help me?" Alex asked. He hated how small his voice sounded in the huge underground room. He wanted to sound confident, sure of himself, but the thought of being a target for Drogan yet again stole some of his bravado.

To his relief, Jaze nodded. "Yes, since you're so determined to do this with or without us. I'd rather us be there than leave you to make your own plans." He speared Alex with a look. "But we will do this during the Christmas break when most of the students are gone. That way, we'll be better able to protect Cassie and everyone else."

"That's a good idea," Alex agreed. "But Kalia will be leaving to go home with Boris."

Jaze's expression was serious when he said, "We don't know for certain that Kalia is the informant. She's had a rough time here already, and if she isn't Drogan's contact, she doesn't need another reason to want to leave. Tread lightly around her and anyone else you suspect, but don't accuse someone if you don't have proof."

Alex dropped his gaze under Jaze's stern stare. He nodded. "Okay." But in his mind, he saw all of the times he and Kalia had talked in a different light. Perhaps she wasn't really a werewolf. Maybe Drogan had gotten her into the Academy as an informant, which is why she couldn't phase. The brief glimpse he had seen of her eyes changing to gold when she looked at the full moon nagged at the back of his mind, but he pushed it away.

"For now, stay within the Academy walls where we can protect you," Jaze said. He gave a small smile. "Private werewolf army or not, I'd rather know that you're safe."

An answering smile reached Alex's face at the dean's tone. He nodded. "I'll be careful."

Chapter Twenty-two

The weeks before Christmas couldn't go by soon enough. Alex felt more on edge. He couldn't get past the idea that someone was watching him, that someone was a spy. The fear that Drogan would attack the school to get to Cassie was never far away. It was hard to participate in the day-to-day classes when his mind kept wandering to the forest and the sound of the helicopter that haunted his thoughts and dreams. He could still hear the percussion of the grenade and feel himself flying backward. Alex pretended for Cassie's sake, but he found it harder and harder to act as though everything was fine.

As Jericho Pack made their way down the stairs to combat training, Alex paused at the sight of snow falling past the windows that lined the hallway to the training room. The sight sent a shiver of anticipation through his body. Wilderness education was the one exception to Jaze's rule to stay within the Academy walls. At least when he was in the forest with Rafe's pack, he could put everything behind him.

"It's going to be cold in wilderness education," Trent noted on his way past.

"You'll be wearing a fur coat," Terith replied.

Everyone groaned.

"What?" Terith demanded. "He set it up perfectly."

"You still shouldn't have said it," Pip replied.

Terith tried to hit him, and the young werewolf ran down the hall with the Lifer close behind.

Alex itched to go outside. Wilderness education couldn't come soon enough. He needed to run or hit something.

"Who volunteers to fight Boris?" Chet asked as Alex followed Cassie into the training room.

It was a joke, the same joke Chet had said every day since

combat training began. No one was stupid enough to go up against the Termer Alpha, and only another Alpha matched him for strength, so there really was no question.

But this time, Alex raised his hand. "I volunteer."

Cassie elbowed him in the ribs. "What are you doing?"

Alex shrugged. "Volunteering," he said simply.

"Alex, Chet was kidding," Dray pointed out. "Jericho will fight Boris."

"Steven got dish duty for throwing plates at a bird that got in the Great Hall," Pip told the professor. "The bird got away, but Professor Nikki said he has to work off the damage by cleaning dishes for the next two weeks. Jericho volunteered to help him get it done faster."

Boris rolled his eyes. "He's an idiot."

Chet looked at Dray. The werewolf quickly shook his head. "No way."

Chet shrugged. "It might be interesting."

"Alex could be killed," Dray replied.

Chet looked at Alex. "You willing to risk that?"

Alex rolled his shoulders. He might have been a Gray, and it was entirely against his instincts to fight the Alpha, but the frustration centering on Drogan had built to the point that he needed an outlet somewhere. "Sure."

"Alex, no," Cassie protested.

Alex ducked under the ropes of the fighting ring. Even Boris looked surprised at the Gray's actions.

Alex stepped from foot to foot, warming up. "Come on," he said to Boris. "Afraid?"

A growl escaped the big Termer. He climbed under the ropes and glared at Alex. "I'm not afraid of anyone."

"I don't know," Alex replied. "You look a little scared."

A vein bulged out of the side of Boris' neck and his face turned red with anger.

"You should probably get that looked at," Alex continued. "You don't want to explode or something."

"Why you little—"

"Gear," Chet reminded them. He tossed up a pair of gloves and a sparring helmet. The gear hit Boris square in the face and fell to the floor as he fumbled to catch it.

Alex caught his and pulled it on smoothly. He avoided looking at the students who watched them. The room was filled with complete silence. He knew he was being stupid, and he didn't need to read it on their faces. All he knew was he wanted to hit something, and Boris had volunteered to become a punching bag.

Time slowed down. Alex heard every strong beat of his heart. A soft brush of a bare foot on the plastic mat surface warned him that Boris was going to be as dirty at fighting as he usually was with Jericho. Alex pretended not to notice the advancing Alpha. He flexed his right hand, then pretended to have all of his attention on adjusting the straps a bit tighter.

One more footstep. The students in front of him tensed. He could tell someone wanted to cry out a warning, but in werewolf fights, it was strictly between the two on the mat. Any interference would be viewed as a weakness and a lack of discipline by both the fighter and the pack.

The step slid again. Alex dropped to his knee, spun, and connected with Boris' right leg as the Alpha attempted to punch him in the head and end the fight before it even started.

Caught off balance by the punch that met only air and the kick to the leg, Boris stumbled sideways. Alex jumped up and slammed a fist into the Alpha's jaw.

Gasps flew through the packs. Pain surged up Alex's hand despite the protective gloves. He watched in horror as Boris rubbed his jaw, then met Alex's gaze. The fury in the

Alpha's stare was enough to send ice through Alex's veins. Not only had he hit an Alpha, he had made the Alpha look bad to his pack. Alex knew he was going to die.

Boris' steps sounded like thunder as he advanced on Alex. Alex scrambled back to the ropes. He spun to the right when Boris threw a fist. Boris landed the second on the back of Alex's shoulder. The Gray flew against the ropes. He managed to protect his face with his forearms for the next two hits, but forgot to breathe out when the third slammed into his stomach. Alex fell to the ground gasping for air.

Boris grabbed the back of his shirt and hefted him to his feet. Alex gathered all of his strength. The Alpha clenched his fist; when he drove the punch forward, it was with the intention of slamming it into Alex's jaw and ending the fight once and for all.

Alex wasn't ready to be beaten. He ducked at the last second, catching only a glancing blow on his eyebrow. He felt the punch split his skin. Warm blood began to drip down his face. Alex righted himself on the ropes, took a steeling breath, and began to jump from foot to foot again.

Boris' eyes widened. "Seriously, dude?" he asked.

"Bring it," Alex replied.

For the first time in weeks, no thoughts of Drogan Carso occupied his mind. He felt alive, free. He still felt free when the strength of the Alpha slammed him against the ropes again. He felt perhaps a little less alive at a foot to the ribs, and argued to himself that perhaps the thoughts weren't so bad when another fist connected with the back of his head.

He lay on the mat trying to fight the dark spots that clouded his vision. His heart skipped a few beats, reminding him that he was pushing it.

"That's enough," Dray called from outside of the ropes.

Boris was grinning at his pack as though he had defeated

an entire army.

The look sent a surge of rage through Alex. A growl of pent-up anger tore from his lips as he leaped at the Alpha, bowling him into the ropes. He slammed a fist into Boris' kidney, wrapped his arms around the Alpha's right shoulder, and twisted as he picked up his feet, slamming the Alpha to his back on the ground. He landed two punches to Boris' face before the Alpha threw him off.

Alex waited near the ropes, his heart thundering in his throat and blood dripping into his eye.

Boris clambered ungracefully to his feet. He studied the Gray. Purple hinted around one eye and there was a small split in his lip. Boris touched the cut, then looked at the blood. To Alex's surprise, a hint of a smile crossed the Alpha's face.

"Not bad, Stray."

Alex smiled back. "Someone had to try."

"I'm not so sure about that," Boris replied. "But you did good."

He crossed to Alex and held out a hand. Alex warily accepted the handshake.

"You got guts," Boris said.

Pack Jericho cheered, and soon Pack Boris joined in. Alex pulled off his headgear and gloves, handing them to Chet as he stepped out of the fighting ring. "You might need to wash those," Alex said.

His pack surged forward. Reaching hands patted his back and tousled his hair. He pushed through to the back where the drinking fountain was. He took a big drink, then sank down against the wall next to it.

"Here."

Alex looked up to see Kalia holding paper towels.

"For your head," she explained.

There was a hint of something in her light blue gaze. Was it worry that Alex had figured out she was the informant? Since his talk with Jaze, he hadn't been able to help avoiding her. Alex couldn't forgive her if she had something to do with the danger Cassie was in. When he saw her walking down the hall, he turned the other way. If she was out at Jet's statue, he went somewhere else. It amazed him how many of the places he cherished she had come to occupy.

Kalia crouched down, her eyes meeting his. "Take it, Alex. I'm only trying to help."

"Are you sure about that?" Alex demanded, unable to stop himself.

Kalia looked taken aback. She rose, her expression unreadable. Cassie stepped around her and handed Alex a paper towel that had been dipped in water. He accepted it and held it to his forehead. Kalia shook her head and turned away, tossing the paper towels at his feet.

Chapter Twenty-three

"You told Kalia we were leaving tomorrow for Haroldsburg to do Christmas shopping?" Alex asked Cassie.

"Just like you told me," Cassie replied. "Though she looked surprised that I was talking to her."

Alex felt a pang of guilt, but if he was right, things would be resolved soon enough. He and Cassie stood at the top step of the Academy watching the Termers load into the buses and cars that had come to pick them up for the holiday break. For the first time, he was glad he didn't have anywhere else to go. He had a chance to help Jaze take care of Drogan. Having a family to go home to and a place away from the Academy no longer mattered.

Cassie waved to Pip and Marky. The werewolves waved back before climbing onto the bus.

"I'm going to miss them," Cassie said.

"I know," Alex replied. "But they'll be back soon."

"See you guys. Take care and try not to burn the place down while I'm gone," Jericho said on his way past.

"We're not making any promises," Alex replied.

The wheels of Jericho's suitcase made double lines in the snow as he made his way to his dad's truck. He tossed the suitcase in the back, then climbed inside.

"It's not like there's a reason for me to come back."

Alex turned at the sound of Kalia's voice. She was arguing with Boris as she pulled three sets of suitcases down the stairs.

"You have to come back," Boris replied, his voice level as though he had repeated the same answer many times.

"No, I don't," Kalia spat. "I hate it here, and I'm not a werewolf. You can tell that to Mom and Dad."

"If they even notice I'm there," Boris replied soft enough

that Kalia didn't hear it over her grumbling about her stubborn luggage, but Alex heard it.

He glanced past them to the limousine that waited as close to the exit gate as it could get. A woman in a white furry hat and coat stood near the limo's door along with the driver in his uniform and hat.

"I brought everything," Kalia pointed out. "That way I don't have to come back." When her suitcases hit the last step, the top piece of luggage flew off and hit the stairs. It opened, spilling clothes everywhere.

Kalia dropped to her knees in the snow. She reached for a shirt, and glanced up at Alex. His heart stilled at the sight of tears rolling down her cheeks. Boris grumbled about delays as he gathered items and shoved them roughly back into his sister's suitcase.

"Alex," Cassie whispered.

"I know," Alex replied as soft.

Boris shoved the suitcase with clothes still hanging out of it onto the top of the luggage and motioned for his sister to continue. She did so slowly, her head hanging and her white-blonde hair hiding her expression from view.

Instead of running up to meet them like Alex expected, Boris and Cassie's mother merely motioned for the driver to put their luggage in the trunk, then stepped inside the open limousine door. A puff of white air rose from Boris. His shoulders fell before he ducked inside the door. Kalia followed as though it was the last place she wanted to be.

"Maybe the Academy's not so bad," Cassie said, voicing Alex's thoughts.

He nodded. "You like it here, right?"

Cassie smiled up at him. "Of course. This is our home."

Alex looked at the imposing walls that rose behind them. He felt a little claustrophobic when he repeated, "This is our home."

Cassie mistook his words for agreement and pulled open the door. "Come on," she called. "You know they'll be serving chocolate cake to cheer up all the Lifers who get left behind. It's the best part of Christmas break!"

She ran down the hall and Alex followed at a more sedate pace. He couldn't get the image out of his mind of Kalia's tears. It wasn't her suitcase she was crying about. It was much more. He wished he knew if it was because of their lost friendship, or because she knew she had betrayed them to something that was worse than death.

He should just ask her. It would make things so much easier. He ran back to the door, but the cars were gone and the last of the buses was pulling out of the gate. Someone inside, probably Brock, pushed a button and the gate slowly closed. The sound of the metal sliding shut reached through the doors. Alex blew out a breath.

"Come on," Cassie yelled up the hall. "You're going to miss the cake, Alex!"

Alex jogged slowly after his sister, his heart heavy with both worry and regret.

***

"You sure you want to do this?" Dray asked for the fifth time.

"I'm sure," Alex replied.

"Just remember," Jaze told him. "If Drogan tries anything, we've got your back. You're being monitored by Brock at the Academy, and my werewolves will have eyes on you at all times."

"You're in good hands," Brock said over the ear set Alex was wearing. The words were followed by the sound of a wrapper being torn open.

"Thanks," Alex replied. His heart hammered in his chest. He was anxious to help take care of Drogan once and for all, and had looked forward to this moment since Drogan's men attacked them in the forest, but now that it was here, he couldn't brush off the nervousness he felt.

Alex walked slowly through the first store. He pretended to be interested in clothes, but he couldn't help looking over his shoulder. The way his senses were tingling, it felt like a thousand Drogan Carsos were watching him.

"Breathe," Dray said with a hint of humor in his earpiece. "You look like you're ready to destroy anything in your path."

"I am," Alex replied softly as he attempted to take interest in a blue shirt. "Hey Jaze, I found you something." He held up the shirt as if looking at the back of it.

Jaze chuckled at the picture of a pink kitty on the front along with the words, 'I'm purrrrfect.'

"Pink's his color," Dray said.

"Definitely," Brock agreed.

"Shut up and pay attention," Jaze told them with a laugh that betrayed the casual way he was trying to observe what a mannequin was wearing near the windows.

Alex glanced around the store. Besides the other werewolves Jaze had brought, it was empty.

"This is a waste of time," Alex said.

"I agree," Brock replied. "Go to the grocery store."

"I'm going to buy groceries during Christmas break?" Alex asked uncertainly.

Brock chuckled. "No one would believe that, but I've got a feed off the security cameras, and they carry toys and things. Maybe you could find something for your sister."

Jaze and Dray left the store in front of Alex. Uncertainty was growing in his chest. He knew something wasn't right, but couldn't place his finger on it.

"I think maybe—"

"Hold on," Brock said, cutting him off. The human's voice was tight. "Are you sure, Rafe?" he asked.

A muffled voice replied.

When Brock spoke again, there was fear in his tone. "Jaze, you've got to get back here. We were wrong."

"About what?" Jaze asked.

The Alpha was standing about a block north of Alex. He could see tension in the lines of the dean's silhouette. Dray was across the street. The same frozen scene showed. It would have been humorous if there wasn't stark worry on both of the werewolves' faces.

"I think Drogan is here," Brock replied.

Alex's heart stopped beating entirely. Jaze moved into action.

"Go get the vehicles," he said to his men.

"I'll pick everyone up," Mouse said into their earpieces from his place in the SUV.

"We'll meet you there," Jaze replied.

To Alex's complete surprise, Jaze tore off his shirt and ran for the alley. Alex and Dray hurried behind him. Jaze broke the rules he had carefully placed for the students and staff of the Academy and phased in the middle of the small city, leaving only a pile of clothes behind. Dray phased, and Alex did the same. He followed the black Alpha and the Gray professor into the forest.

***

The Academy was reached by a winding road through the heavy forest. The closest path was a straight line from Haroldsburg through the thickest, oldest part of the forest to the Academy. Alex's paws drummed along the soft loam as he followed the two werewolves through the forest. The scent of dew that lingered in the shadows failed to chase away the worry that pounded through Alex at every step.

Thoughts kept rushing over and over in his mind. His sister was at the Academy; the Academy was being attacked. Cassie was in danger. Who knew Cassie had stayed behind? Cassie had told Kalia that both of them were going to Haroldsburg. That meant Kalia wasn't the snitch. Alex shook his head, clearing the thought away. He didn't have time to think about that right now. All that mattered was Cassie's safety.

They reached the school just as a helicopter was flying away. Rafe's wolves ringed the front of the courtyard, and Vance and Chet stood on the steps.

Chapter Twenty-four

Jaze phased and grabbed something from a tree. By the time Alex and Dray ran out of the shadows, the dean had already pulled on a set of clothes and crossed to the waiting werewolves.

"What happened?" Jaze demanded.

"They cut into the surveillance feed. We didn't know they were here until it was almost too late," Chet explained, fighting to catch his breath.

"They must have been dropped a ways back," Vance said, "Even the wolves didn't hear them coming. They came in shooting."

Alex loped past Jaze and the others into the wreckage that was the Academy's main hall. Glass, broken marble, and sheetrock littered the floor.

"Cassie's with Brock," Vance called after him. "She's okay!"

Alex skidded across the floor; glass and debris proved to give poor footing to paws. He scrambled upright and darted for the closet. It opened just as he reached it.

Brock burst through as though he had been pushed. He looked affronted as Cassie hurried past. Her eyes widened at the sight of Alex staring at them. She dropped to her knees heedless of the mess and wrapped her arms around his neck. "We were wrong," she said, and he could hear the tears in her voice. "We were very wrong."

Alex stepped back and looked her up and down to make sure she was alright. Nikki walked out of the closet and Jaze gave her a tight hug. His hand lingered on her stomach.

"Are you alright?" he asked quietly.

"Bullet holes everywhere," Brock said, shaking his head.

"At least no one got hurt," Jaze replied. "How did you

guys chase them off?"

Chet's eyes narrowed. "They appeared to know exactly where they were going. They took off to the students' quarters," he said, pointing up the stairs. "They searched Pack Jericho's rooms, and we met them as they began to sweep the school. One of Rafe's wolves took a bullet. Lyra is tending to her in medical. Rafe and Colleen are sweeping the forest to see where Drogan's men were dropped off."

Jaze shook his head. He leaned against a marble column. The top broke off and plummeted to the floor. The sound made everyone jump. Jaze looked at it. "We can't have students back here."

"We have the funds," Vance replied. "We can have it fixed before the break is over."

"The students won't even have to know," Brock agreed.

"No." Jaze looked up from the broken pieces littering the floor. "It isn't safe. They got through our surveillance and we had no idea they were here until they were in the Academy. Our students would be in danger." He looked at Alex and Cassie. "We have to find a place for our Lifers, too. Thank goodness they were with Rafe touring the forest."

Cassie's hand gripped Alex's fur.

"Where would they go?" Nikki asked softly. She set a hand on Jaze's arm. "They have nowhere else, Jaze."

He gazed down at her. "They're not safe here, Nikki. No one is. I don't want you and the baby here, and I don't need anyone to be killed because of my stubbornness."

"Your stubbornness?" Nikki replied, a hint of surprise in her voice.

Jaze nodded. He made a small gesture that took in the entire Academy. "Why else is this place here? Maybe it was foolish to think that we could protect everyone under one roof. Maybe werewolves are better off fending for themselves."

"You don't really believe that," Vance answered. The tone of his voice said how he really felt.

Jaze was silent for a moment. He finally let out a sigh and shook his head. "No, I don't. Wolves stick together as packs for protection. We just happen to have the largest pack of werewolves ever imagined." He looked around at the hallway. "We have some work to do."

The vehicles from Haroldsburg arrived out front. Mouse came running in. "Is everyone okay?" he asked. His glasses were skewed and his hair stuck up.

"Everyone's fine," Jaze told him. The dean looked at his wife. "Check on Lyra. Let Rafe and me know if the wolf's condition worsens."

"Will do," Nikki replied. She kissed Jaze on the cheek.

"What was that for?" he asked with a smile.

She gave an answering smile. "Because every time you think I'm in trouble, you have the same look on your face. I just wanted it to disappear."

He pulled her close and held her against his chest for a moment. His smile grew. "He's a regular little kicker now," he said, putting a hand on his wife's stomach.

"You can feel it?" Cassie asked with awe in her voice.

Nikki nodded. "He likes to hear his daddy talk. Come here; you can feel him kick, too."

Cassie approached cautiously. Jaze set her hand where his had been. After a moment, Cassie gave a little squeak.

"I felt it!" she exclaimed. She looked at Alex. "You've got to try it!"

Alex was about to shake his head, but the look on Nikki's face let him know how much it meant to her. He walked over and set his hand near Cassie's, expecting not to feel anything. He laughed when something tapped his hand.

"That's the baby?" he asked.

Nikki nodded. She beamed down at the twins. "I think he's going to be a handful."

"How do you know it's a he?" Cassie asked.

Nikki and Jaze exchanged a warm look. "Just a feeling," Nikki replied. "I'd better go help Lyra."

"Be careful," Jaze said.

She gave him another kiss and hurried down the hall.

"So about our surveillance shortcomings," Jaze began, meeting Mouse's gaze.

The little werewolf looked at the floor. "I, uh, think I know where they might have gotten in to blind our feed. I'll make sure it's foolproof by nightfall."

"Will you also give Agent Sullivan a call? I need the Global Protection Agency's input on this." Jaze said. "It wouldn't hurt to request some GPA agents to hang around when the term starts back up."

Mouse nodded and hurried to the closet with Brock close behind.

Jaze turned his attention to Vance. "About those repairs," he began.

Vance held up a huge hand. "I'll start making calls. You know my mom's just dying to pump more money into something. It might as well be the Academy."

Cassie and Alex walked up the stairs. To Alex's surprise, Jaze followed them. Alex's nose wrinkled at the smell of Drogan's men that hung on everything. Humans were seldom smelled inside the Academy except for Brock, Professor Thorson, and Nikki. There had been more when the school was being built, but the scent had faded long ago. Now, the scent of human strangers clung to everything.

"We may have to get thorough with bleach," Jaze noted, pushing the door open.

Pack Jericho's quarters were in shambles. Apparently, Drogan's men were not told to be gentle in their search. Alex entered his room to find the mattress sliced and his clothes strewn across the floor.

"They thought I was hiding in there?" Alex asked, disbelief in his tone. "What am I, a weremouse?"

Cassie giggled at the door. "That sounds intimidating," she said.

Alex rolled his eyes. "Oh, go clean up your own mess," he snapped, but the heat of his words was taken away by his grin. She nodded and disappeared to her room.

"We'll get you a new mattress," Jaze said, picking up a few of Alex's clothes.

"You don't have to do that," Alex replied. He gathered them from the dean.

Jaze nodded. "I know you can do it." He paused, then met Alex's gaze. "I shouldn't have let you go to Haroldsburg today."

"You couldn't have stopped me."

"Yes, I could have," Jaze replied, his expression stern. "You're a fourteen year old boy, Alex. I have no right to ask you to be in that situation, even if it had worked."

"You didn't ask," Alex reminded him as he picked up another shirt. It was a gray one that was one of his favorites; perhaps he liked the symbolism. One of Drogan's men had sliced it with a knife. Alex began to twist the fabric between his hands. "I was the one who came up with the plan. I wanted to find Drogan. I thought it was foolproof." He ran a hand over his eyes. "But I was wrong."

At his silence, Jaze asked softly, "About what?"

"About Kalia," Alex replied, his heart heavy. "I accused her, and I was wrong. I avoided her, and I could tell when she went home with her family for Christmas that it hurt her." He clenched his hands into fists. "I don't know how to make up for it."

The look of understanding that brushed Jaze's face almost undid Alex's carefully constructed composure. Jaze sat against the wall, and motioned for Alex to do the same. He slid down among the wreckage that was his room, his attention on the dean.

"Did I ever tell you about the time I accused Nikki of hanging out with me only because she wanted to get back at her parents?"

Alex shook his head, his curiosity piqued. A footstep in the hallway matched Cassie's gait. The slight tilt of Jaze's head said that he had heard it, too.

He smiled. "You might as well come listen, Cass. It's a good story."

Cassie entered the room with a sheepish look and sat down by Alex. "Sorry for eavesdropping," she said.

"It's a little hard not to when you're a werewolf," Jaze answered. "But standing in the hallway makes it a bit easier." His tone made them both laugh.

Jaze's voice took on the cadence of one who liked to tell stories. "She was my neighbor; that's how we met. I found out later that her parents were Hunters, and that was before Hunters and werewolves made their alliance." A shadow crossed his features. "For as long as that alliance lasted." He shook his head to chase the emotions away and kept speaking, "We snuck away to a place where there were a bunch of storage sheds that were used for a giant swap meet on the weekends. We used to climb on the roofs and look at the stars. That's when she told me about her parents."

He smiled at the thought. "She was afraid that I would laugh at the fact that her parents hunted werewolves. Instead, I was terrified!"

Alex and Cassie laughed at his exaggerated expression.

"Imagine, us moving next door to werewolf Hunters. It wasn't ideal, especially considering that I was falling in love with their daughter." Jaze tipped his head against the wall. "My heart was already hers, and that scared me. I tried to chase her away, telling her that the only reason she was hanging out with someone like me was because she wanted to get back at her parents."

"What did she say?" Cassie asked.

Jaze smiled. "She said for me to take my oh-so-composed self-confidence and shove it."

Alex laughed. "No wonder you liked her."

Jaze winked at him. "Just you wait until a girl steals your heart. When you find someone worth fighting for, you won't let anything stand in your way."

"How did you win her back?" Cassie asked, excitement in her eyes at the story.

Jaze's smile deepened. "I let her think my heart was broken. She's too compassionate to let someone deal with heartbreak on their own." He grinned. "I used that against her."

"Heartless," Cassie said, shaking her head, her eyes sparkling.

"I know, right?" Jaze replied. He grinned. "I apologized for being an idiot, and she forgave me."

"It was that easy?" Alex asked doubtfully.

Jaze shook his head. "Apologizing isn't easy, especially when you do it right. It's got to come from your heart, or else she'll see right through it."

"Who?" Cassie asked, looking from Jaze to Alex. Her eyes widened. "Kalia?"

Alex dropped his gaze and nodded. "I was wrong, and it hurt her. I've got to make it right.

"I trust that you will," Jaze said. He rose to his feet and held out a hand to help Alex and Cassie up. "I guess we'd better get started in here," he said, looking around at the mess.

Chapter Twenty-five

Christmas morning was always a quiet affair at the Academy. Though Alex had fond memories of him and Cassie tearing into presents with their parents looking on, he was grateful for the holiday routine for the Lifers. They woke up at eight o-clock, which was sleeping in at the Academy. The cooks had egg nog, biscuits, and a rich meat gravy ready as the Lifer orphans stumbled into the dining room.

After breakfast, Nikki and Jaze gave everyone presents. Alex was grateful for his new jacket and pocket knife. Cassie showed everyone the new princess book series Nikki had picked out for her. It was the most outgoing his sister ever became. Alex knew it was because she had grown up with most of the orphans at the Academy. Without the Termers around, she was no longer shy. He smiled as she and Terith looked through their new books.

"I have something I want to show you guys," Rafe said quietly.

Alex looked up at him in surprise from where he was experimenting with his knife on a piece of aspen Jaze had found for him. The teacher of wilderness education very seldom entered the Academy. Colleen, Kaynan, and Grace had flown home to visit their family for the holidays, but Rafe hated confined spaces and usually stayed in the forest.

"Meet me out back with your sister," Rafe said. He left through the doors as silently as he had entered.

Alex hurried over to Cassie. "Come on, Rafe wants to show us something."

Cassie left her books with Terith, promising to return as soon as possible. She didn't ask questions as Alex led her outside. The twins knew how rare it was for the professor to reach out, and neither of them wanted to miss out on whatever Rafe thought they would be interested in.

Rafe was waiting near the gate already in wolf form. With his dark gray coat, he blended almost perfectly with the bricks of the wall. He vanished through the gate as soon as they saw him. Only paw prints in the snow told where he had been.

"Let's hurry," Alex said.

They ran to the forest and quickly phased into wolf form. Cassie pranced around Alex, glad to be a wolf again. Alex grinned at her. He knew exactly how she felt. Living in human form without phasing into a wolf felt like eating food without drinking water, or having a day without night. It had been a few days since the siblings had phased, and Alex had truly missed it.

He took a deep breath of the crisp winter air. The scent of fresh snow, dormant trees, and frozen sap filled his senses. His breath fogged the space in front of him when he let it back out.

A low bark caught his attention. He looked up to see Rafe waiting for them a few paces away. Neither sibling had heard the wolf return. Alex and Cassie exchanged an excited look before following the wolf beneath the trees.

They traveled to a different part of the forest they had never seen before. The trees were older and larger. Snow didn't penetrate to the forest floor in places, leaving patches of white and shadow. The light was fainter. Alex found himself relying on his sense of smell and hearing. He padded quietly past an ermine hiding in its burrow waiting for them to pass, and heard the soft rustle of an owl adjusting its wings on a low branch overhead.

Alex was concentrating so much on his other senses that he almost ran straight into Cassie when she stopped walking. He looked up to see Rafe pause on a small rise. His head lowered when he met Alex's gaze and his ears flattened, indicating for the wolves to go slowly and quietly. They padded softly behind him, intent on what was ahead. A strange smell filled Alex's nose. He ducked beneath a bush, then froze.

A female cougar stared directly at them. Alex's heartbeat quickened. It was no secret that the scars that showed in Rafe's hide were from saving Colleen from a mountain lion. Alex worried for a second that he was about to be attacked.

Cassie let out a little snort that sounded like a laugh. Alex glanced at her, wondering if she had gone crazy. She was looking intently at something beyond the cougar.

Alex followed her gaze. Three baby cougars played just beyond their mother. The cubs tumbled over one another on wobbly legs and huge paws. They had spots and were covered in downy tufts of fluffy fur. One chewed on a stick that poked from the snow. The other two saw what had caught its attention and pounced. The tumbling ball of cubs rolled into their mother. She broke her attention from the wolves long enough to lick them before they scampered back to their stick.

The female cougar yawned. It was then that Alex realized she wasn't alarmed by their presence, just watchful. Perhaps Colleen and Rafe came often to check on the cougar cubs.

The cougar's ear flickered. She turned her head slowly to the right. Alex saw a flicker of movement in the shadows. His wolven eyes made out the form of a cream-colored wolf watching them from the shadows.

Rafe gave a little bark. The three cougar cubs looked up in surprise. The female wolf lowered her head slightly in acknowledgement. Rafe padded softly back the way they had come. Alex and Cassie fell in close behind. In a few minutes, the cream-colored wolf joined them.

Her scent touched Alex's nose. He felt a surge of

happiness when he recognized the scent of pine and mint he had learned to associate with his aunt. Meredith followed them beneath the trees to the cave that Rafe and Colleen used as a go-between from the cave further in the woods that was their home.

Rafe went in first and phased. When he came back out, he gestured to Meredith. "I set out a change of clothes for you. The twins will be happy to wait."

She gave another nod of gratitude and disappeared inside. Rafe leaned against a tree, his golden eyes glittering.

Meredith stepped out, and Alex's heart skipped a beat. He scolded himself, telling himself again that his mother was gone. It just amazed him how much Meredith looked like her, especially with her dark hair and light blue eyes. She gave them both a shy smile. Alex tried to be patient when Cassie ran in to change, but a tingle ran down his spine. He didn't know if it was his wolf instincts trying to tell him something, or the crisp breeze that tickled his fur. Either way, when he felt his aunt's gaze and he turned to meet her eyes, he couldn't help the happiness that filled him.

Cassie shocked them all by running straight back out of the cave after she was dressed and wrapping her arms around Meredith in a big hug.

"Well, hello," Meredith said with a surprised smile. Her head jerked up when Cassie's scent touched her nose. She looked at Rafe in surprise.

Before she could say anything, Cassie burst out, "I'm so sorry. I shouldn't have done that. I've just been waiting so long to meet you. We didn't know we had an aunt, and Alex has been watching over you; now here you are!"

"An aunt?" Meredith repeated, clearly shocked.

"Yes," Cassie said, her excitement clear in her flushed face and sparkling eyes. "You're our mother's sister. When our parents died, we thought we were orphans. We didn't know she had a sister. I'm sure there was a good reason she didn't tell us, but it's so good to see you now." Cassie paused, aware that she was babbling.

Alex stared at her. It was more than his sister ever said in the presence of a stranger, even if that stranger was their aunt.

"Are you going to phase?" Rafe asked, his tone one of polite inquiry.

Alex realized he had been watching his aunt and sister without moving. He snorted and trotted into the cave. He phased quickly, then pulled on the clothes Rafe had set out for him. It took a few more minutes for him to gather himself before he stepped back outside.

It felt strange to know that in one moment, he would have family again. Jaze and Nikki had been there for the twins since the Academy opened, taking care of the siblings as if they were their own, but there was a feeling that came with knowing you had no true relatives, no one who shared your blood and your bond with kin. It was especially painful as a werewolf, because packs were made of families and the blood bond was extremely strong; having no one hurt.

To know that stepping beyond the cave and truly meeting his aunt for the first time would change that made Alex's heart give a painful beat. He put a hand to it. He knew he couldn't stay in the cave forever. He took a steeling breath, willed his heartbeat to settle, and stepped outside.

The awkwardness he had feared vanished when Aunt Meredith hugged him. He held her tight, denying the tears that burned in his eyes. He realized she had no such reservations as answering tears fell on his head.

"I can't believe you're here," she said. "I can't believe you made it." Her arms shook as she held him. She motioned to

Cassie. She joined them in another embrace. Tears showed in Cassie's dark blue eyes as well.

"When Jaze told us our mom had a twin sister, we could barely believe it," Cassie said, sniffing as she stepped back and wiped away her tears with the corner of her sleeve.

"I always hoped I would see you," Meredith said. She looked them up and down with a proud, watery smile. "You are so much more beautiful and amazing than I ever could have hoped. Mindi said you were perfect. I never imagined just how much that was true!"

Cassie laughed. At Meredith's questioning look, she said, "You called Alex beautiful."

Meredith gave him a warm smile. "I meant handsome."

"It's okay," Alex said, dragging the toe of his borrowed sneaker across the snow.

"Do you want to join us for Christmas dinner?" Rafe asked.

Meredith stared at him. "I, uh, I'm not sure if Jaze would want me there."

Rafe gave her a kind smile. "Of course he would. Please join us."

Meredith glanced at the twins. Alex and Cassie both nodded eagerly; neither wanted to let her leave now that they were together. She finally gave in.

"Alright, I'll go with you."

"Yes!" Cassie said. She slipped her hand into Meredith's. "You'll love Christmas dinner. They always make it so beautiful, and now we have our aunt with us!"

"That will be nice," Meredith said. "I'm excited to share it with you." She walked on ahead with Cassie.

Rafe smiled at Alex as they followed close behind. Rafe's wolves fell in around them. Alex let his hand rest on one of the younger male's backs. The wolf walked beside him as they made their way through the trees toward the familiar silhouette of the Academy etched against the sky.

STRAYS

***

Jaze welcomed Meredith with open arms. As soon as they entered the dining hall, Nikki rushed to greet her. They hugged awkwardly over Nikki's pregnant belly, then laughed like sisters about it. The rest of the Lifers were introduced, and by the time they sat around the table, it felt like a family group.

Alex watched Meredith and Cassie talk as they ate. Cassie told their aunt about life at the Academy, and Meredith shared little stories about what she was learning as she lived at the safe house.

"You should stay here," Nikki said.

Meredith looked surprised. "I thought you'd want me to wait until the beginning of the next school year."

Nikki nodded. "Jaze's team has been helping to relocate werewolf families, and our student body has been growing so much each year we're going to have to take on more staff members if we have any hope of keeping up, so the sooner, the better." Nikki patted her stomach. "And I'm definitely going to need more help around here when this little guy's born."

"Are you sure?" Meredith asked.

"Only if you're comfortable with it," Jaze replied. At the growing shock on Meredith's face, the dean continued, "We were going to ask you to move in when this school year is over so we could prepare for the next one," he smiled at Nikki. "But now's as good a time as any."

Meredith looked from Jaze and Nikki to the twins. Cassie and Alex nodded encouragingly. "I'm not sure if I'm good with kids," she said hesitantly.

"We'll help you," Cassie replied. "You won't be thrown to the wolves." She giggled.

Alex rolled his eyes, but smiled. "Everyone here is nice. You would make a great teacher."

"You think so?" Meredith asked. The answering nods made her smile. "I guess I can try it."

"Wonderful!" Nikki exclaimed. "We'll help you get settled in. It can give you a chance to get to know the students before you start teaching."

"I don't need to stay at the safe house?" There was relief in Meredith's voice.

For the first time, Alex realized she might have been lonely there. Jaze's guards rotated often, but it was probably hard to be away from everything she knew, especially after being taken by Drogan. Alex's heart went out to her.

"You are welcome to move in here whenever you are ready," Jaze replied. "We have plenty of rooms for staff. You'll be comfortable here."

Meredith looked like she wanted to hug all of them at the same time. She settled for kissing the top of Cassie's head. "That's sounds wonderful," she said.

"We can eat lunch together!" Cassie replied. "I can show you my room, and you can meet the rest of the pack. They're crazy sometimes, but really nice. I think you'll like them."

Alex found himself watching them so closely he barely ate his dinner. It was amazing to see Cassie open up; it felt as if he was seeing a whole different person. She glowed as she told their aunt about learning history with Professor Thorson, and how much she was enjoying reading 'Romeo and Juliet' in Grace's English class.

By the end of the evening, sorrow began to crowd the happiness from Alex's chest. Dinner was over, and everyone was finishing the last remnants of the chocolate mousse pie that was a tradition to close Christmas dinner at the Academy. Most of the other Lifers had fallen away into groups talking and laughing around the room. Cassie and Meredith still sat in their seats, catching up over the last years.

"It's absolutely wonderful," Cassie was saying. "You'll have to try it. Grace taught me that you don't always need your sight to create something beautiful."

"I'd love to," Meredith replied. "You'll have to show me."

"I will," Cassie promised.

Alex couldn't take it anymore. He pushed away from the table and walked as calmly as he could manage to the hall. As soon as the door shut behind him, he took off running for the training room.

He ran straight to a wooden practice dummy, slammed it against the wall, knocked another in the chest with a two-handed punch, and then kicked the first so hard it bounced off the wall again, leaving a dent in the sheetrock.

"What's going on?"

Alex spun at Jaze's inquiring tone. Jaze leaned against the doorframe with a calm expression on his face. Alex's chest heaved. He looked from Jaze to the dummies. "It's not right," he finally forced out.

"What's not right?" Jaze asked.

Alex gritted his teeth. It was a moment before he could answer. "Cassie is up there telling our aunt all of the things we do here."

Jaze's forehead creased. "That bothers you?"

Alex shook his head, then changed his mind and nodded. "No. Well, yes. It bothers me." He took a calming breath and let it out in a rush. "It bothers me that Meredith is there hearing about how much Cassie loves school and my mom and dad should be there, too." His eyes burned. He blinked quickly. "They should hear about how she's learning to make friends, and night games, and the time Pip got his head stuck in the banister." His chest heaved. He felt his heart protest.

"Do you want me to ask Meredith to go?" Jaze asked quietly. There was no judgment in his voice, only understanding that cut Alex to the quick.

He shook his head. "No. I'm glad she's here. I just. . . I just want Mom and Dad to be, too." It was the first time he had spoken those words aloud to Jaze. Jaze and Nikki had tried so hard to make Academy life easy for the twins, and Alex had never complained or told Jaze how much he ached to see his parents again because he knew it would never happen. Seeing Aunt Meredith laughing with Cassie nearly broke his heart.

"I know what you mean," Jaze said. The Alpha stepped into the room and crossed to the boxing ring. He leaned against the ropes facing Alex. He met the young werewolf's gaze. "I wished a million times that I could bring my dad back after my uncle killed him. I replayed his death over and over in my head, wishing I could have been there, that I could have stopped them."

The fire left Alex. He sat down against the opposite wall and studied his worn sneakers. "It's enough to drive someone crazy," he said in a voice just above a whisper.

He saw the dean nod out of the corner of his eye. "It really is. But you couldn't have stopped them. Not all of them."

"We can stop Drogan now," Alex said, looking back up at the dean.

Jaze nodded. "We can, and we will."

"When?" Alex asked. He knew he was being belligerent, but he couldn't help himself. The words spilled out. "We have to stop him before he hurts anyone else. I don't want other kids to end up like Cassie and me. I want him locked up or dead where he can't destroy lives anymore. If he's gone, this world will be a better place."

"It will be a safer place for werewolves," Jaze concluded softly. At Alex's nod, he gave the young Gray a searching look. "We know that Kalia's not the snitch. Can you think of anyone else who might be working with Drogan?"

Alex shook his head. "I've thought through everything I said, and I can't think of anyone who knew where we were during the times when Drogan attacked. I'll ask Cassie to be sure, but I can't figure it out."

Jaze nodded. "Don't worry. We'll find him. And for now, I think Meredith might be safer here, especially if she's been wandering the forest on her own."

"You might have to talk to your security team at the safe house about that," Alex suggested.

A hint of a smile touched Jaze's mouth. "I'll do that." He rose somewhat stiffly from the ropes. "Care to join us for the last hours of Christmas?"

"I'd be happy to," Alex replied, rising.

They walked together back up the hall, the attacked dummies lying forgotten on the floor of the training room behind them.

Chapter Twenty-six

Alex searched through the students that wandered back inside the Academy. The buses and cars that brought them back looked out of place amid the snow-lined trees and gray brick landscape. The air was filled with the acrid scent of exhaust. His nose wrinkled.

Students pulled their luggage across the snow, leaving tracks in the expanse of white. Stories of what each had done during the break made laughter and shouts echo off the walls. Alex forced a smile when Marky and Steven walked by.

"Good to be back!" Marky exclaimed, pulling a suitcase that was held together by thread and duct tape.

"My mom cried when I left," Steven said by way of greeting.

"That's, uh, that's too bad," Alex replied, unsure of what to say.

"See you inside, chief," Marky said. He ducked inside the door just as a snowball sailed through, missing him by inches and instead splattering on Vance's chest.

The glower the huge werewolf gave the crowd of students rushing inside sobered them up a bit until another snowball took residence where the first had been.

"Alright. Who did—" Vance's words cut off when he saw Jaze standing outside the door packing another snowball. "You're dead," the huge Alpha exclaimed. He shoved past the students out the door.

The dean hit him squarely in the face with the next snowball. "You sure about that?" he asked.

Vance bent down and gathered a snowman-sized snowball and began to pack it. "Oh, I'm sure."

"Excuse me," a familiar voice said, breaking Alex's attention from the ensuing battle.

He looked over to see Kalia brushing by, her head lowered and her blonde hair hiding her expression from view.

"Kalia, wait," Alex said, hurrying after her. "We need to talk."

She spun around. "Really, Alex? Somehow I lost the only friend I had before Christmas and I don't even know what I did because he won't take the time to tell me, that's how much he cares."

Alex stopped in his tracks, frozen by her hurt and the way her eyes flashed gold in anger. Students swarmed past them, but it felt like they were the only two people in the hallway.

A tear trailed down Kalia's cheek. "What is it, Alex?" she asked, a bit softer.

"Come with me," Alex implored. On impulse, he took her luggage and slid it to the wall out of the crowd's way, then caught her elbow. "Trust me."

Kalia followed without a word as he led her out of the throng to the backdoors of the Academy. They walked through the gates and beneath the trees. Alex's head felt clearer without the chaos of Termers coming back. He led her through the trees, and stopped when he felt her hesitate.

"What is it?" she asked, her voice guarded.

"I need to apologize," Alex replied.

"For what?" Kalia demanded. "What did I do that ostracized me?"

"Nothing." Alex quickly shook his head. "It wasn't you. I thought I knew something, and I was wrong. I'm so sorry it hurt you."

Kalia looked up at him through lowered lashes. Her hands trembled. She put them in her pockets. "What did you think you knew?"

Alex let out a breath that fogged in the chilly afternoon air. He forced the words out that he knew would hurt her even further. "I thought you were Drogan's spy, telling him where Cassie and I were so that he could try to kill us."

Kalia gasped. She put a hand over her mouth and turned away from Alex. He wanted to comfort her, but when he touched her shoulder, she ducked away from his grasp.

"Kalia, I—"

"Don't talk to me, Alex. Don't even look at me," Kalia snapped. Her blue eyes were filled with ice when she met his gaze. "I can't believe you could think I would do such a thing. You think I'm a traitor, a snitch? Is that why you thought I was trying to be your friend?" More tears broke free. She wiped them angrily away. "How dare you assume something so terrible of me?" The next words that left her tore Alex's heart in two. "Why does everyone assume I'm a monster?" she demanded more to herself than to him.

"You're not a—"

"Don't talk to me, Alex Davies," Kalia snapped. "Don't look at me, don't sit by me, and don't presume we're friends, because we're not." She took a step closer, her boots crunching in the snow. "If you so much as try to sit next to me at lunch, I'll have Boris tear you apart." Her eyes gleamed. "And you know he can," she said, reminding him of the practice bout in the training room.

She turned and walked away.

Alex stood there listening to her stomp angrily back to the Academy. He ached, knowing he had lost her through his rashness, and had hurt her as well. He longed to go after her, but with the anger on her face, he knew it would be a bad decision. He was about to walk deeper into the forest when a quiet howl broke through the air.

It was against the rules for anyone to howl when the buses were still out front, but Alex recognized Cassie's voice. He took off running for the Academy.

Kalia had paused near the gate at the sound of the howl. Alex pushed past her.

"Is everything—"

Kalia's voice died away as Alex ran through the door and up the stairs.

He found Cassie in her room. Her window was open, and she sat near it with tears on her face.

"Close the door," she said in a voice that quivered.

Alex did as she requested, then hurried to her side. "Cassie, what happened?"

She tried to talk, but no sound came out. She shook her head and more tears ran down her cheeks. Alex crouched in front of her and took her hands.

"Cassie, you need to tell me what happened," he said in a tone that was cajoling and commanding at the same time.

She looked at him, and the sorrow in her dark blue eyes made a pit in his stomach. "I know who betrayed us."

Alex's breath caught in his throat. He waited without speaking for her to continue.

The door opened behind them. Alex glanced back to see Kalia in the doorway. He nodded for her to enter and turned his attention back to Cassie. He heard the door shut quietly as Kalia stepped inside.

"It was Pip," Cassie said in a strangled voice.

Alex stared at her. "Are you sure?"

She nodded. "I'm positive. Remember the first time Drogan's men found us?"

"He said we should look for the Alphas in the forest," Alex replied. The pit in his stomach deepened.

"And the second time?" Cassie pressed.

"I talked to Kalia," Alex said, glancing back at her. Kalia watched them without speaking, her gaze jumping from one to the other. Something about that night struck Alex. "But I spoke to Pip first. He asked me if I was going to be late for P.E."

Cassie nodded as if she had guessed as much. She wiped the tears from her cheeks with a steady hand.

"How did you know?" Alex asked, hoping by some miracle that it wasn't true. He really liked Pip; the thought that the young Second Year was the source of the attacks ate at him. Even though it all made sense, he wished it wasn't true."

"You know how nobody's supposed to bring cellphones from their homes?" Cassie asked. At Alex and Kalia's nods, she explained, "I was wandering down the halls and I saw Pip hiding one in a hole in his mattress. When he left, I snuck it out." She met Alex's gaze. "There was only one number on the phone. He didn't call with it, he used it to text, and the last text said, 'He's gone. He'll be back in about three hours through the woods.' That was on the night of the last attack."

Alex let out a slow breath. He leaned against the wall, his gaze on the forest outside.

"We need to turn him in," Kalia said. "We've got to tell Jaze."

Alex shook his head. "Not yet. I need to talk to him."

Both Kalia and Cassie stared at him. "That's a bad idea," Cassie said. "There's a reason he's spying on us, some sort of motivation. He could get defensive."

"And what, beat me in hand to hand combat?" Alex replied incredulously.

"If he's working with Drogan, he may have other ways to defend himself," Kalia said reluctantly. It was obvious she didn't want to get involved with anything relating to Alex, but she couldn't let him walk into a battle blind.

"Give me ten minutes," Alex said.

He walked out without waiting for them to argue.

Alex found Pip in the dining room. It took all of his self-control not to attack the kid and demand why he was setting them up. Instead, he grabbed Pip's arm and led him from the room. Pip walked beside him without a word as if he knew what was coming. Alex escorted him to the boys' bathroom, then shoved the garbage can under the door to jam it shut. It wouldn't keep an Alpha out, but it might slow a Gray down or convince them to use another restroom if necessary.

"Why did you do it?" Alex demanded, spinning to face the boy.

"They have my family," Pip replied. He forced himself to meet Alex's gaze.

Alex's hands were clenched into fists. He wanted to hit Pip so badly, to make him pay for almost getting Cassie killed and for getting him shot. He drew his hand back. Pip flinched. Instead of hitting him, Alex punched the brick wall next to the boy's head as hard as he could. The bricks cracked and sent down a shower of dust.

"I'm so sorry," Pip said. Tears showed in the young boy's eyes. He blinked quickly.

Alex shook his head. He bent down so he could meet the ten-year-old's gaze directly. "I need you to tell Drogan where I'm going."

Pip sniffed, his eyes wide. "What?"

"Listen to me," Alex said. "This is very important. I'm going to go to the safe house again, and I need you to tell Drogan where I am."

"B-but he'll kill you," Pip replied.

"Don't worry about that. Do you know where he's holding your family?"

Pip nodded. "He made me stay with them at Christmas."

Alex flinched at the pain in the young werewolf's voice. "Okay. As soon as I leave, I want you to go with Cassie and tell Jaze what happened. Let him know where your family is. Whatever you do, don't tell Jaze where I am. We need Drogan away from his hideout so Jaze can get your family free. If he's worrying about me, your family will still be in danger."

"But you'll be in danger," Pip argued.

Alex shook his head. "I'll be fine. Just do what I say. If we can get your family out and destroy Drogan's base, we'll put a huge hitch in his ability to hurt others. I'll keep him distracted; you tell Jaze where he is. Do you think you can do that?"

Pip nodded, speechless.

Alex patted him on the shoulder. "Good."

He pulled the door open and found Cassie and Kalia waiting in the hall.

"You're not going," Cassie said.

"I've got to," Alex replied, shouldering past them with Pip close behind.

"You can't go alone," Kalia protested.

Alex paused and turned to the three of them. "I've got to. He wants me, Cassie, and Meredith. Now that Meredith is here, all he has to do is hit the Academy. Everyone here will be in danger. I don't want that, and I know you don't, either. If he thinks I've gone to the safe house to visit Meredith again, he'll think he can, as his man said, kill two birds with one stone. He'll get greedy and careless. That'll give us the time we need to get Pip's family out of there."

"What if Jaze can't get them out?" Kalia asked.

Everyone stared at her. "You don't know Jaze very well, do you?" Alex said.

Kalia shook her head.

Alex took a steeling breath. "Look," he said, addressing all of them. "If you want to help me and protect everyone in the Academy, you've got to do what I ask. I'm leaving now. Pip, deliver the message. Cassie, see that Pip gets to Jaze and the others. Kalia," he paused, hesitating. "Kalia, please protect my sister. If I fail, Drogan might be coming back here anyway."

"I will," she said. The girl's icy blue eyes flashed gold for the briefest moment.

Alex nodded. "Take care you guys."

Cassie broke free from the others and wrapped her arms tightly around Alex. The students walking past them in the hallway who had no idea what was going on gave the siblings strange looks. Alex shrugged out of his sister's grasp. "Be careful," he told her. "I love you."

"I love you, too," she replied with a sniff.

Alex nodded at Pip. The three of them headed for the stairs. Alex took off running toward the back doors.

Chapter Twenty-seven

Alex ran through the snow, pushing himself faster than he ever had before. His paws flew in front of him, creating a quiet shush as he loped along the snowy landscape. He was grateful for the way his huge paws allowed him to run above the snow instead of sinking beneath it and slowing his progress. A rabbit darted past. He ignored it as he focused all of his attention on reaching the safe house.

Drogan might not know where the safe house was, but Cassie knew, and she would tell Pip. He only hoped he could get there early enough to make the few preparations he needed before the man with the mismatched eyes arrived.

He was running to his death. He knew that. He only hoped he could take Drogan down with him and end the threat once and for all. If he could protect Cassie and the others with his life, it would be a life well spent. The words repeated over and over in his mind as he leapt frozen streams and ducked beneath snow-laden boughs. Given Drogan's earlier response times, it wouldn't be long for them to find Alex, then the base would be exposed and Jaze could take Drogan down from the inside.

Alex's heartbeat thundered in his ears as he paused on the rise where he had stood many times overlooking the cabin nestled in the valley below. It was empty. No smoke rose from the chimney, and no tracks of cars showed since the last snowstorm. Since Meredith was no longer there, and Jaze had successfully relocated the other families to safe houses throughout the country, this one was abandoned until further need. Well, Alex had need.

He loped down the hill without bothering to hide his trail. He wanted Drogan to know he was there alone. He hoped it would provoke the man into meeting him alone as well.

Alex phased on the porch. The chill of the crisp evening bit his exposed skin. He shoved the door open with his shoulder and stumbled inside. He glanced around quickly. A pair of dressers against the far wall looked promising. He raided the dresser on the right and found women's clothing. While the thought of Drogan finding him in a dress might have caught the man off-guard, Alex chose not to humiliate himself in his final moments.

He searched through the other dresser and found a pair of jeans and a sweatshirt with a howling wolf on the front. Alex rolled his eyes at the irony and pulled on the shirt. He found several pairs of shoes beneath the dresser, picked the pair that fit best, and pulled them on. He turned one of the arm chairs so that it faced the front door and waited.

***

The sound of a chopper cutting through the air came to Alex much sooner than he expected. Alex watched out the window as six men dressed in black slid down ropes. He willed his muscles to relax as he made his way back to the chair. The chopper flew away.

"Is this some sort of trap?" Drogan called out.

Alex's chest tightened at the sound of the man's voice. He kept silent.

"If it is, you better be a much better fighter than the last time we met," Drogan continued, goading him. "Because you're all alone, and I've got six men. You don't have a wolf pack ready to protect your back when you realize you're too weak to take us all on."

"Are you too weak to take me on alone?" Alex called.

Silence followed. Alex could hear their footsteps outside the cabin.

"Clear," someone called softly from the back.

"Stay out here," Drogan ordered. "If I'm not the one who comes out, shoot."

The door opened and Drogan stepped inside. He squinted at the sudden darkness. Alex crossed the space between them in a heartbeat and slammed several punches into the man's stomach. Instead of doubling over, Drogan laughed.

"Thought I would come unprepared?" he asked. Drogan pulled up his shirt, revealing a black shiny material underneath. "Kevlar," he said with a light of triumph in his eyes.

"You should have worn it on your face," Alex replied, throwing a quick punch at the man's head.

Drogan tried to block it, but the werewolf's fast reflexes

snuck the punch in to land a glancing blow on the side of the man's head. Drogan staggered back.

Alex stepped in to take the advantage, but when he threw a second punch, Drogan blocked it and followed with one of his own. The man had fists like steel; Alex's head snapped back. A growl tore from his throat. He punched Drogan twice in the ribs hard enough that the man felt the impact despite the Kevlar; when Drogan winced, Alex threw a haymaker at the side of Drogan's head.

Drogan ducked at the last second and slammed an answering punch to Alex's chest above his heart. Drogan attempted to kick him in the stomach, but Alex blocked it and rammed his shoulder into Drogan's chest, barreling him against the door.

Something seared across Alex's back. He stepped away in surprise at the fierce pain.

Drogan held up a knife. "As much as I would like to fight you, I have to question why you would come here by yourself." He let the knife catch in the light that filtered through the window. "This is silver and made to splinter. Every time I cut you, it will leave silver shards in your wounds, bringing you that much closer to dying. You'd best tell the truth."

Alex grimaced at the sensation of blood dripping down his back. "Why would I need anyone else here with me?"

"You don't expect me to believe that you left Cassie at the Academy without protection, do you?" Drogan replied.

"Who says it's unprotected," Alex shot back. "Jaze and the others will defend her with their lives."

Drogan nodded. "If you believe in my nephew so much, why isn't he here to fight beside you?"

"Because I wanted to kill you myself," Alex replied in a growl.

Drogan's eyebrows rose. "So Jaze has no idea you're here?" He laughed at the thought. "Well that's rich. How's Cassie going to feel when I ship your dead body to the Academy doorstep?"

Alex's heart clenched. He replied through gritted teeth, "Leave Cassie out of it. This is between you and me."

Drogan lunged with the knife. Alex spun to the right, punched Drogan in the shoulder as he passed, then jumped on him. They slammed into a couch and rolled over the back. Pain sliced along Alex's side. He let out a cry and pushed back to his feet. The knife Drogan held glittered darkly with blood.

"I'm happy to kill you first," Drogan said. "Then I'll go for Cassie. I'll know when she's unprotected."

Alex knew he had to stall as long as he could to give Jaze the best chance of rescuing Pip's family. He clutched his side in an effort to slow the flow of blood. "I know you have a vendetta against Jet, but why try so hard to kill us? We're just kids."

Drogan's mismatched eyes darkened. "I have my reasons."

He made a swipe for Alex's chest. Alex ducked under the knife and spun, sweeping Drogan's legs out from under him. The man hit the floor and rolled to avoid Alex's punch. His fist hit the floorboards so hard they splintered. Drogan jumped back to his feet and kicked Alex in the stomach. Alex rolled with the blow and reached his feet in time to jump back as Drogan slice at his chest.

"What do they teach you at that academy?" Drogan demanded.

Alex gave a humorless smile. "How to avoid being murdered by low-minded beasts intent on killing children."

Drogan gave a growl of disgust. "I'm the beast?" he

asked. He fainted once with the knife, dodged to the right when Alex blocked it, and landed a sharp kick to Alex's thigh where he had been shot.

"You're the one who killed my parents," Alex shouted. He slammed a fist into Drogan's chest hard enough to propel the man against the fireplace. "You killed Jet." His second punch landed on Drogan's stomach. Though it was protected by Kevlar, the man let out a gasp of pain. "And you took away everything that was good in my life," Alex concluded. He grabbed Drogan by the shoulders and spun to the right, using his strength to throw the man across the room.

Drogan was up faster than Alex expected. He threw a lamp, and when the Gray knocked the lamp away, he threw the knife by its point so hard that when it struck Alex's left shoulder, it knocked him back a few steps. Adrenaline rushed through Alex, numbing the pain and sharpening his senses. His left arm refused to respond. He ripped a drawer from the dressers with his right hand and threw it at the man.

Drogan blocked it with a forearm. Alex used Drogan's own tactic and followed the drawer, bowling the man to the ground. He punched Drogan twice in the face and was about to land a third when his heart stuttered. He paused, fighting the strength that fled from his body.

Drogan took advantage of the weakness and threw him into a wall. Alex slid to a sitting position. He blocked a punch. His heart stuttered again as he tried to block a kick. Drogan slammed a fist through Alex's guard, connecting with the knife that stuck out of the werewolf's shoulder. Alex let out a cry of pain as the blade was forced deeper.

The need to phase surged through his skin. He had to defend himself. Phasing would send the silver shards from the knife deeper into his body. If they reached his bloodstream, he knew they could reach his heart.

"Not so tough, huh?" Drogan said. He tore the knife out of Alex's shoulder.

Alex managed to grab his hand before Drogan drove the blade into his throat. They struggled, Drogan pushing the knife down with all of his strength, and Alex fighting to hold it back as it wavered inches from his skin. His left arm shook and he fought to keep it firm despite the blood he felt pooling down his chest.

"Give up," Drogan said.

"Never," Alex growled. But he didn't know how much longer he could fight. If he phased, Drogan would slip the knife in before he was in wolf form.

He had to get back to Cassie. His heart stuttered again.

Drogan smiled as he felt Alex's grip weaken. Alex knew he had lost as the man with the mismatched eyes shoved the blade down. Alex closed his eyes so Drogan's face wouldn't be the last thing in his mind.

A crash sounded on the porch. Two yells followed and were quickly silenced.

Drogan looked at the door. Alex took advantage of the distraction and kicked, shoving Drogan back against the couch. Alex rolled to his feet and staggered to the wall. The door crashed open. The sight of the fierce, protective rage on Jaze's face filled Alex with relief.

The Alpha attacked Drogan before the man could move. Within seconds, Drogan was pinned to the floor with the silver knife held to his throat.

"You're finished, Drogan," Jaze growled in a voice that sent a shiver down Alex's spine.

"I have your boy Pip's parents," Drogan replied with a note of triumph. "If you kill me, they're dead."

"They're already safe," Jaze told him.

Drogan's eyes widened slightly. "You're lying."

Jaze glared down at the man. "Next time, don't try to reiterate your threats by forcing the boy to visit his parents over Christmas. Werewolves tend to remember where they've been."

Happiness spread through Alex at the thought of Pip's family safe again. His knees wanted to give out. He leaned heavily against the wall, willing them to hold. The silver in the wounds was preventing them from clotting and healing as a werewolf's should. He had already lost a lot of blood.

"Stay with me, Alex," Jaze said, glancing at him.

"I'm alright," Alex replied, forcing himself to stand up straight.

Jaze gave a nod of approval and turned his attention back to Drogan. "With your help, we'll take out the General's bases one by one. Your father won't have any legs to stand on."

"I won't help you," Drogan snarled.

"Oh, you will," Jaze said. He pulled Drogan to his feet and shoved him toward the door. The man was no match for the Alpha's strength. "Vance, where's the chains?"

"Got 'em," Alex heard the huge Alpha respond beyond the door. The sound of chain links clinking together followed.

Jaze stepped back inside. He crossed to Alex and ducked under his arm. "Let's get you outside," he said in a voice much softer than he had used with Drogan.

Alex allowed himself to be helped out of the small cabin. He squinted at the sudden brightness of daylight on the snow. Somehow during their battle, he had forgotten the sun still shone. Now, it bathed his shoulders, reminding him that he had survived. He closed his eyes and absorbed the sensation of warmth amidst the white-washed world.

Voices made him open his eyes. He smiled at the sight of

the professors who surrounded the tiny cabin.

"I told you we should have taken the helicopter to the Academy," Mouse said, adjusting his glasses as he gave Drogan a disapproving look.

"Where would we have put it?" Kaynan replied. His red eyes looked unsettlingly intense. "Do you have a helicopter hiding place we're unaware of?"

The shrug and smile that was Mouse's reply let Alex know that the professor did indeed have secrets.

Chapter Twenty-eight

"How are you holding up?" Jaze asked, his tone concerned.

"Fairly good," Alex replied. He pushed away from the wall of the cabin he had been leaning against, then stumbled.

Jaze caught him. "Mouse, Alex needs you," Jaze called over his shoulder.

Mouse hurried over. "If you choose going after the number two man on the werewolf most wanted list instead of attending Biology, I would recommend Biology," the professor said, checking Alex over. His hands came away bloody. "Take off your shirt," he directed.

Alex gingerly pulled the wolf sweatshirt over his head. His thoughts were foggy, and he found it hard to focus on the werewolves who checked his wounds.

"They're filled with silver shards. They won't clot until we get them out," Mouse said, his words tight.

"Can you do that here?" Jaze pressed.

Mouse shook his head. "The shoulder wound is too deep; I need better equipment. We need to get him back to the Academy."

Jaze's face loomed into view. Alex tried to focus. "Do you think you can make it to the Academy?" he asked as Mouse wrapped bandages over the wounds from the backpack he carried. "Vance wouldn't mind carrying you."

Alex shook his head, forcing his mind to clear at the thought of being carried again by the huge professor. "I'll walk."

Vance chuckled behind them. "I don't mind. You're like carrying a twig."

Alex rolled his eyes. "Thanks, Coach. I think I'll walk."

"It's your funeral," Vance replied.

"Really?" Kaynan responded. "That's what you choose to say? The kid's bleeding and you say it's his funeral?"

"What?" Vance argued. "It's a figure of speech."

"An idiom," Mouse said.

"What did you call him?" Kaynan asked with a laugh.

Vance rolled his eyes and indicated Drogan. "Let's get this garbage back before his men start to wonder at their radio silence."

"I'm hoping they're a bit preoccupied with the destruction Chet and Dray brought on their base. Brock said they were thorough," Jaze replied, shoving Drogan forward. The chains around the human's arms and legs rattled.

Vance gave a snort that took the place of a laugh. "When Brock says thorough, it's like him describing the way he devours a donut. There's nothing left."

"Did you hear that?" Jaze asked, focusing on Drogan. "Nothing left. How will your dad feel about that?"

Drogan glared at the werewolf. "He'll kill you."

"He's already tried and failed," Jaze replied. "Now it's my turn. Let's get moving." He pushed Drogan again. "Walk."

Alex saw the still forms of Drogan's men beneath the trees. Jaze's attack had been deadly and stealthy until he reached the cabin. Alex wondered if Jaze had known he had been in danger, which was why the last two men had fallen so noisily.

He had to force himself to put one foot in front of the other as he followed Jaze and Drogan. Kaynan scouted ahead while Mouse and Vance protected the rear. If there was to be an attack, the werewolves hoped to have the advantage beneath the trees.

Alex's wounds throbbed with each step. He shoulder hurt the worst, while the slice down his back and the shallow one across his side burned, especially when sweat brought on by the silver broke out over his body. He shivered despite the fact that werewolves seldom got cold.

"You alright?"

Alex glanced up to see Jaze walking beside him. Vance had taken the dean's place holding Drogan's chains. The man would be stupid to try anything with the hulking werewolf at his side.

"Just ready to be back at the Academy," Alex replied. His teeth chattered.

Jaze shrugged out of his jacket and put it over Alex's shoulders before the young werewolf could deny the help.

"Take it," Jaze said, reading his expression. "I don't know why I brought one and it saves me from having to carry it."

Alex slipped his arms into the sleeves and zipped it up, grateful for the warmth. "Thanks."

"We need to talk about why you went to the cabin by yourself," Jaze said. "But that's a discussion for a later date. For now, concentrate on making it back to the Academy. Nikki and Lyra were on standby when we left."

"Pip's family is really safe?" Alex asked quietly so Drogan wouldn't overhear.

Jaze nodded. "As soon as Pip told me what happened, I sent Chet and Dray out to the location he described. I imagine they'll have quite the family reunion tonight."

"I'm glad," Alex said.

Jaze glanced at him. "Me, too."

Snow crunched beneath their shoes. It was much harder to walk silently in human form, especially when the snow was thick enough to walk across with paws, but shoes broke right through. They followed the same trail Alex had run earlier. Three sets of tracks lay on top of the one, showing that the professors had used the same trail to reach the cabin.

As the silver wreaked havoc on Alex's body, his found his

ability to do more than walk hampered. He stumbled and Jaze righted him. At the werewolf's question, he shook his head though he was only vaguely aware of what the dean had asked. The minutes dragged on until he felt like they had been walking through the snow for hours and days. As the daylight faded and darkness stole through the trees, he began to believe they would never reach the walls and halls he thought of as home.

***

"Look," Jaze said.

It was the first word Alex recognized after what felt like hours in a foggy haze. He lifted his head and saw the Academy spires just visible through the darkness. Hope filled his chest. He was almost there.

The pounding sound of a helicopter cutting through the air reached them.

"Can we make it?" Kaynan asked, falling back to join the group.

Mouse shook his head. "It's too far."

"You've lost," Drogan said with a humorless smile. "Give up."

"Pull together. Guard the prisoner and Alex. We can take them," Jaze replied, his tone confident.

The pounding grew nearer. They couldn't see where it hovered, but a few seconds later, men appeared between the trees armed to the teeth with guns and ammo. Their black outfits shone dully in the sunlight, letting Alex know they were made of the same Kevlar Drogan wore.

Alex's heart fell. "They're bulletproof," he said.

"Don't worry," Kaynan replied over his shoulder. "We're not exactly helpless." He pulled the wristband from his wrist and snapped it open. The blade caught the afternoon sunlight.

"A knife?" Drogan asked with humor in his tone. "That's supposed to save you?"

Kaynan grinned at him. "In a manner of speaking, yes." He pushed something black on the top of the knife. A little blue light began to flash.

"Let Drogan go," one of the men surrounding them called out.

No one in Jaze's group spoke. There was a tense silence as each waited for the other to act. Jaze's head tipped slightly to the side and a smile spread across his face. "It's here," he said.

Bullets tore through the air. The men around them scattered and shot back at the drone that hovered above the trees. It looked like the werewolves were winning until the sound of a louder gun began to pulse. The drone was hit twice. It spun in a half-circle, hovered for a moment, then exploded.

"Run!" Kaynan yelled.

Gunfire peppered through the trees. Jaze ducked under Alex's arm and the dean practically carried him away from the men who swarmed forward. Bullets hit the bark around them, chipping away pieces that stung the werewolves' arms and faces. Alex glanced back in time to see Drogan trip Vance. They rolled against a large boulder. The silver knife flashed in the moonlight.

Alex put his hands to his mouth and howled. Before his voice even died away, answering howls echoed through the forest as though the werewolves had been waiting for his signal. Shadows began to appear, gray and black forms that blurred past them, intent on the strangers that attacked in their forest. The students were fast, darting between the trees and taking down the men.

"You good?" Jaze asked.

At Alex's nod, the Alpha tore off his shirt and leaped, phasing to the form of the black wolf before his paws touched the ground. He loped through the forest in pursuit of the attackers.

Alex leaned against a tree with his hands on his knees, fighting to keep standing as he searched through the trees. Drogan was nowhere to be seen. Screams of the men being pursued by the werewolves reached Alex's ears. He wanted to be there with the rest of the students, to drive away the men who dared to attack. Instincts demanded that he keep those who looked to him for protection safe from men like Drogan. He didn't want to fail them, but he couldn't focus through the pain enough to put one foot in front of the other, let alone phase and attack with the rest.

The sound of a wolf's quiet huff made him glance over his shoulder. The sight of Cassie in her wolf form made him want to cry. Until that moment, he hadn't been certain he would ever see her again. He dropped to his knees. She ran to him, butting her head softly against his chest. He hugged her, entwining his fingers in her soft cream-colored fur.

"I tried to stop him," he said. Tears broke free. "I wanted to avenge Mom and Dad. I wanted him to pay for what he did to Jet." The tears were lost in Cassie's fur. She gave a quiet whine. "But I didn't want to leave you," he concluded. He sat back on his heels, but the pressure was too much on the wound across his side. He sat down in the snow.

Cassie gave a worried whine at the smell of blood.

"I'm okay," Alex reassured her. "It's just a bit of silver. Nikki and Lyra will get it out." His tongue felt thick. He wanted to talk to her more, to promise her that he would never leave again, that they would be safe and he would make sure no one could ever hurt her, but his mouth wouldn't obey. He had to content himself with listening to the helicopter as it pulled away.

He wondered how many men had survived. He hoped Jaze would come back with the news that Drogan was among the casualties, but deep down, he knew it wasn't true. After all the man had done to him, and all Drogan had taken from him, he knew Drogan wasn't gone. The fist around his heart was still strong. He had to live to fight again.

"Come on, Alex," he heard a voice say. Strong arms lifted him up.

"I can walk," he said past his thick tongue.

"Yeah, but I need a workout. They left too quickly," Vance replied.

Something licked Alex's hand. His head lolled back and he saw Cassie padding beside them in her wolf form. He smiled and closed his eyes.

Chapter Twenty-nine

Alex and Cassie watched the Termers load into the buses.

"Good riddance," Cassie said, though there was a hint of question in her voice.

"I'm not so sure," Alex replied. The Lifers who lounged around them on the Academy front steps looked at him in surprise. Alex shrugged. "It wasn't really that bad this year."

"Say that again and I'll make you eat your words," Torin threatened from where he leaned against a pillar.

"I'd like to see you try," Alex replied. It was stupid to say, but he had done his share of stupid things this term and he figured why break the habit.

Torin merely lifted an eyebrow, surprised at the Gray's bravado. He eventually sat back against the pillar again. "I heard Boris gave you a pretty good beating."

"We both bled," Alex replied, his attention on the buses.

Torin snorted, but didn't reply.

Alex watched the brother and sister with white-blond hair as they walked to the limousine at the front of the circular lot. The woman who waited appeared to be talking animatedly on a cellphone despite school policy that they not be used within the grounds. She merely waved Boris and Kalia into the car, then climbed in after them.

Alex felt horrible for the way things had ended up with Kalia. She had barely spoken to him the rest of the school year. Though Kalia and Cassie hung out on occasion, as soon as Alex appeared, Kalia found a reason to be elsewhere. When Alex asked Cassie, his sister said to give the girl time to recover. She had been hurt by someone she trusted. They both knew how that felt.

"Think Pip will be back next year?" Cassie asked quietly.

"I hope so," Alex replied. He was surprised to find that

he meant it. He had actually missed the little werewolf when he went home with his family. He wished he could have been there for the reunion, but Jaze had suggested it would be best to give them space because it was for Cassie and Alex that they had been imprisoned.

Alex fought back the guilt that filled him at the thought of what everyone had gone through to protect the twins. The entire Academy had been in danger, and still was. Though Drogan's base had been destroyed, he had indeed vanished in the forest, and Brock hadn't been able to locate Drogan or the General. Alex knew deep down that he hadn't seen the last of the man with the mismatched eyes.

"He's here," a quiet voice said from behind Alex.

Alex and Cassie both turned to see Jaze's smiling face. The pride that shone in his eyes said everything.

"The baby!" Cassie exclaimed.

Both twins darted through the doors and took off running down the hall. Jaze was right behind them. He caught the door that Alex threw open and walked beside them more sedately through the medical wing. The door at the end led to the huge private rooms reserved for operations and, apparently, deliveries.

Alex hesitated near the last door.

"Go ahead," Jaze urged.

He pushed it open and stepped quietly inside with Cassie close behind. Lyra turned to them dressed in purple scrubs with gloves on her hands and funny blue socks around her shoes. To Alex's surprise, his aunt Meredith was there as well. She was dressed like Lyra and had apparently been assisting her in the delivery.

"Come on back," she said, waving for them to step around the curtain.

Alex felt completely out of his element. The sterile scent

of cleaners and soap crowded out any other smell. His sneakers squeaked on the linoleum. The air was a bit colder. Since his prolonged exposure to the silver during the walk back from the cabin, he had become a bit more sensitive to changes in temperature. A slight chill ran down his spine.

"Faster," Cassie whispered excitedly.

Alex bit back a smile and stepped around the curtain. The smile he held back spread completely across his face at the sight of the little baby in Nikki's arms. The baby had Jaze's blond hair and Nikki's blue eyes.

"He is so cute!" Cassie exclaimed.

"Do you want to hold him?" Nikki asked.

Cassie's eyes widened. She looked from Jaze back to Nikki. "Can I?"

Jaze nodded. "He's your little brother."

Cassie held her arms the way Lyra showed her and gave a huge grin as Nikki positioned the baby within them.

"He's perfect," she said softly.

"What's his name?" Alex asked.

Nikki and Jaze looked at each other. "William," Jaze said.

Alex's heart gave a little stutter as he looked from Cassie to the baby. William had been Jet's name before he had been taken away from their family. Jet and Jaze had been more than friends. They had been brothers who had fought together through more dangerous situations than Alex even knew. It felt right that the baby would carry on Jet's name.

William gurgled and looked up at Cassie. "Hello, William," she said, smiling down at him. "I'm your sister Cassie, and I'm going to take care of you." She looked up at Nikki. "With your mom's help, of course."

Nikki smiled. "No brother has ever had such wonderful siblings." She looked up at Meredith. The twins' aunt gave her a warm smile, her eyes sparkling.

"We'll protect him," Alex said. He looked at Jaze and Nikki; they held hands and smiled adoringly at their new son. Alex's gaze traveled to Aunt Meredith who watched lovingly over Cassie and baby William. Alex's heart burned with the need to keep them safe, to protect them, to always make sure they were happy. A smile spread across his face. He had a pack, and he would fight for it.

About the Author

Cheree Alsop is the mother of a beautiful, talented daughter and amazing twin sons who fill every day with joy and laughter. She is married to her best friend, Michael, the light of her life and her soulmate who shares her dreams and inspires her by reading the first drafts and adding depth to the stories. Cheree is currently working as an independent author and mother. She enjoys reading, riding her motorcycle on warm nights, and playing with her twins while planning her next book.

Cheree and Michael live in Utah where they rock out, enjoy the outdoors, plan great adventures, and never stop dreaming.

Check out Cheree's other books at www.chereealsop.com

***If you liked this book, please review it online so others can find it!

Look for Werewolf Academy Book 2: Hunted

Printed in Great Britain
by Amazon